THROUGH MY LENS

SHRUTI JOSHI

Made with ♥ on the Notion Press Platform
www.notionpress.com

To Sheedo...

To Cheeku...

To Molly...

To Scout...

You are all extremely wonderful and delighfully charming. I love
you all, and this is for you!

Contents

Acknowledgements

Thank you, Ananya, for being my first reader, editor, critic, voice of reason, mentor, and sister! More than anything, thank you for listening to all my crazy ideas and (not, *sigh!*) calling them crazy. There aren't enough words to truly express my gratitude or to tell you how wonderful it is to have you!
God bless you, today and always!
And to Molly and Scout—I love you both.
Always have and always will... maybe from a distance, but I love you both deeply!

Prologue

She paced restlessly within the confines of her studio, the walls seemingly closing in on her as frustration echoed from her every word. Jiya's voice erupted through the studio like a storm, her rising anger palpable. She searched through the cluttered space, shouting at no one in particular, as the interns scattered around her. *"I simply cannot find anything useful in this rubbish,"* she exclaimed, her voice rising with each word.

They frantically searched for the small golden ring prop she was looking for but to no avail. *"This place has become nothing but rubbish,"* Jiya declared fiercely, shooting a terrifying glare at the closest intern. The intern tried to hold back tears amidst the chaos, but it was clear that they were not having much luck, either finding the object of Jiya's desire or being able to withstand her anger.

The studio, once a haven for creativity, had metamorphosed into an organized chaos—evidence of the myriad stories the room bore witness to. When Jiya initially moved in, the space was expansive and well-ordered. Now, an assortment of objects lay strewn haphazardly on all surfaces, each narrating a tale of the numerous assignments the team had triumphantly completed. And despite the annual space-cleanup initiatives her assistants ran before Deepavali, none had ever succeeded in sorting out everything—the pile was just too huge with objects of varying sizes. Jiya's habit of asking for random items at any point of the day had always prevented them from throwing things. Hence, the initiatives usually ended with dumping everything into the two cabinets to make space for the Deepavali celebrations before restoring the space to its former chaotic shape.

Jiya marched through her cluttered studio, looking over various items such as makeup, clothes, props, camera equipment, lights, and a collection of miscellaneous objects strewn all over the barely visible floor. Although she was mainly responsible for the creation and rapid growth of this diverse collection of useless artefacts, nobody dared remind her of the same.

It was after all Jiya's dedication and expertise that had made her the successful person she is today. She had focused every living moment of her adult life on making her dream come true—to be the best photographer. She had even largely achieved it. She had her own space, and a few international assignments, and was counted as one of the best in the country. Her work had occupied every bit of her life to such an extent that she had hardly any time to even eat.

Even though the interns knew that their futures were dependent on Jiya's current successes, it did not make their time with her any easier. Not only were they managing every other bit of her life, as well as their own, to help her focus on her work, but Jiya's temper also had a reputation of its own. She could work for days without catching a break. She could demand any item at any time of the day. And she had extremely high standards of work that everyone needed to conform to.

Jiya had two rules when it came to working with her. Firstly, she expected her interns to never take their work for granted, no matter how small the task assigned. Even if it meant getting water, they needed to take care of which glass would go with the mood and infuse some lemon and mint into the water—to overcome the tiredness of a long day. Secondly, her interns needed to avoid getting her angry at all costs. Although Jiya was known to get irritated and angry quite easily, her interns tried their best to not give her more excuses for the same or, especially, become the reason for her outbursts. These were not the rules set by Jiya but passed down by the several interns who had worked with her over the years, and those who followed these two rules were sure to have a successful career ahead.

Over the last seven years, Jiya has taken on more than a hundred interns, a few of whom have become her assistants and moved on to set up and own independent studios or be headhunted by some ridiculously rich ad agency. Jiya still looked out for them, passing assignments that she did not have the bandwidth for or recommending them for an assignment that she knew they would handle better than she could. However, more than fifty per cent of her interns quit the profession altogether, realizing that the speed and hard work required were not meant for them. The remaining small percentage would take internships under other professional photographers, knowing that being around Jiya was always going to be an added difficulty to their already difficult profession. But the ones who stayed to complete their internship or be her assistants were a few of the best photographers in the industry. Not only did they know their profession extremely well and were talented beyond measure, but working with Jiya had also given them an unparalleled experience.

Even today, the only people who ever attempted to clean or organize the studio were Jiya's current two assistants. They were both not as messy as Jiya but understood her abstract organizational system well. They kept the place sorted enough to know the approximate location of everything Jiya could demand at any point. It might take one a little while to get used to Jiya's 'unconventional' organization scheme, but once someone got used to it, even the heaps of seemingly rubbish objects started to make some sense.

Unfortunately for the interns, both the assistants had gone off for a shoot in Dubai with a few interns, and the remaining interns were left to assist Jiya, which was proving to be a highly demanding task in itself. Every moment of working with her was challenging and rewarding at the same time. There was always something to learn, always a new challenge to solve. Today's challenge? Finding a ring—a seemingly simple task that had everyone on edge. Firstly, no one knew what the ring looked like. Secondly, there were almost a few thousand things in the room—combining the heaps for a small ring was going to be a long and meticulous task. This was the cost of working with one of the best professional photographers in the country. Every little detail mattered, and every small object was important, even if you could not understand the reason. The studio, typically a hub of artistic energy and creative exchange on most days, now crackled with tension and the sounds of scurrying footsteps.

No one, however, could imagine the reward for finding the ring. They were sure of the repercussions of not finding it, though.

After a tense thirty minutes, one intern unearthed a dusty box buried under heaps of clothes, dug out a small golden ring from a weird collection of broken objects, and claimed his discovery. Jiya's eyes gleamed as she took the ring, and finally, the calm returned to her face. A wave of relief swept through the room, which was, however, short-lived. Jiya examined the ring closely for a few nervous seconds while rotating it between her fingers before finally declaring it to be of the wrong fit for the purpose and tossing it away on the floor to be lost again in the assortment of objects scattered all over. *Get me another one that will give us the desired effect,* she spoke with an uninterested tone to one of the interns along with the instructions to pack for their shoot before leaving.

The interns exchanged bewildered glances as Jiya exited, her silhouette disappearing as she exited through the narrow door into the narrow corridor. The room remained silent for minutes after the echoes of Jiya's heels had silenced. They marvelled in admiration and fright at the complexity of the thirty-two-year-old, highly talented woman. Jiya was an enigma—an artist whose brilliance shone through the chaos she seemingly thrived on. Even after working with her for over a year, most of the interns could not decipher her thoughts and wishes. The less experienced had no chance. Every new intern would attempt a couple of times to ask for reasons behind Jiya's extremely impulsive and mood-driven decisions but soon learned to simply trust the mad genius. No one knew how Jiya got her ideas, but they always worked well.

They all stood perplexed, rooted to their spots, before one of them was brought out of the horrid enchantment and helped others snap out of it as well. Aware of the ticking clock, the studio again transformed into a chaotic space with interns running in every direction, packing and throwing instructions. Jiya, very unlike herself, had accepted an unplanned shoot in Lonavala, and the team was to leave in a couple of hours. They geared up and switched to their highest operating efficiency levels, each trying to not be the reason for Jiya's annoyance.

As everyone rushed all over the studio room, the lone intern, who was asked to find '*a ring that will give the desired effect*,' stood rooted to the spot, unsure of what each word in the request meant and where to begin his quest for the right ring from.

ONE

"*For once, could you hold the light steadily?*" Jiya snapped at the intern while wrestling with the various wires attached to the light the intern was holding. The wires had not been fixed properly, causing the light to flicker, and even though it was well-lit with the sun shining brightly in the clear sky, the model kept complaining. Two other interns had to step in to keep the light from falling off the stand as the first intern had let go of the light, frightened of merely finding himself too close to his boss. The shoot that was envisioned to be a regular portfolio shoot for an ad agency was proving to be more difficult with every passing second. The agency had recruited a bunch of fresh faces, and the photo shoot was meant for their breakthrough into the world of modelling. It had been long since Jiya had stopped taking on such projects—for a long time, she had only worked with selected models and brands. This one was her refresher into portfolio photography—something she could have done even blindfolded. Yet, it was, without a doubt, the one testing all her strengths and patience.

To begin with, Jiya never took on any project on short notice or on an ad hoc basis. Being one of the best in her profession, she had months of planned work ahead of her at any point in time. Currently, she was scheduled to shoot a veteran actress's return-to-movies portfolio shoot. However, the actress's secretary had called to cancel a day before the shoot's start date. That was when things started to go downhill. Jiya was not great with the sudden change of plans and was definitely not good at sitting idle. As a result, she made a few calls and ended up picking up the assignment, much to the ad agency's astonishment, which she not-so-subtly considered way beneath her skills. While there was nothing wrong with the job, it was merely not worthy of the "*Queen's time,*" as the interns called Jiya owing to her tantrums. She would usually not take up such assignments, mostly because the ad agencies could not afford her budgeted work, and neither did she feel it added any value. In dire situations where she could not deny an assignment she did not wish to take up, her assistants would complete the shoot on her behalf. Unfortunately, both her assistants were taking care of another such assignment for a private client.

Moreover, it had been some years that Jiya had been on such a project all by herself. She had worked on big-budget projects for quite some time and had become habitual in getting the ad agency or other hired staff to arrange the logistics. Her assistants and interns were trained to check off all items on their standard requirement list before the beginning of any shoot. But this assignment was outdoors—in a resort in Lonavala with no staff from the ad agency, except a coordinator, to help. The models were all new—most were facing the camera for the first time. Her interns had to manage all the setup. Jiya wished she could walk out of the situation, but she had never left an assignment after accepting it, and the group of interns accompanying her were not trained enough to handle the entire project. Blunders on assignments even as menial as the one she found herself in were not seen in a good light in her profession.

Luckily, the shoot would finish in three days, and then they would be back in Mumbai. She would have three days to prepare for her next shoot—the thought of which kept her going. When in Mumbai, the interns would get some hours of Jiya-free time to relax and unwind. Being onsite in Lonavala prevented them from banking on that solace as well. They were in a shoot from nine in the morning till nine at night. They had to spend two hours before the start of the shoot to arrange everything and then another two hours post-pack-up to wind up everything. They would then need to spend another hour with Jiya to understand the next day's requirements.

This would leave the interns with very little personal time to perform their non-productive tasks, such as eating, sleeping, and getting ready. Most of them were already exhausted, and it was just the first day of the shoot.

Jiya turned around, making the three interns jump back, and walked back to her camera. Two other interns, standing by her camera, jumped out of her way, colliding with each other and falling down. Jiya looked at them in contempt but did not say a word. She was finding the work as challenging as her team. As much as she enjoyed being behind the lens and capturing phenomenal stills, she had little or no people skills. Without her assistants, she despised every moment that she was forced to be on the set. The ad agency team had their issues—the coordinator kept shouting her inputs and suggestions to the models directly, causing the newbies to change poses and expressions. Two of the models, who claimed to have had a portfolio shoot done priorly, were giving their own endless stream of inputs. And her own interns were working at the speed of snails—that too clumsily. She could have finished the shoot in one day, only if these people would let her. It had been quite some time since she had not been the queen of the room while at work, and it was not suiting her well.

A distinct thud followed by some indistinct chatter, somewhere from behind, told her that one of the experienced models was having another disagreement with the coordinator. Jiya let out a long sigh and shook her head, expressing her annoyance. She pulled out a cigarette from her jeans pocket and turned towards the nearest exit, uttering a single word in a tone of finality, *"Break"*.

ᗷᗷᗷ

The morning routine was completed after a lot of hindrances. Despite all odds, Jiya finally managed to capture a few good pictures; combined with image editing and enhancement skills, these pictures would be perfect to flaunt over several hoardings and newspapers all over the country. She needed to shoot the next set of pictures by the swimming pool. Despite the fact that she did not understand the reason behind shooting pictures in different locations in a world where photo editing software was practically free, she refrained from registering a verbal complaint. She had deliberately kept a small routine and intended to get it over with before the evening.

Jiya's team had coordinated with the hotel staff and secured access to the poolside. It should not be a difficult task, as people do not prefer swimming during peak noon. The noon manager had also appointed a person from housekeeping to stand by the pool to arrange any items that might be required during the shoot and to prevent any guests from visiting the pool.

All the interns had started an internal bet on how long it would take Jiya to lose her temper and abandon the project. Only the intern, the newest girl to join Jiya's crew, who had spoken to the hotel management to secure access to the pool, did not find it funny and stayed away from participating.

Luckily for everyone present, the second half of their day's shoot started well. The sequence was pretty straightforward—the models would sit by the poolside, under the sun. Since the agency wanted a few sun-kissed pictures, the models did not have much to complain about except requiring the makeup artist to touch up their makeup every ten minutes. Jiya's anger with the morning shoot had subsided. She had devised a clever strategy during lunch—the models needed to be stationary; she would move around and take shots. It called for most equipment to be fixed as well—giving her interns less chance to fall, collide, or break objects. The strategy was working well. She would take pictures of a model for a couple of minutes before dismissing her to get her makeup fixed, during which she could take the pictures with another model.

After doing one pose with all the models, Jiya would retreat behind the small screen setup she had arranged to review her work. It was difficult, though, to check the pictures with her usual precision and eagle vision as the light glistening off the pool's surface was landing right in Jiya's vision. Once or twice Jiya did look towards the pool, only to see the silent water in the vast pool, the hotel staff guiding guests to some locations, and the sign that read '*Silence Please*'. She pulled out a cigarette from her jeans pocket and kept rotating it between her fingers. Satisfied with the arrangements and, above all, pleased with the photos, Jiya was finally able to get into her element and got engrossed in filtering pictures for final deliverables. She was so deeply engaged in the screen that she never got the moment to light the cigarette.

She marked the pictures that she wanted to recapture. Her interns, who usually surrounded her as she reviewed and edited her work, were taking notes. Halfway through the shoot, Jiya decided to take the recapture shots as the sun was slowly changing position. Instructing her interns to get the models ready, Jiya walked to her camera, conscious of losing light with every second. It was almost four in the evening, and if she was not able to get the desired shot in the next few minutes, she would need to shoot by the pool the next day—something no one wanted.

The cigarette stayed in her hands. Jiya had a problem—her work kept her high, and in times when her work failed to give her the stimulation she needed was when she would turn to external sources. Right now, she was not sure if she would need the cigarette or not. Calling out to everyone to take their positions, Jiya started to focus her lens on the right angle, pushing the cigarette back into her pocket.

Focusing on the model's face against the perfect azure sky kissing the sparkling water and creating a picturesque backdrop, Jiya knew she would not need the cigarette. She would get her perfect shot. And as she put her eyes behind the camera, a lot of things happened. The model screamed and humped. Suddenly the tranquility was shattered by an unexpected splash and the introduced commotion to calm the model. Instinctively, Jiya snapped towards the disturbance, still holding the camera in her hands, ready to click.

The sudden commotion had been enough to cause the impact. Jiya looked around and then moved two steps closer to the pool as she noticed the ripples emerging from the farther end. As if the interruption had not been enough to stun everyone around, the shock on Jiya's face increased as a figure emerged from the pool, a few feet from where she stood. Her fingers tightened around the camera, clicking pictures in succession. Not that Jiya needed these pictures; the man was too good-looking to be forgotten. Time seemed to freeze as the drops of liquid sunlight cascaded down the masculine figure. He stood there, emerging from the pool, a living sculpture carved by the gods, and Jiya found herself looking at him, momentarily breathless and unaware of anything but the man who now steadily emerged in front of him.

As the man's torso rose out of the water, he wiped water out of his eyes and opened them. As fate would have it, the man's gaze locked with Jiya's. The man's eyes, a mesmerizing shade of deep, mysterious brown, were deep with experience and yet gentle with warmth and love. They were windows to a soul that had weathered both storms and sunshine. Jiya could not help but notice that they sparkled. He ran his long fingers through his dark hair to tame his tousled look. Each moment, whether intentional or not, unveiled the strength beneath his hunky exterior and a heart full of love and wisdom.

The man broke off the connection to look around and then could not help but again look directly at Jiya. It gave her a moment of relief to take notice of him as a whole rather than just as a pair of mesmerizing eyes. As he wiped the water from his face, Jiya noticed the sinewy strength of his arms, admiring the perfectly chiselled torso and built shoulders. He exuded a magnetic pull, and she felt its pull. She stood there, as a lone spectator, admiring the most perfect piece of art in a huge but empty museum. Neither the man nor Jiya blinked or made any attempt to look away from one another. The world was just comprised of the two people, and that is all that mattered.

In the background, the constant clicking of the camera filled the otherwise silent background. No one dared interrupt Jiya. Her interns were patiently waiting for her to tell them how the interruption had been their fault and shout at them as well as the man in front of her. With every passing moment, the aura of fear became denser. Yet, Jiya was oblivious to anything such. She stood there, the camera still clicking, clutched between her hands, as the man jerked his head to the side, breaking their connection at last. The housekeeping staff was the one responsible for that. He had walked over to the edge of the pool and called out to the man until the man was forced to break the connection and give him his attention. However, the man kept looking back at Jiya, reluctant to lose the connection completely. Finally, acknowledging the intrusion, but not before casting a parting look at Jiya that lingered for a long moment, the man took the towel from the housekeeping staff and allowed him to escort him out of the pool area.

Gradually, the world around Jiya materialized. Foremost, she looked at her hands and immediately lifted her fingers off the camera to stop the clicking. She was finding it difficult to juggle between the world that was now materializing versus the one she was being reluctantly forced out of. Conscious of keeping her camera safe, she placed it carefully over the stand and then craned her neck in the direction of where the man now stood, half hidden behind the partition. He was patting himself dry with the towel before tying it over his wet shorts. A group of men surrounded him as he stood conversing with the housekeeping staff who had ushered him away. He was nodding and probably, Jiya thought, smiling.

The housekeeping staff rushed to fetch a duffle bag that he handed to the man. Before leaving, the man turned his head to get one last look. The two pairs of eyes interlocked into a kind of intense dance before the man took another step over the threshold and walked on. Jiya stood, still transfixed on the spot, reliving the last few seconds over and over again. She found herself captivated not only by the incredibly handsome man she had seen but also by the uncharted emotions stirring within herself. She could not explain the reason behind the urge she felt to meet the man and talk to him. It felt like the only thing worth doing. Their encounter was not over. She was going to make sure of the same.

Jiya was smiling as she turned once more. She picked her camera off the stand, picked up her laptop from the table, and walked away without a word. No one had ever seen her leave without a single word—it was the first time. Everyone had expected her to be extremely angry at the intrusion, and they were shocked to see her smile and behave in such an un-Jiya-ish manner. Not only had she not shouted at anyone for the disruption, but she did not seem to mind it at all. Rather, a few of her interns could have sworn that she was smiling.

If there was one person who seemed equally, if not more, happy as Jiya, it was the female intern who had instructed the hotel management to not allow any intrusions. Since the splashing noise, she was sure to get the worst scolding of her life and possibly lose her internship. When Jiya walked without a word, the girl decided that it was the divine helping her and made a mental note to visit a temple first thing the next morning.

ᐁᐁᐁ

Jiya's strange behaviour did not end at that. When the interns went to her room to get further instructions for the shoot, she simply handed them the camera and asked them to complete the shoot. Unlike her usual self, she did not share any storyboards or ideas that she had. Closing the door, she returned to the several pictures she was browsing through on her laptop.
She was still unsure if the encounter had been real or if she had been dreaming. An alternate reality replaying the moments of the encounter played right before her eyes. The man was perfect. Every small detail was engraved in her memory, and it played like a movie, which she could zoom in on at any point. Droplets of water had clung to the strands of his dark hair like liquid diamonds, glistening in the sunlight as his strong and long fingers navigated the dark waves. At the moment, when his hair surrendered to the gentle

command of his fingers, taming down to give him a surreal look, the world seemed to hold its breath. The veins on his forearms are subtly accentuated by the play of light. His broad shoulders narrated his long journey of becoming the hunk that he was. And yet, he moved with such poise, composure, and grace that the elements of the world seemed to flow along with his perfect strides and posture.

She remembered the delicate flutter of a thousand butterflies taking flight within the confines of her stomach as their eyes locked in a surreal embrace. And though there was nothing about the stranger that had not drawn Jiya towards him, it was his eyes that drew her the most.

It was not the first time that Jiya had seen a handsome man. Her profession required her to be surrounded by models and other well-groomed and well-dressed men. Rather, if she had to compare, she probably knew twenty better-looking men than the man she had earlier witnessed. Yet she could not explain the pull she felt. It was much more than a mere carnal desire. She did find the man extremely sensual and appealing and would not pass any opportunity to lay a finger on him, but she wanted more. She wanted to sit with him and talk. She wanted him to tell her everything and for her to listen to him. She wanted to have dinner with him and then breakfast and then the next dinner and everything in between.

She sat in her room for hours, reliving the encounter in her mind. She had lived that moment for so long that she had not realized that it was barely a minute that the two of them had stood with their eyes interlocked. She had barely seen the man for two minutes in her life. All Jiya knew was that she could not wait to see him again.

TWO

Chirag's world was simple—well, as simple as it could get with two successful companies to manage. Chirag Kapoor—the man said to have the Midas touch. After completing his graduation, he and two of his friends found it extremely difficult to settle in a new city where their jobs had taken them. Barely surviving the heat, traffic, food, and expensive cost of living of the IT hub, they decided to quit and start their own venture. The trio set up their first Working Professionals Hostel in the very city where, like them, many others came to work and found the other challenges overwhelming. It was simple—they rented several accommodations, hired staff for basic amenities, and rented out the rooms. Soon all rooms were taken, and the requests for more kept queueing outside their makeshift office. Maybe their idea was very good, they were at the right place at the right time, or they did spend countless hours in their business, but their business took off. All they ensured was to remember the challenges they had faced when they first came to the city and were determined to not let their customers face the same. Within three years, they were not just a start-up but a business with a twenty-million-dollar valuation. They expanded their operations to premium hostels for corporates and affordable long duration stay family hostels. By the end of the fourth year, they received a proposal from a hostel chain group to buy their start-up. Though Chirag thoroughly enjoyed the entire process and did not like the idea of selling off his business, he was outvoted by his friends. Having received a little over twenty million dollars each, his friends retired. They invested their share of the money in big organizations and relocated to the US to act as directors in those firms.

Chirag was not going to rest. He took a break to pursue an MBA degree and then invested his share to start a logistics firm. Luck favored him one more time, and he won several big contracts. By the age of forty, Chirag had done enough to feature in several national and three international business magazines. His firm generated direct employment for over ten thousand people in the country and approximately twenty-five thousand globally. The firm that had started as a simple logistics firm now handled international transfers for several big companies, partnered with international agencies, and had thousands of vehicles of different sizes and capacities running all over the globe. His firm was rumored to have all kinds of vehicles available—scooters, cars, jeeps, bikes, ferries, boats, private cargo planes—and even had permanent booking on several Indian Railway cargo routes.

It was on his forty-third birthday that someone sold Chirag the idea to start an e-commerce platform. Chirag, who had already been intrigued by the idea, gave it serious consideration. While he wanted to set up another business, he simply did not wish to do it for money—he already had plenty of that. With a lot of brainstorming and guidance from his selected trusted advisors, Chirag started a digital distribution platform that would source products from rural areas in the country, partnering with several artisans, farmers, and skilled individuals and organizations, labeling the products, packaging them, marketing them, and selling them internationally. This was his quest to not just understand the rapidly evolving dynamics of the digital market but also to give back to his country. Most of the domain was completely alien to him—though his logistics firm had a website, he had rarely navigated it entirely. It was very exciting for him as he was back to being his twenty-year-old self, working through day and night to learn and strive.

Meanwhile, his logistics business supported immensely in spreading the presence of his digital distribution business at an accelerated rate, making it an instant success. Within three years of its launch, the platform had recovered all the investment and was generating considerable profits. At the age of forty-six, Chirag got the title *'The Man with the Midas Touch'* from one of the National Business Journals.

While the achievements sound very good when narrated one after the other, everything comes with a price tag. The journey was not this simple. There had been challenges and countless sleepless nights for Chirag to bring his businesses to a respectable stature. There was just one constant thing—he never gave up. Even when things became extremely difficult or harsh, he might take a step back or slow down but never stop. But the biggest cost that Chirag paid for his success was the love of his family.

He had married Amita at the age of twenty-four. His 'Hostels for Working Professionals' were already all the rage then, and they had expanded their offerings considerably. His parents had found him the perfect girl, and he had liked her a lot. She was supportive of his work and encouraged him to not give up. She, herself, was teaching in a government school. Things looked good. At the age of twenty-five, the couple was blessed with a baby girl. Things were smooth for a couple of years, but then, at the age of thirty-two, both his parents met in a car accident while visiting a temple and died. The loss drove Chirag crazy. He immersed himself in enormous work and secluded himself from the world. It only became worse with time. His travels were frequent, and each one was longer than the previous. Amita was restricted because of her job and their daughter's education. As a result, things between the couple took a turn for the worse, and before Chirag turned thirty-seven, he was divorced. Together they shared the custody of their only daughter, but the person who was the sole heir to all his earnings, businesses, and assets, who was his one reason of survival, did not bother speaking with him after the divorce. Rather, he had not even seen her for over five years.

His daughter was another one of his failures—one that no one really knew about. While the couple shared the custody of the little girl, she grew up to blame Chirag for everything. Chirag knew that she was not wrong. He may have lost his parents, but he should have been there for his wife and daughter. With the passing years, not only did she grow up with his negligible involvement in her day-to-day life, but she also grew up to be as unlike him as possible. They would just talk once a year when Chirag would call to wish her on her birthday. Amita would sometimes share a few pictures with him.

His daughter had enrolled herself in a fine arts course and decided to follow her passion. Chirag had several times offered her to join his business in any capacity, but she had never agreed. When she announced her decision, Chirag had even offered to fund her college—but there had been a lot of distance between them by then. She was, after all, his daughter and adamantly declared that she would work to earn her fees rather than take it from him.

Now all Chirag had left was his two successful business ventures and no one to share all the success with. He spent most of his time working and looking for new opportunities to grow and expand his businesses. In any free moment, he would find his thoughts wandering to all the things that he should have done differently and all the times that he should have prioritized his family over his work. But there was little he could do to fix the damage. Things were broken beyond repair. He had accepted his fate and made it a personal mission to not let other families struggle the way he had. He made it his priority to check the well-being of his employees as well as the families of his employees. And in whatever little time that he got, he spent it on the only person in his life—himself. He took his health and well-being quite seriously. It was his only hobby, recreational activity, and source of entertainment. Most importantly, it kept the negative thoughts away.

When he returned from his lunch meeting with a potential distributor in Lonavala to his hotel, he found out about a shoot going on in the hotel. The news was of no interest to him. He retired to his room to catch up on some pending emails and reviews. He was going to spend the remainder of his day in Lonavala and leave early the next morning to go to Pune to meet another potential distributor.

These meetings were a less desirable but highly necessary part of his job. This is something he had done since day one of his professional career and always mentioned it as the root cause of his success—to meet people personally. People connect better when they can see you. If they feel comfortable and involved, they tend to be loyal and more hardworking. That is the situation where you both profit together.

After going through a few of the emails, Chirag felt dizzy. His morning meeting had been a slow drag. He decided to go for a quick swim. It would refresh him and also bring back some energy. He went to the locker room and surprisingly found it completely empty. Well, not a lot of people would come to Lonavala and go to a pool in the hotel when there were so many pretty sights to be seen and places to be visited. Pushing any suspicions aside, he changed into his swimming shorts and climbed up the diving platform. From the height, he could see the shooting that was happening by the pool. It looked to be on pause as no one was taking pictures but concentrated behind the monitor. However, he could not be sure. The rising heat, the height, and the sunlight being reflected off the water's surface were making it very difficult to concentrate. Chirag considered his options for a few moments before jumping off the platform. He had never learned swimming when he had been younger—it was something he had picked up not so long ago. However, this was something he enjoyed. The platform was high enough to make his dive exciting, and without another second's delay, Chirag took his position and bent his knees.

The pool, with its rippling and shining surface, was both intimidating and inviting. Chirag, in a moment of suspended anticipation, spread his arms wide, embracing the freedom that the impending dive promised. In one fluid motion, he launched himself into the air, his body becoming a study in elegant motion. Time seemed to slow as he brought his legs closer to his torso, mid-air, before stretching himself to a perfect form to cut through the water with minimal splash.

It was not the water but the entire experience that made it exciting. As Chirag emerged from the refreshing embrace of the pool, he had a feeling that there were several eyes drawn to his sudden intrusion. He wiped the water off his face and eyes and opened his eyes naturally, adjusting to the surroundings. Before he could look around and take it in, his gaze met with something unexpected—a girl with a camera in hand, poised near the shallow end. Slowly he made his way toward where she stood, without realizing that he had been looking only at the girl.

Unaware of anything or anyone else, he could not break the connection that had deepened. It was as though their eyes were locked in an unspoken dialogue. He kept looking back at the girl's hazel eyes—eyes that hid several stories behind the layers of kajal, liners, and mascara that she was wearing. The unnatural nature of this connection gave rise to an unusual tug of curiosity within him.

The girl, beyond being beautiful, exuded an air of confidence that held him captive. There was something about her that extended beyond the physical and visible realm. And now that he was caught in the visual exchange, Chirag hesitated to be the first to look away. He could feel a surge of emotions arising—curiosity, concern, happiness, excitement, longing, and more—that he could not discern.

With each second, the connection only grew deeper. The world around them momentarily faded, leaving only the silent connection. Chirag's usually focused mind found itself contemplating the enigma before him. He had stepped outside the pool and stood before the girl, transfixed. He simply could not turn away. The girl with the camera became more than an observer; she became a puzzle, a mystery that piqued Chirag's interest, a magnetic force that made him oblivious to everything and everyone else, compelling him to linger in the unspoken dialogue. And then, after what seemed like several minutes, or maybe after a single second, Chirag was forced to be back in the real world by a man calling out to him quite persistently.

As if jerked awake from a beautiful dream, Chirag turned to his left to find a man calling out to him. It took Chirag a few seconds to comprehend what was being said. Age was taking its toll on him. It was someone from the hotel staff informing him that the pool was currently unavailable for the guests owing to the shoot that was taking place. He was informing about some schedules and announcements that were put up at the reception. Well, it did not really matter.

Chirag turned back to get another look at the girl, who was still looking at him. A few of his assistants had spotted him in conversation with the hotel staff and had come to aid him in case of an issue. The hotel staff had to repeat everything—words that fell onto Chirag's ears but did not make any sense. Chirag heard them but could not comprehend. His mind was stuck on the large hazel eyes that he could still feel watching him. He took the towel from the man to wrap around himself. This was the first time in a long time that Chirag was conscious of how he looked or how the girl would see him. The others did not matter. He had grown accustomed to the feeling of being invisible in the spotlight. There were always onlookers for some reason or another. Some people recognized him and stared; others stared at him, intrigued with the two bodyguards and the personal staff that accompanied him to most public encounters. None of them cared for who he was. But the girl was neither. She was not looking at him but seeing him.

Once his assistants were happy with the situation, he found himself being ushered away from the pool. Finally, being forced to come out of his thoughts, Chirag asked to collect his clothes from the locker room. He turned to look at the girl one more time. Their eyes locked again, but this time he was more aware of the surroundings. He did not stop or pause but kept walking towards the locker room. He reached the edge of the room and took the door leading him away from the pool.

Even when he was not looking at the girl, he could see her clearly. He could see the girl wearing a faded brown top and tight jeans with a chocolate-brown scarf rolled around her neck. Her image was imprinted in his mind quite distinctively and clearly. And the magnetic pull of those hazel eyes was still strong and something he could not deny. If only he were younger, he would have felt what others called "butterflies in his stomach." He laughed the thought out of his mind but could not deny that he did feel an odd sensation running through his body.

He could not describe it, but he kept reliving those few moments by the pool. He kept rehearsing a conversation in his head that he should have had with the girl. He did not even ask her name. And yet, he felt as if he had known her for a lifetime. She did not seem like a stranger. She was not just pretty, but she was someone who made him feel good and made him smile for no reason.

Chirag mechanically dried himself and wore his clothes as his mind wandered over to all the thoughts that he would have otherwise pushed away. Once ready, he exited the locker room from the other side.

ᐟᐟᐟ

The girl with hazel eyes and the entire scene at the pool were soon driven out of Chirag's mind owing to the several files he had to review before meeting with the distributors the next day. He made two important calls, dictated a few letters to his secretary, and reviewed some more files. Habitual due to the strict regime Chirag employed, his stomach made him aware of the time at quarter past seven. Happy with the work he had done during the day and positive that the meetings he was having were going to be productive in the longer run, Chirag closed the file in his hand and made his move towards the restroom.

Dressed in his impeccable three-piece suit, Chirag looked quite handsome and professional. This was how he liked to look every second when he was not in bed or in a place that warranted special dressing. He washed his hands thoroughly, ensured his hair did not have any flyaways, and then made his way out of his room towards the restaurant where the dinner buffet was served.

He could not help but feel happy. And though he usually followed a very strict fitness regime, today he was going to deviate—he did not feel hungry but longed for a dessert. As he made his way towards the restaurant, he let his mind wander to all the sweets that he wanted to taste tonight.

THREE

Jiya was as different from Chirag as possible. Life was never going to give you things decorated on a platter—she had learned that at quite an early age. If you wanted something, you needed to go and get it. The key was to never stop and never shy away from hard work and learning new things. There was nothing called luck, and it was just what hardworking people said to dismiss the lazy. At the early age of sixteen, she knew that she was not just a face behind countless photographs; her true place was behind the lens. Her board exams, her parents' constant reminders to score well, and a foreign city did not dissuade her from pursuing her dreams and applying for an internship under several famous photographers in different parts of the world. Since then, Jiya had managed to earn just enough to pay off her school fees and have a little amount to spend each month. Soon after school, she started accepting freelance assignments, which helped her buy her first DSLR camera. She had enrolled in a Mass Media graduation course, which soon proved to have little or nothing of photography. Yet, she decided to finish her education, as per her parents' wishes. Post-college, Jiya rented a small studio apartment that, though small, was large enough to accommodate all of her requirements. It was her house, party place, and work studio. She worked another two years assisting other photographers and taking freelance gigs before she had enough savings to open her own setup. Most importantly, she now had sufficient contacts and assignments to keep her afloat for a year. Luckily, she has never had to look back. It was still not luck; she had simply refused to give up.

Her latest obsession was the man she had seen in the pool. While she had dated a few guys during her twenties, none of her relationships had lasted over a year. The simple reason was that no one understood her passion and the drive that she had towards her job. Most of them considered her crazy or not ready for a relationship. After her fourth breakup at the age of twenty-eight, Jiya knew that relationships were not meant for her.

Jiya had met her first boyfriend in school at the age of fifteen. They both got together sometime before their tenth-class board exams but broke up before their twelfth-class board exams. Their relationship seemed to be taken out from the pages of some teenage romance novel that she had then so often read. Her boyfriend, whom she believed was going to be the only man in her life, had constantly complained of her being negligent of him. He had broken up with her abruptly, arrogantly thinking that she would return to him apologizing. But before she even realized it, she was over the relationship. Her internships, freelance work, and exams kept her quite occupied and happy.

The second time that Jiya had felt a tinge in her stomach created by fluttering butterflies was at the age of twenty-two when a handsome and upcoming model had asked her out. She was working as an assistant to one of the big photographers at that time. He took her around the streets of Europe every day for three weeks while they were shooting together. It was also with this boyfriend that she had made love for the first time. Things had felt so right. Everything was perfect. Jiya could not even remember feeling anything remotely close to how she felt for the model. She had dismissed her first relationship as nothing more than a desperate attempt to be popular in school. This was the real thing. The model made her feel cherished and cared for. It was all perfect until the three weeks lasted. Once they were back in Mumbai, the two became busy with their lives and saw less and less of each other. The few moments that they did get to spend with each other were either consumed in having meaningless sex or complaining to each other. In under four months of beginning their courtship, Jiya found out that the model was dating two other women at the same time. When she confronted him about the same, he asked her to make other boyfriends if she liked and added that this is how things worked in his world. Silently, Jiya turned and never saw the man again. The butterflies in her stomach had turned into worms that were eating her alive from the inside. Every day was more difficult than the previous one. She kept herself immersed in work—giving up on men.

While Jiya did not believe she would find love again and immersed herself in her work, she met a cute architect. They had been introduced by mutual friends at a house party at twenty-three. The two talked through the night and then for the next few days, realizing that they both felt a connection and attraction towards each other. The guy was a little older than her and had already established his own construction and interior design firm. It was difficult, but he was driven. Jiya had just then gotten out of an internship and was considering opening her own venture. Things were quite exciting on all fronts for the first year. They both found it exciting to sneak off from their busy schedules to meet. But after the first year, things started to become difficult. The guy had pressure from his family to settle down. On meeting with his parents, both of them realized that she did not fit the caricature of the wife he had envisioned for himself. He was looking for a wife who would support him with his work and life. While Jiya was more than happy to be his cheerleader, she never thought of herself as a homemaker. Arguments broke out, first occasionally, then quite frequently. Words were said. And before they both could say it, they knew it was over.

Jiya was already deep in work at this point. She did not have the time or the strength to be involved with anyone else. She refused to get herself set up by any of her friends and declined any advances, not that there were many. Things were working well till she met a director.

He was a year older than her and had studied filmmaking. Currently, he was assisting some of the big directors in Bollywood but has a lot of ideas that he is working on. They met when Jiya was twenty-six. She was mature enough to understand what she did and did not want for herself. Her priorities had been well-defined and clearly chalked out by this time. The director was good with everything. He was very handsome, did not want to rush into anything, his parents were not forcing him to marry, he did not wish to settle before thirty, he understood her work and appreciated her, and the sex was great. It was perfect. They dated for three years, went on two vacations, and even exchanged keys to their apartments. Jiya was happy with him. They did have their fights occasionally, but both prioritized the relationship over petty arguments. After every fight, they took some time off and then came back stronger. She was sure that in a matter of a few years, they both would be married. Life was becoming better than a dream. It was all good until one of their arguments happened right before the director had to leave for an outdoor shoot for a week. To Jiya, this would provide them with the time needed to cool down, and once he was back, things would be back to normal. But things did not return to normal. Coincidentally, he met with the executives of a company for which Jiya was shooting the following month. Conversationally, the topic went over to the photographer who was going to handle their upcoming project. In his anger and negligence, he said a lot of words that cost Jiya the biggest contract of her career. It was the opportunity that could have given her international exposure but became the one that made her take several small assignments just to scrape by. It was a mistake, but it was a mistake that she could not put behind. This was her longest relationship. Once she knew that she was not able to make a home with the director, Jiya was sure she would find no other person for her.

She never felt the giddy feelings she had often heard other girls discuss nor felt the need to be by someone at all hours. Her work, her studio, and occasionally her parents—this kept her life going. There was no requirement for any drama. Of course, this excludes all the harmless flirting and the rare picking up of a guy from a bar to relax and rejuvenate after a long and hectic shoot. She had been on a secretly 'Only Benefits' policy for some time, and it was working well for her.

It was probably the first time that Jiya felt the need to speak to someone and to know him. As her passion for her work grew, she found most of her friends settling down to have their families and others becoming her competitors. Her mother had often asked her about her friends, and every time, she had given generic answers. The man had been different. He was handsome—he was freakishly handsome! And Jiya wanted to keep him around. But she wanted much more than just benefits—for once, she wanted to be friends. However, she was too proud to accept it. To her, it was no different than meeting a guy in Goa, having a good time, and saying farewell on the last day, never to meet again. This was a tourist spot as well, after all!

She pulled on her plain white crop top and blue high-waist jeans. Completing her look with a metallic belt, a long, grey shrug, a light blue scarf, and heeled boots, she set out towards the reception. She was going to find the man, no matter what it took. The quickest way was through the reception. She could simply describe him, and someone might just help her, or she could look for the housekeeping staff who had ushered the man out of the pool. He would surely know. And when nothing worked, an offer to include her in the shoot as an extra model or some cash would surely get her a room number. She felt her pockets to ensure she had securely hidden a few hundreds in there.

As Jiya entered the lift, she checked her well-crafted look in the mirrors. One could never go wrong with a white top and blue denim jeans. This look had survived centuries and was sure to stay in fashion till the end of time. This was not a look that Jiya would ever get to shoot, as the fashion industry's idea of fashion was nowhere near to the clothes that people could actually wear. However, the man was more mature. He did not look like the kind to care for the skin show or the high slits. It would be a good move to meet him in a look that he would find attractive.

Touching up the lip balm through the reflection on the metallic interiors on the left, Jiya walked out into the lobby. She was looking frantically around for directions when she spotted the golden signs telling her the way to the 'Reception,' 'Lift,' 'Swimming Pool,' 'Bar,'" and 'Restaurant.'. He could be at the bar! Jiya made a mental note. The man would have to be rich to afford to stay at the hotel, and one would find rich, middle-aged guys in bars during most evenings. As she checked the direction signs again, the glimmer of light moved across the golden backdrop. Someone passed behind her. She moved in the opposite direction, towards the reception, thinking of how to approach her unusual request, when her brain told her to turn back.

Jiya turned back to register the head of a man going out of sight, behind a wall, as he turned left on the other corner. She turned back just as soon as she had turned and resumed walking towards the reception when she stopped again. It was the head of the man she was looking for. She turned back one more time. Her brain had taken too long to identify the man, and he was now gone. A beautiful smile spread across Jiya's face as she realized this was going to be her lucky day, or night, as she rushed in the direction that the man was headed.

ᗽᗽᗽ

The hotel's main restaurant was unusually crowded owing to the large number of guests made up of Jiya's interns, models, and the attendees of the two conferences that had coincided. Rarely would one have a problem finding a table in a large enough restaurant at seven thirty, but today was no other day. Today the restaurant was overcrowded. Jiya stood at the door, scanning and skimming, looking for the man who she believed was somewhere in the room.

The restaurant manager recognized her instantly and came to offer help. He had barely finished greeting her when Jiya raised her hand to stop the man from breaking her concentration and kept scanning the room. Offended less than he was intrigued, the man joined her in her quest, but since he did not know the object of Jiya's search, he was not helpful at all. He waited for a minute before making another attempt at asking her if she was ready to dine. He had already greeted a few others while Jiya kept craning her neck to look around, blocking a few more who were patiently waiting for her to move aside before they could direct their queries to the restaurant manager. Their chatter was making it difficult for Jiya to concentrate. "*317*," she whispered her room number without a single look at the manager or acknowledging his response. With a wave of her hand, she walked away, still looking around. She was certain that she was going to meet that man in the restaurant—she did not know when or could not explain how she knew, yet she knew.

The restaurant was a culinary masterpiece, a grand elliptical expanse, a little more elongated than it was wide, that beckoned guests from all over the country and even internationally. The menu was wittily crafted for people with refined tastes and aimed to provide a unique, opulent, and vintage ambience for a hard-to-forget culinary experience. Stepping into the dining space was a stimulating experience for all the senses—the mulberry circular expanse, intricately adorned with gold-patterned curtains and copper and brass statues, was the perfect contrast against the tasteful and colourful array of dishes stocked in the centre.

The interior exuded a timeless charm, with muted vintage tones reflected through the numerous rich canvases adorning the high walls, illuminated with ambient lighting casting a soft, inviting glow. The magnificent chandelier in the centre of the room cast a warm light all over. Its length filled the entire height of the room barring the seven feet distance from the ground, allowing the sparkle from its multi-faceted crystals to give the desserts underneath an additional shimmer. Rich mahogany furnishings, complemented by golden accents, added a touch of regality to the setting. The elliptical layout unfolded a grand spectacle, with tables spread three-fourths of the expanse and food emanating from the centre and expanding to the remainder of the room, ensuring that every guest was treated to an intimate yet expansive dining experience.

Tables of varying capacities adorned with fine vintage scarlet-coloured linens were strategically arranged along the perimeter in multiple rows, enabling people to enjoy a private dining experience and allowing ample passage for movement. The air, heavy with the tantalizing aroma of spices and the tunes of the soft jazz played by a live performer, beckoned the approval of even the most difficult people to please.

The attached rectangular outside dining area contrasted with the interiors. It was a simple white-walled and brown-tiled expanse, with no adornments but a breathtaking view of the city and the nearby hills.

Jiya did not have time for any of the above. She had heard her interns discussing these while perusing the hotel's pictures on the internet during their nearly three-hour journey to the hotel. She navigated through the restaurant oblivious to the chandelier, the rich warm tones of the linen, and the hums of the conversations combined with the frequent clink of cutlery or the soft music. On an ordinary day, she would have been very interested in all the details—after all, this was a perfect example of a place that could be, with very little effort, converted into a beautiful backdrop. She would have, normally, taken inspiration from it and made mental notes to use during any of her future assignments. But her current desire was as far from her work as possible. She did not notice two of her interns who had rushed to meet her. They believed that she had come looking for them, but Jiya crossed past them without even a glance.

Her presence in the restaurant was quite unusual. Her presence in the hotel had been unusual in itself. Jiya had a reputation for either being behind her camera or being at parties. Today, she had already surprised everyone by choosing to step away from behind the camera, and now, she was in the hotel's family restaurant for a very early dinner. Her interns, amazed to find her suddenly asking them to complete the assignment, had split into two groups—the first group was still finishing the shoot, and the second group was going to burn some midnight oil to review the work. These two interns were part of the second group and immediately raised an alarm about their queen's unusual evening activities.

Jiya wordlessly kept looking for the man. She moved graciously between the stacked tables, carefully scanning the people. She chided herself for not paying attention to any more details about him. She had only managed to look into his deep brown eyes. If she were tasked with finding the man from a lineup of blindfolded guys, she doubted if she would be able to with absolute surety.

Three of the models, who were finished shooting for the day, had spotted her in the restaurant and walked over to greet her. Jiya did not hear them call out to her—not only was she focused entirely on a different thing, but the models spoke quite softly, and the noise of the restaurant made it difficult for anyone to listen to them. When a model came and stood right in front of her, did Jiya notice her? Even then, it took her some time to bring her focus onto the person standing in front of her. The Model. Not important.

"Why don't you join us, Jiya?" The model spoke in an extremely sweet voice. Do they all sound this fake? Jiya thought to herself. Unfortunately, she could not remember the name, let alone the voice, of any other person on the planet. Jiya looked on both sides, desperately looking for a reason to excuse herself. She spotted two of her interns standing a foot away. She called them and asked them to take care of whatever the models were asking of her. She watched the disgruntled models leave without a word.

As she watched the three women leave, she noticed how heavy her feet were feeling. She had been in the restaurant for less than fifteen minutes, but the smartwatch on her wrist was asking if she was doing some workout with all the moving around. For a moment, Jiya considered taking a seat herself—the man might not be an early diner. She was not sure how long she would have to wait. There was a chance that he might have already left. Either way, the food did look tempting.

While she had no alternative but to wait, she decided to multitask and took a plate. Lost in her own thoughts, with the plate resting on both her hands, Jiya made her way towards the restaurant bar. She closed her eyes for a moment longer than a blink to relive a few moments from the afternoon. She needed a gentle reminder of the prize she had been looking for.

And then a lot of these things happened at the same time. Jiya closed her eyes for hardly over a second, but that was enough to look at the image of the man that had been embedded in her mind. Just as Jiya had been smiling, lost in her thoughts while walking through the restaurant, she bumped into a man emerging from behind a counter. The impact from the collision made Jiya lose her balance, drop the plate, and made her stumble backwards. The man grabbed Jiya's outstretched arms and pulled her close. The sudden movement caused several pieces of raw salad to fly around from the man's plate, and cut vegetables and leaves landed on both of their hair and clothes. Jiya did not open her eyes until she was sure that she was not going to fall. When she did open her eyes, she saw the man she had been looking for was the one who was standing close to her, supporting her still slightly bent body. Her smile broadened to a grin.

Time froze. The man gave his plate to a waiting staff member who had rushed to help them. He caught hold of her right shoulder with his strong left hand. Jiya could feel a ripple of warmth spread across her entire body, starting with her right shoulder as the focal point. Their eyes locked for the second time that day. They both stood there, holding onto each other. The chatter had subsided, and even the live performance halted for a minute as the loud sound of the collision echoed. The other guests and staff looked at the two, unsure if they needed any help. At this moment, however, Jiya could not help but notice the man's impeccable attire—a full-sleeve off-white shirt with sleeves folded up to his elbows to reveal his sturdy and muscular forearms, paired with a muted earthy shade of midnight blue-coloured waistcoat and matching pants. He wore a deep blue tie. The entire outfit complemented his complexion quite well. Rather, Jiya could not help but think that there would hardly be a shade that would not complement the man. He was perfect. His deep brown eyes, contrasting with his clothes, showed no inclination to break their connection.

As Jiya's eyes scanned the rest of the man's face to her heart's content and with the increasing chatter as people found their non-verbal encounter less interesting with every passing minute, the effects of the spell reduced. A playful salad leaf had found its way onto Chirag's handsome face. Jiya delicately raised her right thumb and index finger and plucked the leaf away from his forehead, her touch fleeting yet tinged with a subtle intimacy. She could feel her heart beat a thousand times faster as her fingers brushed against his skin. The man must have felt something as well, as he released the hold on Jiya's arm. She held the finger in front of him, assuring him of no ill intentions. He smiled, mirroring Jiya's broad grin, creating a lightness in the air that broke all inhibitions and awkwardness between the two.

They both straightened up and found themselves to be the object of amusement to the hotel staff, still waiting to help them, and the several guests, who were being blocked by the couple. Jiya's interns stood right behind the man, close enough to be by her side in under a second, yet hidden behind the conveniently tall man to avoid being shouted at. The models even stood up from their table to get a better view of the two. Several men in two-piece and three-piece suits were surrounding them. They looked like people who might be waiting for the man. It did not matter. The man seemed to be in no hurry. Neither was Jiya. She noticed the haphazard amalgamation of different items on the plate he had kept to the side, salad along with some baked beans and jalebis. All of them had no natural affinity but came together in a beautiful harmony of colours, and even though Jiya would never want to taste it, she found it quite alluring.

"I am sorry about the mess" she said apologetically to the man. One of the men, dressed neatly in a three-piece suit, who had been mere spectators till now, pulled out a large handkerchief from his coat pocket and handed it out to the man. Jiya beamed as she took the handkerchief from the other man, leaving him quite shocked at the fluidity and authority of her actions. She wiped her own face, with

the man smiling at her, before removing the pieces of his face and hair.

The two of them had still not taken their eyes off each other. An invisible force kept them rooted to their spot while another force obliviated their surroundings. While they were no longer a sight interesting enough for the majority of guests, they were causing enough blockage in the passage. A few people at faraway tables had started to stand to get a better glimpse of the holdup near the salad counter. The hotel staff, in distress, was trying to help them clear up but were being restricted by the invisible barrier. The staff was also concerned on account of the two most unlikely people to be together in the collision and did not want either to find a reason to discontinue their stay in the hotel. People who did actually know either one of the pair stood aghast with shock.

The man was the first to become aware of the curious and eager glances fixed on him. He, with neither a desire to be the centre of attention nor the intention to make this encounter any longer, stepped aside. Jiya, who had been cleaning his hands now, sensed his unease as he pulled his hand away. She looked around, rolled her eyes, and let out a perfectly audible sigh. Couldn't you just give us a break? She thought, barely able to keep herself from speaking the words aloud. The man seemed to be politely excusing himself out of the frame. Now that she had finally found him, there was no way that she was going to let him disappear.

Pushing the handkerchief back into the hands of a curious onlooker, who was shocked at being handed something, she held out her right hand, now perfectly clean, and introduced herself, *"Hi, my name is Jiya. Jiya Thakkar. I am a professional photographer, mainly into portfolios and fashion shows. You might have seen some of my work."*

Jiya found herself at a loss for words—not only was she still mesmerized by the man, feeling unusual emotions at being in close proximity to him, but she had not had to introduce herself in a long time. Most people she had met in the last few years were either people seeking to work with her or had done their basic share of research on her before the meeting. The rest comprised random strangers she met in bars or her relatives, neither caring for her profession.

Her smile extended all the way to her eyes as she patiently waited for the man's name. He, who had not expected this sudden turn of events, was taken aback and could not think of the best response to Jiya's move. Jiya could hear his brain churn out thoughts one after the other. She had always found it amusing to observe people. Most people liked to show off—they would introduce themselves to portray them in a better light. This man, however, was different. He sure was taken aback by Jiya's sudden gesture, but his face did not lose the smile that had already melted Jiya's heart, and neither did he take a step back. He stood there, weighing his words.

Finally, he extended his hand and said, "*Chirag Kapoor. Nice to make your acquaintance. And I should apologize for -*" He paused for a moment, looking around at the evidence of their collision. He let out a sigh and continued, "*Well, for the inconvenience, I should have been careful.*" Gently, he held Jiya's extended hand, gave it a firm shake, and released it immediately. Waves of warm emotions, as she had previously felt, raced through every nerve in Jiya's body. She heard the words in the man's deep voice but could not make any meaning out of them. The voice was as magical as the eyes—deep and melodious. He was a soft-spoken person, but his voice reverberated with authority.

Even as the man released her hand from his, Jiya's hand remained suspended in midair. She felt the remaining tingling sensations weaken. She was determined to take as many details about the man as possible. Her eyes were gazing fondly into his. Her ears strained to catch more of his calming voice. Her nose was smelling his perfect cologne that, she knew, was now her favourite smell. And she could not wait to taste the unusual combination of items on the man's plate.

The man was still speaking something. By the few words that she managed to catch, he was asking her whether she was hurt. Or so she comprehended as he kept pointing to the debris of the broken china scattered on their feet.

"*I am perfectly fine*" she assured the man. And before she realized it, she had placed a reassuring hand on his arm.

She saw the man look toward where Jiya's hand touched his arm. Conscious of not freaking him out, she picked up his plate from the adjoining counter and handed it to him.

The man was a bit confused. A person from the housekeeping staff had come with all the cleaning mops and was waiting for them to move aside. As he had not witnessed any of the previous moments, he was as alien to the activities as could be, and the additional hold-up did not amuse him. The man took the lead as Jiya stepped aside to allow the housekeeping staff to clean. After a few paces, he asked where she was seated. Oblivious to the models, waving frantically to capture her attention, Jiya replied, "*Wherever you are sitting.*"

FOUR

Chirag had met several interesting people in his career, but the girl in front of him, Jiya, had managed to amaze him more than he was willing to accept. The moment he had properly seen her walking through the restaurant, he knew she was the same girl who was holding the camera by the poolside. Something about her had caught his attention then; he had been so caught up in following her that he got careless and collided with her.

They had had another silent yet beautiful encounter. Something about her had made him speechless every time he had found himself close to her. And now as she walked by his side, he was finding it still difficult to talk. He was not sure if he had heard her correctly and asked again politely if he could escort her to her table. When Jiya beamed and repeated that she was going to have dinner with him, he had no alternative but to comply. He usually dined alone—unless you counted his several assistants who occupied the nearby tables. Though he could not help but feel happy to be in her company, he did not care to express it out loud. However, unlike him, she seemed not to care for the onlookers.

Once they reached the table, Chirag kept his plate and pulled out the opposite chair for Jiya. Jiya's eyes lit up at his gesture. Ensuring that she was comfortable, he took his own seat across the small table. It had been a long time since he had shared his meal with anyone who was not a business associate. The experience was refreshing and slightly frightening. He realized that he was happy for no other reason but to have someone to share his meal with.

It was a small table, designed to seat two people only. Once the hustle of settling down died, Chirag grew conscious again. Apart from his assistants, who had seated themselves at a little distance, he could not see anyone else interested in the two of them. However, he was sure that the gossip would carry out from the restaurant and flow into all the rooms before the end of the day. He kept glancing at his table, stealing looks at Jiya, who had been constantly looking at him. Chirag had no clue about the next steps. His brain was constantly chiding him for not knowing something so simple. He had forgotten how to share a meal. Despite trying, he could not think of anything to do other than stare at his plate.

A waiter swiftly walked in to save them from the awkwardness and placed a plate in front of Jiya. Not wanting to create another scene, or avoid another hold-up, the waiter returned almost immediately with a plate full of different kinds of salads to their table. Chirag smiled as Jiya took generous helpings from the tray. He slowly picked up his fork and started eating the remainder of the items from his plate. Over the last two decades, Chirag has travelled to every continent and most countries. He had met people from different and diverse backgrounds. He had spent days in places where everyone spoke a foreign language. Most of his travels mandated him to accompany a translator. And once, he had had a very amusing encounter with the children in Africa who did not understand his language, and he did not understand theirs; yet, somehow, they had all managed to play a jumping game together. And here, sitting across from a girl who looked absolutely beautiful, extroverted, and spoke the same language as him, he had no idea what to speak. He forced himself to keep his focus on the plate.

After all the beans on his plate were finished, he could not help but sneak a look. To his astonishment, Jiya had not touched her food at all. Rather, her elbow was placed on the table, her palm supporting her head. She was looking at him with all her attention. He could not help but notice her eyes were sparkling and there was a warm smile on her face. For a moment, he got lost in the sparkle of those hazel eyes. The girl was extremely beautiful. Apart from being physically beautiful, he noticed that she radiated warmth and glow from within. This was something he had observed over the years—people with a good heart radiated with warmth from within. He could not explain the reason behind this, but he just knew that she was a good person. The aura around her was of a go-getter and an authoritative person. But underneath all the façade, she was an extremely simple person.

Realizing that he had been again captured by her mesmerizing presence, Chirag focused back on his now empty plate. Several members of his team, who were travelling with him, were staring at him in shock.

"*Is there something on my face?*" Chirag asked politely as he put down the fork and picked the napkin to his face. It could be a simple reason that made everyone stare at him. Chirag looked around once more. His team members turned away slightly after getting a look from him. He returned his attention back to Jiya, and she simply shook her head.

Damn. She is so beautiful and cute. He would lie if he were to deny the strong urge he felt to talk to the girl, but the voice in his mind constantly kept making him look away. He kept making arguments against himself sometimes winning and sometimes losing. Chirag could not believe that there was a second voice inside his head. He had either never heard it before or had forgotten how it sounded. Lately, all his words and thoughts had been for his work. He did not understand what was wrong with meeting someone and liking them. He could do with a friend.

Allowing the original voice in his head to take control, he forced himself to do anything but look back into the girl's eyes.

"*Are you not hungry?*" he asked. The untouched plate in front of the girl seemed like the perfect excuse to look away from the girl to her plate and then to his plate.

Jiya shook her head for a second time as she pushed the plate away from herself. Her smile was briefly replaced by a cute face showing her dislike of salads.

"*Do you need anything else?*" Without realizing it, Chirag raised his hand to summon a waiter. He did not even realize that he had placed the fork down on his plate, and all his attempts to avoid the girl had been in vain. He was concerned about her food. The second voice in his brain was all that was left, and he knew it was right—he had a chance to meet a new person and make a friend. He was not going to let the opportunity go.

As a waiter walked over to their table, Jiya straightened up, looked away from him for the first time, and recited a long list of dishes that she would like served. Chirag sat on his chair, transfixed at her transformation. With every gesture of hers, every head tilt, every hair flick, and every word that she said, he felt the connection deepen. It had been a while since he had seen anyone be excited about food, and the way Jiya was asking questions and placing orders, he could tell that she was someone who enjoyed food. Occasionally she would turn to him to ask if he was fine with some item. Chirag would merely nod.

"*I am sorry. I guess I am just not a salad person.*" Jiya exclaimed after the waiter left. Picking the two plates with both her hands, she added, "*And it would be rude to not share the dishes with me. So, I guess we do not need this.*" She stacked the plates in the corner for the waiter to clear.

The two sat there, facing each other, without any distractions and with a world full of topics to share with one another. Jiya was the more talkative of the two. She asked him all sorts of questions about his favourite foods, salads, sauces, and so much more. Chirag was quite pleased to be interrogated. He kept answering her, and she proved to be a very patient listener. She would allow him to complete and then add her answer to ask a follow-up question.

Over the wide range of assorted appetizers, Chirag got to know a lot of her likes. Jiya was a non-vegetarian, though she did not enjoy it so much. It was more of an occupational choice than a preference, as she had to travel a lot for her work, and vegetarian food was difficult to find. There were a few years when she enjoyed alcoholic drinks a lot. Not anymore. A glass of wine or a freshly prepared sangria was all she would need at parties. And even after eating at some of the best restaurants all over the world, her go-to food was Spicy Garlic Chow Mein and Diet Coke from a Chinese takeaway food truck near her studio. Her favourite dish was probably Butter Chicken Masala or Dal Makhani—she could not ever pick between the two and Laccha Parantha. The dish she ate most was eggs, as that was the only food she knew to cook, courtesy of the egg boiler she was gifted by a friend.

The surprising bit was that Chirag did not know all these things about himself either. When Jiya asked him, did he think about what he liked and what he enjoyed. During his younger days, he had frequented a burger-selling chain. He enjoyed their vegetarian burger. However, he had not visited any of their outlets for years. Before that, he enjoyed his home-cooked meals. Now, he probably just liked his salads, considering he ate them the most. He was a vegetarian by choice. It started as a bet in college when he wanted to prove to his friends that vegetarians had as many, if not more, options as the non-vegetarians. It turned out that he had never agreed on the expiry date for the bet, and it had simply continued over the years. He could cook a lot of vegetarian curries, rice, and rotis. Chirag paused for a moment. There had been a time when he used to cook for his daughter. Even that had not happened in a long time. Now, as most of his meals were just for himself, he asked the chef to cook everything at once, and he could eat it in appropriate portions throughout the day.

Luckily for him, the main course arrived just then. Jiya had ordered mostly vegetarian options with the exception of Fried Fish Curry and Chicken Masala Tikka. As the waiter placed the dish on the table, Jiya picked it up to return it.

"*I can be a vegetarian by choice too.*" She added with a wink, looking at Chirag. Just as he heard her words, Chirag reached out, grabbed her hand, pulled it back, and shook his head.

Jiya turned back with mild surprise in her eyes at his bold action. He was not sure what made him do it either. Instinctively he released her hand and apologized. "*Sorry. You should eat it. Do not change yourself for anyone. You are too good, and no one is worth changing yourself for."*

Chirag was not sure what had made him grab Jiya's hand. Or speak those words. For a few seconds, he could not believe he had done either of the two. He looked at her with mild embarrassment in his eyes. Jiya's hand was again stuck in midair, just where Chirag had released it. She probably understood his hesitation and blinked to assure him that it was right. Her slow wink was accompanied by the warm smile that Chirag had now gotten used to.

"What if I want to bring the change?" she asked, adding lightness to the moment.

He smiled back, relieved that the tension had broken. *"Would it matter if I insisted?"* he added in a playful tone. Even as he felt his lips move and his larynx vibrate to say the words, he could not believe his daring. He had never been this candid to anyone in his life. Rather, he had no idea that he was capable of being this person. The girl was having a deep impact on him.

Jiya picked up the dish with both her hands and placed it in front of her. Her eyes lit up with mischief as she pushed the vegetarian items towards him. Letting out a fake and loud enough sigh, she said, *"Looks like someone will have to finish all the vegetarian curries by himself."*

▷▷▷

Their meal was extended for over three hours. Neither of them was in a rush. Both relished every morsel they ate, every word they said, and every moment in each other's company.

People after people came in to occupy the nearby tables, had their dinner, and left. Nothing bothered them. Jiya was explicit about what she wanted and did not shy away from voicing it. Chirag could never believe he had finished the enormous amounts of dishes that she had ordered. The food had been extremely good—he wasn't sure if it was the preparation or the company. Chirag's assistants hung around for some time, unsure of how to proceed in this foreign situation. When over an hour had passed, one of them approached the table to talk to Chirag. It was his routine to review the files for the following day before retiring to bed around nine every night. He would wake up early the following morning, go for a long walk, and then begin his day by eight in the morning.

However, Chirag seemed to have forgotten all about his routine. Chirag's senior assistant approached the table and greeted the two. He had clearly intervened in some important discussions. It took Jiya and Chirag a second to focus their attention on the man standing close to Chirag with an iPad in his hand. Before he could speak, however, Jiya cut him off.

"*Hi. My name is Jiya.*" She extended her hand to shake his. The man had not expected this. He looked at the outstretched hand, dumbstruck. Unsure what he needed to do, he turned to his boss for instructions. Chirag smiled, bemused at his senior assistant's expressions, thinking if he had given the same expressions when Jiya had introduced herself to him.

The senior assistant had known him the longest. He had joined Chirag's logistics business as a junior analyst. But had shown great skill and interest in understanding the business. Chirag had noticed the young man right from his first year at the firm. After five years of operations, when Chirag's business had spread to several other countries, he decided he needed help to meet the ever-increasing demands of his time. He handpicked ten long-serving employees from his office who had shown the character, morals, and attitude to grow. He called this team his '*assistants*'. Their titles were largely misgiving. These men had been his trusted advisors and, in most cases, had taken decisions on his behalf—decisions Chirag believed he could not have taken better.

In return, Chirag had not let them down from his end either. He respected their counsel and made sure to share his thoughts and thought process with them before making any crucial decision. He took an interest in their lives and was elated to be a part of their extended families, while they were his family.

Some of his assistants had been strategically promoted to head country operations in the new countries where his business was expanding.

However, his senior assistant had chosen to willingly stay with Chirag. Having been with him for a long time, he had mirrored Chirag's thoughts and actions the most. Rather, on several occasions, a few of the employees were more scared of his decisions than Chirag's. Others would try convincing the senior assistant of an idea before taking it to Chirag, as it was always sure to get acceptance from Chirag if the senior assistant approved.

The interaction between the two extremely different people was quite amusing. At this point in their dinner, Chirag had become a veteran at expecting the unexpected from Jiya. Rather, anything remotely normal had lost its charm. And he knew his senior assistant well enough as well. He was the exact definition of an introvert. Rather, it was amusing to see his expression seeing the unexpected handshake invitation from a complete stranger. Chirag nudged his head, suppressing all his desires to burst into a hearty giggle, encouraging his senior assistant to shake Jiya's hand.

Slyly, he extended his hand, which Jiya grabbed and shook firmly. This was a brief and unwilling handshake. It was awkward at all stages and ended as abruptly as it started. The assistant pulled back his hand as if he received some form of shock emitting from Jiya's hand. Jiya and Chirag exchanged looks and giggled. They had both seen the senior assistant flinch as he pulled back his hand. Controlling her smile, Jiya turned back to the assistant and said, *"I am sure you have some urgent work to share with your sir."* She stressed the last word, giving a chuckle in Chirag's direction.

The senior assistant nodded, *"Chirag sir."* He started to address Chirag, but was cut again.

"Yes, Chirag sir is on his personal time right now. And I recommend you do that too. I promise he will not bother you for the day. And I also promise that I will personally make sure that your Chirag sir reaches his room safely." Jiya cut short the man with her monologue in a single breath. She kept stealing glances towards Chirag at the right moments for a dramatic effect.

For several years that Chirag was running his businesses, he had been the sole person issuing instructions. He liked to review all the files personally and kept on top of things. Even with a vast staff to support the different operations, Chirag liked to be involved. He trusted his people, but it had become more of a habit than a need to pick up a file from any desk and start working on it. He knew his assistant would never take instructions from Jiya. But he was enjoying getting bossed by someone, for a change.

"*Go on. I will see you in the morning.*" He said, adding weight to her words.

The senior assistant nodded, hiding his surprise, which would definitely be there, wished them both goodnight and turned to leave. Chirag watched as he dismissed the other assistants and all of them left quite reluctantly.

"*And now time to dismiss mine,*" Jiya spoke to Chirag. It was the first time during the evening that his attention was divided. His mind raced through the files that he had read not so long ago. For some reason, he could not recall everything that he had been working on. He tried his best to remember if there was anything urgent that his senior assistant might have wanted to discuss. His focus was brought back as Jiya spoke suddenly. He saw her pull out her phone from her jeans pocket. Still smiling at him, she dialled a number and allowed it to ring two times before cutting the call.

Before she had replaced the phone back in her pocket, a group of five young individuals arrived at their table. Unlike his assistants, they were all wearing jeans and tops. Two of them were wearing ripped jeans. Only one of them had shoes on; the rest were in sandals. All of them had coloured their hair to varying levels and supported multiple earrings—even the boys.

"*Stop wasting the memory stick on clicking my pictures. Rather, go edit the ones from today's shoot. I hope there are at least a hundred good ones.*" She addressed the group, staring at each one of them in turn. Her voice had a no-nonsense and commanding tone. Chirag chuckled, thinking how scared her interns looked.

She dismissed them with a flick of her hand. As they returned to the outdoor seating area, he noticed that they joined a few others, who indeed were holding cameras and appeared to have been clicking the two of them. Chirag could not comprehend how Jiya had managed to notice their actions without looking at them.

"*So where were we?*" Jiya asked, bringing him back to their conversation.

The two were left undisturbed for the remainder of the hours, except for the occasional visit from the waiting staff to clear some dishes. Jiya had ordered a variety of her favourite desserts that she insisted Chirag try.

For every dish that Jiya had ordered that evening, she had insisted on adding her own personal touch. She had added lemon juice to some of the curries, Italian seasoning to his Dal Makhani and lavash crumbs to the ice cream before adding a hot Gulab Jamun.

While Chirag had not been experimental with his food before, he had thoroughly enjoyed each of the combinations that she served him. He was not sure if it was Jiya's special ingredients or Jiya herself, who had made them all a delight for the tongue. He could not remember enjoying and relishing food this much before.

It was undoubtedly the best and the most food that Chirag had ever had. He had completely forgotten about the lonely jalebi that had been hidden partially by the baked beans on the plate that he had placed on the table and was cleared by the waiting staff more than two hours previously. He could not remember eating so much food, having so much conversation over food, or discovering himself. Unsure where he got his appetite from, he was still glad. Maybe the appetite had always been there, waiting to be accompanied by good food, conversation, and emotions.

FIVE

Jiya had not been able to take her eyes off Chirag. Thanks to the other man who had come with his iPad and called out his name; else she might have never found out his name. It would have been embarrassing to admit that she had not heard a word when they had introduced themselves shortly after they had collided. That seemed like ages ago. A lot has happened since then. The Earth had spun a lot and moved further along its orbit, and Jiya had gotten to know so much about the man—about Chirag.

The last few hours had been surreal. Jiya and Chirag remained in the restaurant till they noticed that most of the tables were vacant and the few occupied ones were taken by the hotel staff. While their stomachs were full, their hearts yearned for more—not food, but words and each other's company. On the pretext of digesting a bit of the excess food they had consumed, Jiya proposed to take a walk by the swimming pool.

Chirag got up, as if on cue, and just like the perfect gentleman that he was, rushed to pull her chair as she got up. The waiting staff tending to their table emerged out of nowhere with Chirag's coat. Placing the folded coat over her left forearm, leaving a generous tip for the man who had tirelessly made several tours to and from the kitchen to get their food, he escorted Jiya outside the restaurant. She had taken off her scarf and left it loose around her shoulders. The two of them were getting more comfortable with each other with every minute. The proximity was no longer sending ripples down their body but giving them a sense of belonging.

Jiya admired Chirag without even looking at him. The way he stood by her side to let her get up, tipped the waiter, held the door for Jiya to pass through, conversed with the evening manager, and shared the adorable laughter that he had shared with Jiya several times over the meal had won her heart. She was a step behind him as they exited the lift onto the lobby; Chirag exited the lift and stepped aside to let Jiya lead the way. This small gesture melted her heart completely.

While several people would talk about equality and woman empowerment, very few imbibed the sentiment in their behaviour and actions. All the men that Jiya had been within the past had never understood her competitive spirit. They often told her to slow down or improve in some aspects. Even the men who sang of their support for feminism had never treated her with the care that Chirag had shown. Her competitive spirit was often seen as the excuse men gave to not treat her like a lady. And then there was Chirag. He allowed her to hijack his meal and was happy to go outside his comfort zone to make her feel comfortable.

She was not just happy but blessed to have met him.

▷▷▷

Now that they were outside the confines of the posh restaurant and away from the tempting aroma, they realized that there was so much more to know about one another. Jiya was restless. As much as she wanted to tell Chirag everything, she wanted to keep hearing from him. She asked him about his business, and Chirag started on about his new venture and the things he was planning on to expand his business. Jiya kept asking questions. She was genuinely interested in everything he did. While she did not have expert knowledge in a lot of the topics he said, she could sense that he was quite good at what he did. She kept asking even the most basic questions, and Chirag would always smile and explain to her with a lot of patience. The way he spoke and explained things in intrinsic detail told a lot about his attention to detail, love for his work, and experience of his years.

The two of them had stopped pacing and sat on the chairs by the poolside. Despite the original temptation of digesting some food, the moment they got up, they realized that they had overdone overeating. Neither of them wanted to walk. Chirag rested against the recliner, with his feet up on the chair, while Jiya sat on the edge of a chair, facing Chirag. And when Chirag stopped speaking, they sat there, basking in the silent moonlight for several minutes. It was not a full moon night; there were a few insects around, and there was hardly any wind—it was the best night possible.

Suddenly, Chirag turned around, opened his eyes, and looked at Jiya. "*So,*" he asked in an inquiring manner. Jiya looked back into his deep brown eyes, not daring to blink. They had travelled an entire circle. From staring at each other by the poolside as strangers to staring back at each other while eager to share their worlds, things could not have been complete in a truer sense.

"*Your turn to amaze me,*" Chirag added in a playful tone. He looked stunned even speaking the words. But Jiya decided to take it a little further. She stood up, playfully knocked the scarf off her shoulders, and pulled her phone from her jeans pocket. She took a seat next to him on the same recliner, causing him to instinctively move backwards.

Both of them laughed before she started showing him some of the pictures that she had captured on her phone. These included photographs she had taken from her last internship. Of course, most pictures on her phone were not part of the professional portfolios but ones she had captured as a hobby. These photographs, which she had captured when she was not under any deadlines or worries, she believed, were some of the best works that she had ever done. While showing the photographs, Jiya was also showing him glimpses of her past.

She had not had such a meaningful connection with anyone in a long time. The last she remembered showing these photographs was her first assistant, who was still a good friend. Rather, she had not even shown these photographs to three of her boyfriends. She met her first boyfriend in college. When she shared with him her passion for photography and shared some of the photographs she had captured, he acknowledged that they were good, but photography was a hobby and not a profession. That memory had prevented her from sharing her work with the rest of her boyfriends. Her colleagues and clients could see her professional portfolio and her personal connections rarely had any interest.

Chirag had taken the phone from Jiya and was scrolling through the images. He spent a few minutes on every image, listening to Jiya's anecdote on the same, before moving to the next. Sometimes he would scroll back to the previous image, looking at some minor detail or asking a question. He did not give her a compliment, but he was extremely interested. Jiya could tell that he, too, shared a love for the craft, as he knew some jargon and techniques. He enjoyed asking questions, and she loved answering them.

Once he had gone through all the photographs at least twice, he looked up from the screen. Jiya was delighted to see the appreciation on his face. With all the words in the world, one could not express as he had done with his simple smile and excited eyes. "I have seen a lot of photographs, but you are a natural."

Jiya beamed while taking her phone back from Chirag and thrusting it down her pocket. For a few minutes, she found herself experiencing what others called blushing. Her cheeks felt hot, and she could not look Chirag in the eyes.

Chirag sat down properly now. His face was still turned towards Jiya, who was looking the other way, struggling to secure her phone.

"But there is one picture missing." He added quite seriously. Jiya pulled out her phone and started going through the photographs again. It took her a while to realize this was her phone and album. There was no chance Chirag would know which photographs were there and which were not. She looked back at him, but he was not laughing. He was quite serious.

Her smile faded a little as she considered the possibility that he was not playing a prank. Maybe he was serious. *"Which one?"* she asked in an uncertain voice.

"Show me." Chirag extended his hand with an open palm.

Unsure of what was going to follow, Jiya unlocked her phone and placed it in his hands. He took it immediately, swiping a few times, and then before Jiya realized what had happened, a flash shone, illuminating the dark night, before fading away as quickly as it had come.

Chirag turned the phone to show Jiya a candid photograph that he had captured of her. "*This one.*" He added.

There was a reason that Jiya did not like getting clicked. Being a professional photographer, she would find some problem with the photograph someone else would take. Moreover, whenever she clicked selfies or self-portraits or got them clicked by someone else, she would see herself as a shallow person—with fake expressions like the models that she instructed to have. She was as awkward in front of the camera as she was confident behind it. As a result, there were hardly two pictures of herself in her phone memory.

But this photograph was different. Clicked too close to the subject with a majorly dark background and an eerie illumination emanating from the lit swimming pool, the flashlight making her as pale as a ghost, the photograph was perfect. She did not look awkward in it at all. She was relaxed, happy, and a bit quizzical. And the photograph captured it perfectly. She felt the emotions that the photograph conveyed—happy, content, a little goofy, and extremely tired.

Jiya turned the phone in her hands, moved a little closer to Chirag, and clicked a selfie. This photograph was even better. A little shy, Jiya switched off her camera and placed the phone in her jeans pocket, leaning ever so slightly away from him.

Neither of them spoke for some time. The click of the camera had not just captured the moment as a snap but frozen a perfect moment in time forever. It would not matter what would happen the next minute, the next day, or the next week, but the photograph was a witness to the perfect dinner and the perfect moment that they both had shared. Jiya sat there, enjoying his silence just as much as she had enjoyed his words. There was constant background music by the bubbling sound of the pool, the chirping of the crickets, and an occasional note added by some birds at a distance. Other than that, it was silent and perfect.

The truth was that both of them knew it was well over midnight. And they were too tired for words. So far, they had managed to steal a couple of hours away from their work and lives to enjoy each other's company. Even if they stayed awake the whole night, they only had a couple of hours more before they would be forced to get back to their routines. Without a word, both of them wished for the moment to stay forever.

Again, it was Chirag who broke the silence with a solution. He had been in the process of onboarding products from local artisans from Pune and nearby areas to his digital distribution business. Eventually, he would need a photographer to shoot promotional photographs of the new items to be added to the catalogue. Additionally, his marketing team had been sitting on an idea to do some video advertising campaigns. He never felt that he needed the extensive advertising as his businesses were doing well so far, but he wanted to check if Jiya was interested and available the following week.

"I would be back in Delhi on Sunday." His tone was calm and practised—as of a seasoned businessman. And yet it felt so much more than just an assignment. It was the solution. The assignment would take at least two weeks to be shot and approved. If Jiya agreed to take up the assignment, they would get to spend that time together.

Jiya closed her eyes. Several voices were shouting in the back of her mind. She was finding it difficult to differentiate one from the other. She knew that she had a planned shoot. Her assistants were away as well; otherwise they could have managed. But that shoot, she could not remember the details—extremely unlike herself—was with someone important. They would expect her to turn up. What if she finished the shoot sooner? But she had never done a photo campaign for a digital distribution website. She had never even done an advertisement campaign. She would not know where to begin! But she could always learn. She knew some of her former assistants had done that. She could always ask them. But what about the next assignment? If she just took off, her subsequent projects will also get delayed. Did she even know a good studio owner in Delhi?

"Do I see you in Delhi on Monday?" Chirag's enchanting voice broke her train of thought.

"Absolutely." Her voice slipped through her tightly pursed lips and against all the logical instructions of her brain.

ÞÞÞ

They exchanged numbers and official email addresses. Chirag assured her that she would get an official email invitation from his team in a day. He would also ask them to share a draft of the contract that she could edit to suit her requirements. They discussed other plans for the products, the shooting locations, some advertising concepts, the accessories required, and other things. Most of the discussions involved the things Jiya and Chirag would do together. Neither of them was interested in discussing things such as the time required for the shoot or the budget.

Once they were quite satisfied, having discussed a few aspects in detail, Jiya looked at her phone. It was a little over two in the morning. Once more, they became aware of the time passing at a speed faster than they would like it to. Yet they both had a busy day planned. Unable to avoid it further, Jiya offered to escort Chirag to his room.

"Your team might not take kindly to me if I left their boss alone in the middle of the night." They both chuckled at the awkward conversation Jiya had had with the assistant earlier.

As they got up, Chirag instinctively reached for Jiya's scarf to hand it over to her, and Jiya reached for his coat. They both smiled at their attempts to still impress each other when it was evident that they were already smitten. Chirag led the way to his room. On the way, he informed her that he would leave early. Jiya, obviously, had to stay to finish her shoot. She was not sure that she would be able to wake up early to have breakfast, but she promised to see him before he departed. She followed him to the fifth floor but stopped midway. She did not trust herself to walk to the door of his room. It would be either too dramatic or something too rushed. And she wanted neither.

As the two stood at the farewell point, Chirag extended his hand to bid her farewell. "*I will see you in the morning.*" She assured him as she turned to re-enter the lift. Chirag was quite certain that their midnight excursion would surely keep Jiya asleep till late, and he teased her about not being a morning person. Playfully, she snapped her fingers and pointed an index finger as a gesture for him to wait and watch.

Then, without allowing her a lingering look, the doors of the lift shut, taking her to her room on the eleventh floor.

ᔭᔭᔭ

There was just one word to define the evening that Jiya had just lived through—perfect! She reached her room without knowing where she was going or what she was doing. Her mind was lost in the words they had shared. Moments from her long and mesmerizing evening kept playing in her mind. Her left hand secured the phone in her jeans pocket. It had his photograph and number, making it the most valuable item in her possession.

Once in her room, Jiya quickly changed into denim shorts, removed her shrug, scarf, and accessories, and jumped into bed. Checking that her phone was securely placed on the bedside table, she grabbed a pillow tightly, as if hugging the pillow. In her mind, she was hugging Chirag.

Jiya had had a few casual hookups over the years. These, she found, were quite effective in relieving stress without getting into the messy details of a relationship. In the afternoon, when she had seen Chirag for the first time, she had labelled her desire to meet him as another potential hookup. But their meeting had been so different. It was the most meaningful connection she had ever had. She wanted to listen to him, to walk with him, to share food with him, to go swimming with him, to click photographs with him, and to hold him—just hold him and never let go. The thought made her go weak in the knees and gave rise to some sensations in her stomach.

She blushed a little under the layers of blankets and the darkness of the room as she drifted off to a sweet sleep.

SIX

Chirag woke up with a heavy head as his alarm buzzed loudly. He could not recall the reason behind feeling so tired. It took him some time to focus on his surroundings. Finally, he reached out under the pillows and the bedcovers to find his phone—the source of the commotion. Reaching on the bedside table with his other hand, his eyes still out of focus, he searched for his reading glasses. Forty-eight was proving to be a bigger number than he had ever considered it to be. Age was taking its toll. Putting on his glasses, he checked the phone screen. It was six fifteen in the morning. Slowly, the things were coming back to him.

Putting back his glasses on the table and the phone back on the bed, he got out. His head was extremely heavy with less than four hours of sleep, but he was smiling. He remembered Jiya, their evening together, and how she had made him feel. Instinctively, he checked his phone for her contact. It was still there. She had not been a dream or a figment of his imagination. She had been real, and so had been their dinner and conversations together.

For several years, Chirag had followed a monotonous routine. He woke up at around five thirty, switched off his alarm, and then took a morning walk—if he was travelling—or did a workout in his home gym—if he was in Delhi. He would then spend the next three-quarters of the hour getting ready. He would have breakfast between seven and seven thirty and then leave for his office by seven-thirty. Usually, the first hour was dedicated to travelling or catching up on important emails. He knew most people did not start their days as early as he did, and since his afternoons and evenings were packed with calls and meetings, he utilized this time to review all items pending his comments. He utilized the remainder of the morning to prepare for the meetings lined up for the day and brainstorm new ideas. This, Chirag found, was the most productive time of his day.

That was not the case today. Every muscle and every joint in his body ached as he forced himself to walk towards the washroom. There was no time and no strength in him for a walk. His team would be waiting for him for breakfast. For the first time that he could remember, Chirag calculated the time he had. He had a little over an hour to get ready, have breakfast, and leave. And by the speed at which he was moving, he was sure he needed more than an hour just to get ready. And he still needed to do a bit of packing. His late activities the previous night had prevented him from doing the bit before he slept. It was for the first time that he had woken up to find his night clothes on the desk chair and his suitcase lying open on the floor.

Yet he slugged through the room with a broad smile. Jiya had been so much more than a dream. She had been his personal inspiration for living life happily. The headache and the body aches were worth an evening like that. He decided to do some multitasking. Chirag messaged his assistants to get the breakfast packed for him, and he would meet them directly at the reception at seven-thirty. He had also asked them to proceed with the checkout formalities as he was running a bit late.

Jiya's voice and words echoed in his mind as he groomed his appearance and packed his bags. He kept replaying their conversations in his mind. The picture that he had clicked of her was imprinted in his mind. He wished he had clicked it on his phone—then at least he could see it whenever he missed her. He could only imagine the reaction of his assistants as he would ask them to send a formal invitation to Jiya for the product shoot. He couldn't help but wonder whether she might have just agreed to humour him. She was, after all, a highly skilled professional and would have her diary booked for months in advance. There was a very slim chance that he would get to see her ever again. And then he remembered her parting words—that she would come and see him off. He felt a sudden jolt of excitement at the thought of seeing her again. The feeling made him move a little faster.

The voice of his boring old self kept telling him that it was for his own good that she remained like a dream—something he had cherished while he was living it but better to be forgotten once awake—for dinners, walks by the swimming pools, and ad campaigns were just excuses to buy some time. The truth was that they were two people belonging to different worlds. And despite the way they made each other feel, they could possibly not incorporate each other on a more permanent basis.

Chirag's mood got grim with his growing negative thoughts. He did not know what to believe or expect. The heaviness he felt had turned to anger by the time he finished packing the rest of his suitcase. Haphazardly he pulled it out and banged the door behind him. A part of him wished for Jiya to be a dream. At least he could call the experience entirely his own. The memories would live within him. But he knew that that was not the case. Jiya had been as real as the corridor he was crossing to reach the elevator. Her words had been as real as the beep sound announcing the arrival of the elevator. And her touch had been as warm as the gush of hot air filling the elevator once the doors closed.

The corridors, the elevator, and the lobby he had walked across just a couple of hours earlier with Jiya reminded him of her. Everything reminded him of her. A loud voice from deep inside him was shouting in his ears, commanding him to call her. She would want to see him off. He could wait for a few minutes.

He checked his thoughts. This was reeling out of control, a little too far and a little too fast. His team was all dressed and ready to depart. His senior assistant had already settled all the accounts. Chirag walked over to the reception and handed over his key card. He waited a few moments with a forced smile, trying to focus on the manager's words. His heavy head was preventing him from listening to anything, and his heavy heart did not wish to listen to any voice other than a specific one. Courteously, he nodded a few times before speaking a few rehearsed words of gratitude and made his way to the door.

Dressed in his dark grey three-piece suit, pastel lemon shirt, and black tie, Chirag was running out of excuses to postpone his departure. He had put on his sunglasses to hide the swelling under his eyes due to the lack of sleep. His luggage had been secured in the car, and his wholesome breakfast meal was packed and placed on the back seat.

Chirag checked his watch, more out of necessity. It was two minutes till seven-thirty. It was time to leave. Just as he crossed the large vase placed in the centre of the reception area and proceeded towards the doors, a loud voice reverberated through the entire reception and lobby.

"Chirag!" Jiya called out as loudly as she could. Her morning voice was coarse, probably due to lack of sleep, and not as chirpy as it had been on the previous evening. "Wait."

He turned around. Actually, everyone turned around. His entire team turned. The hotel staff turned around. The guests who were heading for breakfast or were returning from breakfast turned. He noticed his driver take a step closer to the door to get a better look. The receptionist even took a step towards the source of the sudden screaming.

It was Jiya, and she did not care for anyone else. She was just as Chirag had remembered. Dressed in the same white top, faded denim shorts, and the same grey shrug on top, she walked over to him, rubbing her swollen eyes. She was walking slowly, like a child learning to walk. She was wearing the hotel-provided cloth slippers, which must be adding to her difficulties. Her hair was no longer in a bun but was flowing down her shoulders and sticking out from all odd places. There were clear signs of unsuccessful attempts at taming them before giving up. If there was a word that Chirag would use to describe Jiya at the very moment, it would be 'authentic.'. There was nothing artificial about her. She was raw, honest, cute, and extremely beautiful. He took off his sunglasses to get a proper view without the dimming effect and placed them in his pockets.

Without realizing it, Chirag had extended his left hand. He had no idea what he anticipated. Did he want to shake her hand or give her support to walk confidently?

Jiya's face brightened at seeing the extended hand. She quickened her pace and reached out with her right hand. But just as she reached close enough to grab his hand, her right hand changed direction and made its way to his torso. Jiya held his extended hand with her left hand as her right hand went behind his back. Before Chirag knew it, she was holding him in a warm embrace.

Chirag felt her gentle but firm grip around half his torso. A warmth was spreading on his front right half—from where Jiya stood, holding his left hand and resting her head on his right shoulder. He felt the grip tighten. He could feel the hot air from her nostrils blow over his collar. He knew that they were both again attracting unwanted attention, but he did not care. Honestly, the hotel reception and lobby seemed to be a part of another universe. His universe was the only one where Jiya held him close to herself.

For some time, he was not sure of what to do with his right hand. It was just hanging by his side. He felt the urge to use it. Without meaning to, his right hand went over Jiya's shoulder, completing the embrace. Jiya's breathing relaxed as he rested his hand on her shoulder.

They stood there, holding each other, for a while before Chirag felt Jiya turn her head up towards his ear. Gently, she whispered, "I told you I would see you off." The softest voice, the low tone, the gush of air after every syllable—it was meant just for him.

It had been considerably long since Chirag had felt anyone this close to him. Rather, he could only think of his mother, who used to hug him in such a loving and affectionate manner when he was a child. Embraces were amazing. All other thoughts had been dismissed from his mind. He did not realize how much he needed to hold someone and to be held. He felt weak and strong, both at once. Having someone care for him in a very loving and honest manner was the most abundant feeling. He had been so used to being on his own that he had forgotten the feeling of the touch of another human. That feeling was beyond words.

Chirag could stand there forever. His chin gently rested against his head. He could feel her breathing become slow, indicating she was going back to sleep. He did not dare move, scared of disturbing her.

It was at this moment that he knew that with Jiya by his side, everything in the world was possible. Through her perspective, things would always be several shades brighter. Every success would grow in magnitude if he got to celebrate with her. It was at this moment, in less than twenty-four hours of meeting Jiya, that he knew that it was not a coincidence. Their inability to take their eyes off each other, meeting over dinner, and the conversations that felt so natural—none of these were by coincidence. Chirag needed to meet her to know what he had been missing and then have her complete him.

She was the question that he needed answering, and she was the answer to all his questions. He could not even imagine how he had managed to scrape by all the years without knowing her. He had been missing out on life when he was living without her. It was just like the business decisions that he had taken without a reason—purely on his instincts. He had no reason for the revelations that he was having, but his instincts told him never to let go.

After a moment, a minute, an hour, a day, or possibly several days, they both moved a bit, then loosened their grip on the other, and then pulled themselves apart.

Jiya's left hand was still in his right hand when he caught the look on her face. She had grown prettier if it was possible. She still had her eyes closed. Even without a word, Chirag knew that Jiya was experiencing the same emotions as he did. The peace and calm on her face were making him grow fonder of her. An unexplained urge erupted within him. He wanted to touch her face with his other hand.

As the air rushed to occupy the space between them, the universe where they were getting judged and the chiding voices inside Chirag's head also returned. He knew his feelings were wrong on so many levels, and yet it felt like the most correct thing. It felt like the only thing that should be done. The voices in his head were growing louder—loud enough that he let go of Jiya's hand and took a step back.

Chirag lost his footing slightly in haste to move backwards. Jiya grabbed his right hand immediately, with both her hands, to prevent him from falling down and regaining his balance. She was smiling at him.

"Sir." It was the voice of the senior assistant that broke the silence of words between the two. He had come forward and placed a hand on Chirag's back to support him. He had been a silent and slightly embarrassed spectator of the entire exchange so far. Now that he was involved, he decided to change the course of things.

"Sir." He repeated it on a louder note to attract Chirag's attention. As he was standing right behind Chirag, he succeeded in getting the desired result. As he turned his head, the senior assistant added, "We are ready whenever you are."

Chirag pulled his hand out of Jiya's one more time. He checked the time. It was seven thirty-nine. Their encounter had not been too long. It definitely felt like a lifetime while it lasted. But now, in retrospect, he longed for more.

Together, with their arms brushing against each other, she walked by his side as he made his way out of the hotel towards his car. Jiya was oblivious to anyone else. She did not care for the onlookers or the questions that conflicted with Chirag's emotions. She held the door open, allowing Chirag to settle. He forced a smile and put his sunglasses back on.

"*We will meet soon*" Jiya added in a confident tone. She was referring to his offer to work together, but the subtext was a challenge for him to doubt her again. Despite the state she had turned up in, she had lived up to her words and met him before he departed. And she seemed to not even care the way she was dressed or looked. Chirag had not cared either. Her presence was all that mattered.

Chirag nodded. If this was the bet, he would want to lose every time to see her one more time.

ᴘᴘᴘ

The day that followed the beautiful morning was the longest that Chirag had to endure in his entire life. He had often joked about the night of his class's tenth results when he had not slept the entire night, anticipating his results. Now every hour felt as long as that night of anticipation.

Chirag wished to catch up on some sleep on his way to Pune. Every time he closed his eyes, he would feel Jiya's presence lingering in his senses. He felt her in his arms and kept his arms closed, holding an imaginary Jiya in a tight embrace. His nose could smell her perfume as he had noticed when she sat close to him while clicking their selfie. He kept his eyes closed, remembering each of her expressions. He could see the sparkle in her eyes that had illuminated the previous night more than the moon and the countless stars. He kept feeling a constant longing to turn the car and go be by her side—a feeling that he neither understood nor could explain. This was the first time he had longed for a person.

He did not care for breakfast that his senior assistant had for him or to review the agenda, as he did before every meeting. For the first time in his life, he was enjoying the moment just as it was. He did not wish to do anything—simply sit there, close his eyes, and smile.

The sudden halt of the car startled him. Before Chirag realized that they had reached their destination, his long-serving driver had rushed to open the door for him. The gust of cold air replaced the warmth he felt holding onto Jiya's essence. Reluctantly, he opened his eyes. Laughing at his own immature actions, Chirag thanked the driver, got out of his car, and pushed the door closed. He slowly entered the office of his prospective distributors in Pune. It was an above-average building—better than what he expected, at least. While he was there for just one meeting, his day was certainly going to be long. He was greeted by their general manager and led into a small cabin for rest and refreshments. The CEO would meet him in the room before taking him to the presentation hall.

The itinerary was enough to keep his thoughts from wandering off to Jiya. Yet he could not help but feel happier for no reason. Twice different people from the distributor's staff asked him if he found something funny, as he was smiling a little too broadly.

There had been a few minutes before the presentation when Chirag took the file containing the research his team had done on the company. As per his own initial research and the report that he held in his hands, the company did not produce goods of sufficient quality. Their products were quite regular and often comprised of details or raw materials. Since he had already agreed to a meeting, he had travelled all the way to meet with the executives. But he had a good mind to politely decline their proposal.

A twenty-four-hour younger version of himself would have kept the meeting short and rejected their proposal without keeping them in any limbo. But the last few hours had changed his perspective immensely. As he had sat through the general briefing, he could not help but consider a few alternate possibilities. He decided to test out the waters before taking the plunge.

After the briefing ended, Chirag insisted on finding his way back to the CEO's office for further discussion. The CEO's office was on a secluded floor with the offices of the other heads. He wanted to go meet the other employees. On the pretext of getting lost while finding a washroom, Chirag, followed by his assistants, found himself two floors below, walking through the aisles where the departments operated from.

While the whole company knew that there had been a rich client visiting them, no one had expected the rich client to walk amidst them. His assistants understood the reason behind this—Chirag strongly believed that the strength of any organization was its employees. If the employees are taken care of and satisfied, the business will thrive. It was also an excellent way to check on the attitude of the leadership.

They could not have had more than ten minutes when the general manager found them and escorted them back. However, the ten minutes were enough. Chirag requested them for a room where he could talk to his assistants in private. It was an unusual request, but the general manager took them to a smaller meeting room and left.

Chirag contemplated for a few minutes, allowing the thoughts to be formed in his mind. He chose his words carefully, and even as he mentioned his thoughts, he could see the shock echo through the room. All the faces reflected clear rejection of his proposal. But Chirag had a good feeling about it, and he had started to have faith in these good feelings.

He did not have any plans. It was not a small thing that he was suggesting. Things like these were not finalized in a small meeting room in ten minutes. Usually, such decisions take months. But they did not have months—all they had were the ten minutes.

Well, the meeting did not end in ten minutes. It took him almost thirty minutes to convince his team. The general manager had come thrice to check on them and stood outside after the fourth time he came to check on them. Chirag did not still have his team entirely convinced, but they agreed to his points. The people working in the company were good. They were unfortunate to be led by poor leadership, but if given proper guidance, they would surely take the company to greater heights.

ᗺᗺᗺ

"Sir, are you sure?" the senior assistant asked, handing Chirag the printed document. His voice was muffled with uncertainty. It was the first time in all his years of service that he saw his boss make such a radical and sudden decision. Acquisitions were never part of any of their discussions or future roadmaps.

And then the senior assistant was stunned some more, for Chirag decided to respond in the most uncharacteristic manner possible—he winked back.

ᕈᕈᕈ

During the general overview walkthrough of the company, Chirag had been impressed with a few of the operations. The processes and the workforce had been pretty productive. Clearly, they had been victims of a sequence of bad decisions.

However, Chirag then had a thought—what if his team could guide them? With global experience and a sufficient pool of funds to modernize a few things, the company had the potential to become one of the finest producers of handicrafts in the country. Of course, they needed to set up their own self-sustaining unit that would prevent the onset of any further acquisitions.

The first step of the process was to gauge if the company was worth all the effort. That is when Chirag had snuck around and interacted with the employees. His assistants had a similar experience—the people were very hardworking and adaptive. They were simple. The company did not have any unnecessary expenses—they did not have any major and regular stream of income either.

"*Do you trust me?*" he called out to his assistants when they kept citing their doubts on his proposal to acquire the company. He had met with a silence—which was a positive response, as until then they all had been voicing their refusal.

Chirag had followed his assistants into the CEO's room. Before they could settle down and be offered some refreshments, he told the leadership of his plans. Chirag did not wish to do any business with the company. However, he was interested in acquiring it. This would be a unique acquisition—he was not interested in firing people or hiring new people. He wanted the company to be branded under his umbrella—that would make it easy to procure better raw materials and sell globally. Additionally, he proposed setting up just one additional department that would act as a liaison between the company and his businesses. They would also review the processes present in the existing departments and suggest changes wherever required to ensure that they operated at the best standards.

He had no intention of sitting himself or getting someone from his team to sit on top of them. He assured them that the hierarchy would not vary and most of their processes would not be impacted.

The senior assistant had taken some time to get the document ready. However, he had been as efficient as always. The drafted contract for acquisition exclusively mentioned all the clauses that Chirag had mentioned. Additionally, he had gone the extra mile and added some figures and percentages. Chirag had gone through the document, and as always, he could not have drafted it better himself.

Presenting the document to the CEO, he asked him and the team to go through the document and think over the entire thing carefully. Chirag had decided to stay an additional day in Pune, waiting for the answer.

The senior assistant had not supported the second decision—to give them time to think. This was too good a deal, and there was very little for anyone to consider. Chirag had already narrated all the clauses and had ensured that everything indicated a smooth transition towards improvement.

He had been right in thinking the same. The contract was signed in less than three hours. Of course, this was just to agree to the process. The contract explicitly mentioned that the entire transition would be gradual. The timelines and desired state would be decided by the collective leadership in the course of the next six months. The senior assistant could not help but think if the CEO had also been an acquaintance of the girl who had had a weird effect on his boss.

SEVEN

It was especially a torturous day, which came with its own sweetness. This was the first time in almost a decade and a half that she could not get herself to focus. Her thoughts kept wandering back to the man she had closely held in his arms a couple of hours ago. Every second, she found herself planning their meals together during their next meeting. Her interns were not getting any better at their jobs, and she had to do everything—from the lighting to telling the models to correct their postures. And while Jiya did feel irritated, it was not because of her assistants not being able to do their job. She did not seem to mind such minor inconveniences. Rather, she had not said a word to anyone all morning. Every time that something had gone wrong, she had very uncharacteristically fixed it all by herself. However, she did feel irritated, for there had been no message from a certain someone.

It was not until after her lunch that her phone buzzed and she received the message she had been waiting for. It was an email from Chirag's assistants officially inviting her for a photo shoot in their Delhi office. It was a standard email, asking for their quotation and sample work. Handing her camera to one of the interns, she immediately went to her room with her laptop. Her phone buzzed another time, and she saw something that made her even happier—a text message from Chirag asking if she received the email.

She playfully replied, "*I did. Let me consider it.*" This was supposed to be a joke, but there could be a small chance that Chirag might not see it as a joke. She thought of the consequences. He would have just read the words and not heard the playfulness in her voice. She did not want him to get any ideas, so hastily she typed another message. *"I will see you in a week in Delhi. Miss me till then."* And almost immediately, she got a smiling emoji reply.

ᐁᐁᐁ

The remainder of the week, they decided to play as many tricks as possible. On some occasions, time would slow down to expand each second to an hour, while in others, she would be missing several hours of her day that she had spent daydreaming.

Jiya kept waiting for a message from Chirag, and when it did come, she would spend the next few minutes having a small conversation with him and the next few hours re-reading their conversations. It was weird that the two had resorted to texting. Regardless of the longing she felt and knew that he felt as well, she never called him, and he did not call either. None of the interns dared voice this out loud, but this was what they called *'being fifteen'* again; except, none of them could imagine 'the Queen' being fifteen, ever.

Jiya returned to Mumbai on a fine Tuesday morning. Her next assignment was for a famous international designer who had come to India for the *"Fashion Festival,"* starting on Friday. He needed his latest collection photoshot, ready to be displayed and advertised, before the Fashion Festival commended next month. Needless to say, it was the biggest assignment of her career so far. It would immediately put her in the league with the international photographers. The designer would be not just a client but also her key contributor to networking. She had worked tirelessly to get the designer's contract, done a lot of free work to influence him, and had finally managed to win the contract. She could not let it slip. She checked up on her assistants' schedules. They would be returning to Mumbai on the following Tuesday—which would not do. She called them in and asked them to be back by Saturday at all costs. They were going to have to fill in for her.

She kept going over the details—the key to a successful assignment was always the planning that went behind it. And this one was the most crucial one so far. Since the shoot was in Mumbai itself, it would be easier to manage.

After pondering over all aspects for almost an hour, Jiya was quite happy with herself. She was going to report a day early—start from Thursday and work as much as possible till mid-Saturday. She would fix the storyboard, decide the dresses, and take a few shots as well. Then, making an excuse, she could take off for a couple of days while her assistants would fill in for her.

She would fly to Delhi on Saturday evening, spend Sunday with Chirag, and start work from Monday. She would have to take as few interns with her as possible and potentially hire a few from Delhi. She could work the week and then return for the weekend to check progress. She could return even sooner if things went the other way.

It meant that she had just one and a half days to deliver the pictures for the ad hoc assignment she had taken. It might be a little extra work as she had not had the chance to review all the images. While the client had not requested any editing, she felt there might be some needed and was happy to do that—if it meant she could get free sooner.

One of Jiya's assistants confirmed that he would return by Saturday, but the other would arrive on Wednesday, owing to some personal work she had. Jiya had forgotten that she had already discussed the leave plan. It did not matter—Jiya was confident that she would take care of most work. She was determined to take as many pictures as possible before leaving—so she could share them with the designer for review. That would buy them an additional day or two.

Working in parallel on the plan in her diary and editing the pictures on the desktop, she lost track of time. It was way past midnight when the last two interns asked her permission to leave. There was still a small batch of photographs pending to be edited. And now that Jiya had a chance, she realized that she had not had any food either. She had purely been running on the memories from two days back, the anticipation of making more such memories, and a few SMS conversations.

By this time, even Jiya was convinced she was, indeed, acting like a fifteen-year-old. There were a thousand things that had the potential to cause her plan to fail, but the thought of seeing Chirag soon enough kept her going. Despite the heap of work lined up for the remainder of the week, she could not help but feel happy and optimistic.

ppp

The week was a particularly good one for the interns. Jiya had given them a lot of work—like always—but was not breathing down their necks—unlike herself. It had all started on the last day of the shoot in Lonavala. She had allowed the interns to wind up and then divided them into teams to pick up separate tasks to ensure all the pictures were properly developed and delivered in two days.

Her contract with the ad agency mandated her to click the pictures, deliver the pictures, and get the pictures approved. The last bit was always the trickiest, and agencies included it just to get some extra *"free"* work done by the photographer. She, of course, came with her own clauses that helped her out of such situations if the client ever got too greedy. She had personally reviewed all the photographs and assigned three of the interns explicitly to get the contract closed and the remainder of the payment made. The instructions were simple. *"Close this. I do not want to work on this anymore."* Jiya had declared.

She chose two of her oldest interns to accompany her to Delhi for the assignment. Briefing them vaguely about the task, she was explicit to ask them to make arrangements. She needed a studio, technicians, accommodation, her best camera and editing laptop, and all the other items that they could think of. The remainder of her team was going to the fashion designer's shoot with her. They were all tasked with different activities with little to no interruption from her end. She would give them an hour each evening to review their progress. This was the only time that she was the same Jiya as before. Even the fifteen-year-old Jiya was very particular about her work. She would not miss a single dot if she saw one out of place. Luckily, there were not many out-of-place dots as she was heavy-lifting most of the crucial tasks.

Life in the studio had changed drastically. Everyone was extremely busy, busier than they had ever been, but no longer were they scared. Jiya spent most of her time behind her screen or over the whiteboard, chalking out details. Sometimes she would run down to buy a few lenses or special lights. She kept picking random items and testing them in various lights and angles.

With the absence of Jiya's anger, not only were the interns more confident, they were learning more as well. Several of them would keep sneaking looks at Jiya, trying to comprehend what she was doing. Asking her questions was nothing any of them had tried, but if they stood close enough, they could hear her explain her thoughts to herself out loud.

Their internship so far had comprised them of helping out Jiya or her assistants. They had rarely been asked to handle an entire task by themselves. This renewed approach gave them an opportunity to outshine. Each of them believed that they needed to do a good job not only to not give Jiya a chance to revert back to her former self but also to get a commendation from her.

ᐅᐅᐅ

Before she had realized it, Jiya found herself waking up on Thursday morning. She had already called the designer and informed him that she would start the work a day earlier to get things started. He had been extremely happy getting a day's worth of her time, free of cost. Of course, she had not mentioned anything about not being present on the shoot post-Saturday. She had woken early—well, not as early as Chirag does, but eight in the morning, for an entire week, was a personal record since she had left formal education.

Since she had woken up early in the hotel in Lonavala to see him off, she had not been able to sleep in late. He would send her messages early in the morning. And Jiya wanted to reply to them as soon as possible. Since Chirag had his morning less occupied than the rest of his day, they would exchange a few extra messages.

His 'Good Morning' message had been waiting for her for over three hours. She replied, 'Barely morning,' followed by a sleepy emoji. Jiya had just managed to pull herself out of the bed when her phone buzzed, and the screen previewed a wink emoji from Chirag.

She had told him all about the shoot she was going to start. But she had craftily hidden two facts. First, she did not tell him the actual duration of the shoot. She had told him that it would end on Sunday. Next, with the first one, she had hidden the fact that she was planning to surprise him on Sunday itself. Monday was too far away.

He had told her about how he had done a crazy thing—acquired a new firm. Due to the acquisition, he had to stay back an extra day in Pune. He had shared all the funny anecdotes of how all his assistants were left puzzled and shocked.

Luckily for her, it meant Chirag had less time to check her travel plans. His team of assistants did not care as long as she confirmed that she would be at their office before nine in the morning on Monday. Happy with her carefully crafted plan, Jiya got ready for the implementation.

Just as Jiya packed her purse, her phone beeped from inside her jeans pocket. Suddenly SMSs had become quite important to her—she might keep sleeping through alarms or calls, but she would know if she received an SMS even in the middle of a shoot. She opened her phone with excited anticipation, "*Best of Luck.*"

Chirag was wonderful in that aspect. He noticed things and made an effort to remember everything. He had even noticed how her mornings had been changed to early mornings and had each evening reminded her to sleep early. Three simple words from him and all the effort behind them made the message something Jiya read and re-read.

"*Break a leg?*" she typed back, as a standard response to keep the conversation going.

"Sorry?" Chirag replied back almost instantly. It dawned on Jiya that he was probably not someone who had used this phrase or even heard it before. She could visualize him standing in his kitchen, having breakfast, and staring at his mobile screen. She fell on the sofa laughing, letting her purse hit the floor. Something about him sitting in his kitchen, in his track pants and a loose t-shirt, with that confused look on his strikingly handsome face, was hilarious. But then, if she knew him, he would already be dressed in his ironed shirt and smart pants for his office.

Before she could control her laughter, her phone rang. It was Chirag. Their unsaid rule about no phone calls was broken.

"Did you break your leg? Are you fine?" he asked with a lot of concern.

His voice was slightly different from what she remembered. It was another charming voice. It took her a moment to get over the shock of seeing his name flash across her phone's screen and then hearing his voice. Things from her daydreams materialized into existence quite quickly. Before she could control it, she was feeling butterflies in her core. It took her over a minute to stop laughing. Through that time, Chirag patiently waited. She could hear his breathing and movements. She spent a few minutes assuring him that she was fine and it was a phase.

She could not have asked for a better morning!

ϷϷϷ

The first day of the shoot was always the prep day. Jiya liked to meet the people, establish her ground rules, tick off items on her checklist, scold a few people, declare several completed tasks that needed to be redone, declare several props as worthless, demand the random-most items, and go over the storyboard. The last was the most crucial, and Jiya usually spent hours getting it perfected—it would provide her with a clear vision of getting things done.

However, this first day was not going as planned. Even though Jiya had focused all her energy on getting things ready, things were not happening quickly enough. Her team was making mistakes as usual. The fashion designer's team was not ready enough. And when Jiya saw the clothes, she wished for a miracle to save the shoot. Not that she was any fashion expert, but the clothes were hideous. Only a miracle could make them look good. However, she was not going to let the challenge beat her up—professionally or personally. It simply meant that she needed to get slightly creative with the storyline. She needed better lighting and better angles. Putting her team to procuring the best lights possible, she sat down with her camera.

It was a bit frustrating as everything was taking a lot of time. No one had understood Jiya's decision to start early. The lights were late. The studio was not set. There were no models yet—the initial phase was to shoot the dresses on statues and take shots of the studio. The team had set up a big green screen that Jiya was going to replace with a bokeh backdrop superimposed on dress materials and beads.

Jiya had divided the work. Keeping her interns in smaller groups helped her. They were more coordinated and efficient. Most importantly, they did not get in her way. She had a few of her assistants take care of arranging the schedule for the next couple of days—coordinating with the models and the designer's team with the requirements and deliverables for each day. Another group had a shouting match with the lighting vendors over getting the new lights delivered fast. The rest of the interns were walking on eggshells around her, straightening up the green screen, fixing the position of the existing lights, and running behind Jiya, holding her laptop.

The days like these when they got to witness Jiya perform some artistic exceptions and pull out the best results were the reason behind the interns putting up with all her temper tantrums. Her focus on detail was unparalleled. Her creative insights and instincts justified her accelerated career progression. Most of the time, even after accompanying her on several shoots, the interns were just as amazed as they were the first time they witnessed her work. And seldom would they agree out loud; each of them agreed that the title of 'Queen' was because of her skills; the condensation in their voices while calling it out loud was because of her temperament.

Jiya, frustrated with not getting the desirable effects, stood up, looked all around, did some mental calculations, and after a few moments of silence, pointed out five locations where the lights should be. As a group of interns ran around to make the changes, the interns behind the laptop marvelled as they saw the enhancements it made.

Jiya got down on her knees and took a couple of shots at an unusual angle. But the pictures were wonderful! The interns ran some pictures to the designer's teams, and they all agreed.

It had taken most of the day to set up the light positions. The interns had drafted a schedule based on the availability of models and dresses from the designer. Jiya made a few tweaks—she did not want the important dresses and the experienced models to be shot during the weekend. Her assistants would certainly have returned by then and settled in. She could try to travel for a day and pitch in as well. Of course, she did not share the reason with anyone, and no one asked.

Jiya had not taken a break. Her interns had run down to pick her up a wrap and a large cup of cold coffee. Unfortunately, they did not get any more than a couple of minutes to finish the half a dozen pizzas that had been ordered for them. Their lunch was cramped in the moments when she had run into the room to check her phone.

Since Chirag was travelling back to Delhi, she had not heard from him after their morning call. It allowed her to concentrate on her work, but she could not help longing for a message while holding her chicken wrap.

She debated the best technique to share her updates from the day for a while. Finally deciding to keep it short, she sent the message.

Morning Run √
Reached venue on time (fifteen minutes delay allowed) √
Lighting √
Audio System Setup √

Lunch √
Discussed the Story Board. √
Discussed the Call Sheet. √
Met the model coordinator. √
Met the Makeup Team √
General Briefing √

All her shoots had a strict '*No-Phone*' policy. Phones had to be submitted to the room outside the studio area. Everyone was allowed to collect their phone at any point but not carry it to the shooting area. This helped maintain the confidentiality and integrity of the shoot, as well as allowing them to focus better. While Jiya was not a fan of the rule at the present moment, she could not imagine getting any work done if she had held that device in her hand, constantly checking the screen for a message or longingly staring at his pictures stored in her phone. As a result, she had hidden the phone deep in her purse.

Going over the pictures of him from the pool, she hurried through her lunch. She needed to keep her focus if she wanted to follow her schedule. She needed to get a couple of shots done before she wrapped up on Saturday. But nothing kept her from getting a bit worried. It was not like him to not message or to switch his phone off-her message had been sent but not delivered. She remembered the time when they had exchanged numbers. Those moments by the pool had been truly magical.

Finally, shifting her thoughts from the conversations they had shared to the conversations they would share soon, she secured the phone in her bag. She couldn't help but think of what he had been doing since his phone was switched off. She tried her best to put the thoughts out of her mind. He would be fine. He would message her any moment and tell her about another firm he acquired or any other big idea he had had.

ϷϷϷ

Jiya walked back to the studio and disappeared behind the laptop containing the pictures. Her interns had arranged to get the better lighting delivered the following day—there was little point in clicking more pictures without them. So, she decided to go over the ones she had taken and sort them out. Satisfied with a couple of pictures, she kept juggling between the laptop and her notebook—where she noted the details she wanted to repeat or eliminate. She had been a little edgy and irritable. Of course, her interns had no idea that the Queen's displeasure was at nothing in the room but on someone whom she had not spoken to. Her best chance to get the worry out of her mind was to emerge herself into work. She pushed herself even more than always and forced to think of nothing but the pictures on the laptop.

It was not until quite late that something disturbed her. She was leaning over the whiteboard spread on the table, writing her notes and schedules for the following days. She was lost in thought when someone's phone rang. She did not need to raise her hands as her interns were already rummaging through the furniture to find the source of the noise. The ringing stopped after finishing its course, only to start a second later. The sound made it very difficult for her to concentrate, and when she had made her fourth unsuccessful attempt at writing the note for a particular golden dress, she turned around. Her interns were standing by the table, looking at a bag. Exasperated as she was, it took her over a minute to understand that it was her phone ringing—which was now through the third call.

And just like that, something snapped in her mind, and Jiya rummaged through her bag to pull out her phone. A smile spread across her face as she saw Chirag's name flash across the screen of her phone. In a moment, all the thoughts of her work melted out. She felt all the emotions at once that she had battled to conceal throughout the day. Even though she had had very little time, she could help feel angry at Chirag's carelessness. *Going off the grid was not acceptable.* And getting consumed with the emotion, she shouted into the phone, "*Where were you? How could you do this?*"

It may not be the day that she had hoped for, but listening to her voice, made it end on a perfect note.

EIGHT

It took Chirag almost twenty minutes to console Jiya. She had burst out in a fit of rage on hearing his voice. He was thankful for being alone at home, lest letting everyone hear her scream at him. He had not expected a cool and witty person like her to have an emotional side. Even she had sounded shocked over her reaction.

With everything that they had discussed over the last few days, and they had discussed pretty much everything under the sun, he had not realized that they were not sharing just words. In the moment, as he heard her tell how scared she had been, he could not help but think of being in her place. He had been extremely worried about her in the morning and before she answered her phone. It had only been for a few moments, but he had been very worried in those moments.

This was a very new experience for him. It had been a really long time before he had cared for someone and in return been cared for. He narrated the events of his day—hoping to buy some time to think of a way to soothe her.

His switched-off phone was put inside the coat pocket, and his coat was put inside the handbag, owing to the souvenir bags given to him by his newly acquired firm, filling up his capacity to hold things. The bag containing the coat had been ignored for a while, as upon his arrival in Delhi, he found that the airline had misplaced his check-in bag.

He had to visit the airline office and meet several officers before his bag was located. It had been mistakenly boarded on a flight to Hyderabad and would be sent to Delhi the following day. Chirag was assured that he could collect his bag anytime the following day. But in all the hustle, he had forgotten to switch on his cell phone.

To add to his troubles, he had a few video calls with his international clients scheduled for that evening. Chirag went directly to his office, as it was closer to the airport in comparison to his home. A few of his assistants accompanied him. Not until quite late in the evening did the calls break, and he left for his home.

Once home, Chirag rummaged through his handbag to find his phone. He anticipated a few work calls, but he was surprised. There was a sweet message waiting for him, and he could laugh at the same.

Without realizing, his fingers navigated to the phone and dialed her number. It went unanswered the first time. He dialed again, without a thought. It went unanswered again. He hesitated before dialing in for a third time. Thoughts of doubt had started fogging his mind. Was it alright for him to call her at the hour?

Before he could cut the call, her voice sounded from the other side. He had just said "hello" when she started screaming at how irresponsible he had been.

Even as his mind raced to find a way to calm her, he noticed his own erratic heartbeat. It could have been because of his worry over her not picking the call, or it could have been the joy of hearing her voice, or it might be both. It was his moment of realization that they were much more than words when they were together.

Chirag had spent the last few days listening to a very charming and attractive person. He was excellent with her work and confident in her approach. Jiya had come across as a go-getter, and though she might feel aloof, he had sensed her gentle heart on their first dinner together. Today, however, he met the little girl who had left home at an early age to be independent and had done everything possible to reach where she was, had her heart broken a few times, and survived all the challenges that life threw her way. He met the girl he was liking more than the girl he had not been able to take his eyes off a few days ago.

They both talked for several hours. He heard as she left the studio, drove to her house, grabbed some food on the way, had her food, and decided to call it a day. Even with the realization and the voice in his head asking him to be cautious, he could not help but feel happy. There was someone who worried for him. There was someone who awaited a message or a call from him. There was someone whom he wanted to talk to. There was someone who did not care about the *whats* and *hows* of his businesses but wanted to know him as a person. There was someone he cared back for.

The voice of caution kept asking him to stop, telling him that he was not meant to care for her. It was not his place to be. His emotions were clouding his judgment, and the connection was never to be. He felt a pang of guilt as he retired into his bed. Was he being wrong? Was he not allowed to have a friend?

It was the first time in over two decades that he had had a friend outside work. Content with his classification of the bond he shared with Jiya as friendship, he let go of all his thoughts.

It did not matter what he called it. He had spent some considerable time talking with a complete stranger. And now the stranger, without him realizing, had become an integral part of his life. Nothing else mattered. He was allowed to have friends—though this was something he had not done for a long time. He felt good knowing that she was out there and he could talk to her whenever he wanted to. He would see her soon too.

He ignored all the signs and warnings of heading into things that were difficult to get out of as he drifted into a sweet slumber.

ᐯᐯᐯ

The week was going at a pretty fast pace—even with Chirag's usual standards. He had to extend his stay in Pune for a day before heading to Indore for his planned visit. As always, the most important documents were being sent across for his review while his assistants were taking care of the majority of matters from the office. He anticipated a lot of in-person calls and meetings to be scheduled for the next two days, but he had not, even in the wildest of dreams, considered the enormous volume of queries that came his way.

While he was the sole owner of the logistics business, he had set up proper hierarchies to take care of all the tiny details. This allowed him to travel without causing any major halt. Additionally, he liked to discuss his ideas with the heads of departments before putting them into action, safeguarding the interests of his teams and employees. His sudden action to acquire another organization had not gone unnoticed. He was swarmed with numerous calls and meetings with his various department and country heads from all over the globe. No one had truly understood the reason. He had told them that this was not something he was considering as a strategy—the company comprised of good people and deserved a chance to excel. Yet, the doubts that had now crept into his people gave rise to several questions and concerns. And no matter how much he tried, they just kept increasing.

For the first time since the start of his career, Chirag found his employees to be divided. Some of them were showing him support, while most of them were unsure about their own future prospects. His sudden decision had left them considering what other changes could Chirag introduce.

He constantly kept getting cornered by the minority percentage of his team, which had already researched a few viable organizations operating in logistics worldwide, but at a significantly smaller scale, for them to consider acquiring. Chirag patiently heard about each of their research projects, though he gradually decreased the duration of his time with every consecutive person to bring up such an idea, before assuring them that as an organization or as a person, acquisitions were not part of their foreseeable future plan.

His mornings were cluttered with going through the abstract emails he received. As the word had gotten out, he was receiving unwarranted media interactions. The emails and calls from various media houses had started adding to his existing volumes of unread emails and unanswered voice messages.

He had already had a delay in getting to the office on Friday morning, and despite all his efforts, he had not managed to do anything significant by eight in the evening. Calling it a day, he asked his assistants to get the stack of files on his desk sent to his home. It was going to be a long night—he wanted to close any pending and urgent matters from the logistics business within the week. Since Jiya was invited from the e-commerce business, he would not want to juggle days between the two offices. He would rather be with her and watch her work. He closed his eyes to visualize her smiling face as he closed a particularly heavy file with a sigh.

He called her over the Bluetooth in his car as he drove back home. They shared a small conversation before she had to return to her shoot. Chirag, too tired to do anything, was grateful for the pot of hot and tempting dishes kept in the oven. He washed himself clean and sat down for dinner, with the reporter from a local news channel screaming his way through his silent house.

Just as he was finishing his late meal, the alarm on his phone buzzed. After being shouted at on the previous day, Chirag had been made to keep an alarm on his phone for every two hours during his non-sleeping hours. If he had not spoken to Jiya at all between two alarm buzzes, he was going to have major problems that Jiya had not elaborated on. He finished his meal before taking his phone to message Jiya.

He could not remember a time when someone had commanded him to do things. His parents had been very trusting, and their conversations were quite mature, even during his growing-up years. Amita had been busy, first with her job, then with the house, and later with their daughter. She had always been self-sufficient and by the time, he realized that he needed to be there, she had already made a separate life for her and their daughter. He had never done a job and had owned all the businesses—no one commanded him there, either. Thus, it was a completely new experience for Chirag to be bossed around. And he was liking it.

He walked around his house as a habit as he texted Jiya.

"Had dinner?"

"You did?"

"Yes. You?"

"Not for another hour. Had coffee just now."

"How many?"

"10th maybe... lost count!"

"How was your day?"

Chirag typed at length about how his day had been. He shared how irritated and amused he felt when the fifth person walked into his room to give him another 'unusual idea.'. She had dismissed it with just a statement, *"You are the boss!"*

He chuckled as he thought of the expression she might have had, had he seen her say them in person. While he would have otherwise called her, he knew she was still in the middle of a shoot. Their pact was that he would text her every two hours, and since phones were not allowed in her shoot, they would use a messaging app with an online interface. He was not allowed to skip messaging her, and she promised to apprise him of the progress of her shoot. If he felt that she was getting distracted with his messages, he would stop.

Conscious of her time and the pending files awaiting his attention, he told her that the following two days would be a little stretched as well. He needed to close a few important matters in his logistics business before heading out to his e-commerce business, where he would have to endure worse. After all, they had been the ones directly involved in the acquisition.

"Two long days ahead..."

"But then you would get to see me on Monday!"

"Cannot wait!"

ᐅᐅᐅ

Saturday was no better than Friday! After the first fifteen minutes in his e-commerce business office, he had already asked his secretary to restrict all unscheduled visits. He had been bombarded with questions from the moment he had stepped foot inside the building. Not only the staff from the office but also his employees from the neighbouring towns had poured into Delhi to understand the further course of action. Understanding that there was a need for some damage control, Chirag asked his assistants to immediately set up a town hall. He needed to share his thoughts and answer their questions.

The stack of files on his desk had grown significantly despite his best efforts to close as many files as possible before retiring the previous evening. He had been away from his work for longer than anticipated, and his desire to be involved in things was not helping. Though he had already set up hierarchies and appointed people to the executive roles, he had decided to keep the business expansion portfolio to himself. Apart from that, he fancied becoming a part of marketing and technology discussions. Often when he visited his e-commerce office, he would find some time to sit with the teams and understand everything that they were working on.

His marketing team was comprised of quite diverse professionals. Most of the employees in the department had experienced between five and fifteen years. He never told anyone, except Jiya, that he not only learned so much from these people but enjoyed working with them as well. He was working with a team of enthusiastic, creative, and talented people who were also helping him understand these concepts that were earlier foreign to him. They were filled with the energy and zeal that he had had when he was a fresh college graduate. Thus, when he informed everyone that he had contracted a professional photographer for a photo shoot for an advertising campaign, the news was received with a lot of enthusiasm along with a mild shock—Jiya was a well-renowned personality in the field and was not known to do advertising campaigns.

Nonetheless, the bigger problem was that they had just a day to make all the arrangements before the start of the shoot. Luckily, Chirag's assistants had taken care of most of the things. Several of their products had been delivered to the office from the warehouse. Jiya's contract had been signed and filed. She had also shared with them the details of the studio she had rented out, and it had complied with their standards.

However, the buzz in the office after Chirag's announcement changed drastically. The topic had switched from the acquisition to a celebrity photographer—Jiya.

He could not help smiling thinking about her. He imagined her gelling up with his marketing team, drafting the storyboard, and setting the schedule. The thought of the next two weeks kept him afloat with joy from within.

Chirag was not one to plan a lot in advance. He liked to keep a few tasks aligned and maybe a week planned. Anything more than that was likely to be altered, causing unnecessary rework. Additionally, the motivation behind it was not to look forward to something but rather to get the most from each day. Yet he found himself planning two entire weeks—not to get anything done, but simply to spend them with Jiya.

ϷϷϷ

"You simply cannot go and buy another organization!" The senior legal counsel stood to emphasize his point.

His legal advisors, the legal department of his e-commerce business, and the executive teams of both his businesses had been inside the meeting room for over an hour. Everyone was given a copy of the acquisition contract. They all read through the contract in the first fifteen minutes of the meeting which had already surpassed its allocated time. His senior assistants had spent the next fifteen minutes going through the detailed plan that Chirag had shared with them. The meeting was then left open to share their thoughts and concerns.

Chirag had never truly gotten along with the legal team. Dreading the meeting, he had even told Jiya the same. *"They use their big legal terms and make me feel small."* But somehow, they were more furious than he had ever remembered. They were not able to understand his vision even after he had explained it to them twice already.

Rather, none of his assistants had understood Chirag's sudden desire or the reason behind it. It was his senior assistant, who had approached him during their flight to Delhi to understand the reasoning. The senior assistant, Ashish, was a wise man with an excellent memory and a keen sense of curiosity. He had sensed the delicate nature of the situation in the distributor's office and avoided making strong protests. However, on the first chance that he could find Chirag sitting by his side for a two-hour uninterrupted session, he was not going to miss his chance.

By then, Chirag had also had sufficient time to go over his thoughts. He would not be completely truthful to blame it all on Jiya. As he had taken a tour of the distributor's office, he had this chance to see the people at work and interact with several of them. Those people were not stupid, uneducated, lazy, or careless. The way they worked—even on the tiniest of tasks—showed a lot of dedication and commitment. Through his conversations, he found out that most of them were restricted by their family or health conditions from leaving their current location. As they did not have a lot of exposure, they found the best job they could get. And the same was true for the leadership—they were doing the best possible based on their capability and knowledge.

His observations had led him to think over everything in detail.

Chirag had countless chances in his career to settle in a foreign land. But that was not something he had ever aspired to do. He did not find the charm to be successful if there were not others who were successful with you. And this was also his thought in opening his second business—he wanted to take the skills of his people to the world and bring the world to them.

So, by the time Chirag had returned back to the cabin, he had already decided to do something to bring a change for the people of that organization. Of course, the decision to buy the organization was sudden and unlike him. And he would give complete credit, for the strength and the confidence it took him to make that decision in a second, to Jiya. Had he not known her that day, he would have never made such a decision in such a short time.

Ashish had made similar observations at the distributor's office. While he had felt that the team was certainly much more talented than the management, not even in his wildest dreams could he imagine Chirag acquiring the organization. After the two-hour-long discussion with Chirag, he was convinced that the *"weird girl"*, as he liked to call Jiya in his mind, had not influenced his boss too much.

Once Ashish was onboard, it was half the battle already won. Ashish was extremely driven, and he would not agree to something for the mere sake of it. And if he agreed, he would make all ends meet to complete it.

Chirag's senior assistant, Ashish, had just delivered their plans for the newly acquired organization. He started by mentioning the points that led to the acquisition, followed by their proposed one-year, three-year, five-year, and ten-year plans for the organization. Somewhere between five and ten years, the processes in the organization would become streamlined, and they would have to do very little to keep pulling it up. Rather, it should start generating significantly higher revenues and profits. Chirag had patiently repeated the points twice post-Ashish's presentation to get his legal team onboard.

Personally, he thought he might then decide to sell it back to the owners. But he did not volunteer that information to the legal counsel, who was already giving him a hard time.

"Well," Chirag replied calmly in the most casual tones. *"I already did."* He did not raise his voice and neither reflect any mark of anger. But there was certainly a tone of finality - he was done with getting questioned about the acquisition. His sentence jerked him back from the flashback that he had been having for the last few days. Surprisingly, he had never said it out loud to anyone, not even to himself, but he had accepted it in a message to Jiya that he had had a good feeling about the acquisition before going ahead with it. Unfortunately, that was not a reason he could have given to any of his team.

No one had expected him to revert with such a response, especially to the legal counsel, whom he had always consulted before making any significant decision. Chirag believed that Ashish had explained all the points quite well—even he could not have done a better job himself. Hence, they should now focus on the next steps rather than fussing over what is done. Since the deal was signed, there was no backing out.

He looked around, bemused to find the dumbstruck faces looking back at him. Yes, he had considered the executive leaders co-owners, given them extra perks, and valued their counsel. But none of this changed the ownership of the organization. And if he had acquired a firm, there was little the others could do about it now.

There was a silence in the room. The senior legal counsel had taken back his seat. No one knew if they were allowed to speak, and if they were, what should they say? Sensing the tension and suddenly becoming aware of the change he witnessed in himself, Chirag got up, announced a ten-minute break and left the room.

ᗡᗡᗡ

Chirag was pacing the length of his cabin. Eight out of the ten minutes had already passed. He was trying to reason with himself. While he did understand the confusion and uncertainty that the acquisition had introduced into the ecosystem, he did not like the distrust. He had never and would never do anything to harm the interests of his employees—that had always been and will always be his first priority. Being asked questions like this made him feel that he had not earned the trust of his employees. And he did not like his reaction either. He had never dismissed anyone's questions, suggestions, or concerns.

He kept shuffling the phone in his hands. There was a voice in his mind that wanted to dial Jiya. She would surely have a way to talk him out of such thoughts. On the other hand, he attributed the change in his behaviour to Jiya. No one had told him in so many words, but he had seen the change in his assistants' behaviour whenever he spoke to or texted Jiya. They all knew about her and had collectively decided never to mention her. But whenever they saw him replying to her text, they all gave him a look of discouragement and disapproval.

No matter how much he thought about this, he could not understand what Jiya had done. She had never told him to acquire that organization. Rather, she had never told him anything about his work at all. But he was an intelligent man. He remembered telling her all about setting up his first business, selling it, setting up his second and third businesses, and a lot of details in between. While she was extremely excited to listen to all the details, she also kept probing deeper into his thoughts and feelings. She kept asking him about his feelings and reactions to various situations that he narrated to her.

And just like that, he found himself feeling all the emotions that he had experienced through his highs and lows. He remembered feeling vulnerable as a newly graduated student in a strange city. He remembered several anecdotes of surviving through each day. These were things he had kept bottled deep inside him. Since no one before had been interested in these, these things remained safely hidden. Jiya's only fault was to remind him of who he was and how he became that person. Nothing more and nothing less.

The thought of Jiya brought certain other emotions as well. He had found himself thinking about her or talking to her quite too often. While he had reasoned with himself that she was a friend and he was allowed to have a friend, he was not sure if it was a good idea to bring her into his professional life. Ashish and his other assistants had made it clear with their reaction towards him asking them to send her the contract that they were not excited about the idea. Additionally, bringing her and her team all the way from Mumbai with his team not trusting him at the moment might cause additional challenges.

Maybe he could ask her to postpone? Or cancel? Did he even need a photo shoot? His marketing team had been thrilled at the idea of getting a proper advertisement campaign. They had been trying to convince him to have one for over six months. But was the timing and the person right? What if the team was hiding their true opinions considering his changed behavior and actions?

There were a lot of questions that clouded his mind. He was unsure of what worried him more—the room filled with executives, the impact Jiya was having on his life, or the thought of her coming to Delhi.

Maybe he should call her. Chirag picked up the phone and dialled her number. He waited for a few seconds for the phone to connect. Just then, there was a knock on the door. He turned to see one of his assistants informing him that everyone had returned to the meeting room and was waiting for him. Without checking if the call had connected, Chirag cut the call and switched off his own phone.

He needed some time away from her—to reflect on his thoughts and actions.

ϷϷϷ

The first day of the weekend was almost coming to a close. It was a little over half past eight in the evening. Chirag was back in his cabin. There was a fresh stack of files waiting for his return. He felt a little optimistic.

The second half of the meeting with the legal counsel had gone better than anticipated. No one had any outbursts or made accusations. They discussed the plans prepared by Ashish, and Chirag decided to appoint him as the lead for the liaison unit between both organizations. He understood why Chirag had acquired it and had made the same observations as himself. Who better than Ashish could be to implement those plans into action? Surprisingly, Ashish had accepted.

It was followed by another two long discussions with the e-commerce business heads, one regarding the usual issues in business operations and another regarding the new department he had suggested to liaise with the acquired firm. The discussion expanded into several verticals—human resource policies, payroll, compliance policies, employee benefits, and several other things. Chirag had given all those things a brief thought. He was able to provide his thoughts on all of them. However, Ashish had done much more than give a thought. He had already prepared a few detailed documents on the various policies and changes both firms would need in order to set up that seamless work environment.

Making a mental note to catch up with Ashish later, Chirag had emerged from the meeting feeling much better.

It had been a couple of hours since his meeting with the stakeholders. He had still not switched his cell phone back on. It was lying inside the pocket of his coat, lying on the sofa in his cabin. He was well aware of the fact and fought the urge to switch it on and dial Jiya's number. He kept thinking of all the messages that she would have sent him. What if she tried calling him? Finding his cell phone switched off, she would have panicked again.

He was going to cross that bridge when he came to it. He decided he was going to stay longer in the office and review the files. His work kept his negative thoughts and emotions at bay. Moreover, he could finish his work and then enjoy the cricket match on television the next day.

Just as he pulled the first file, there was a knock on the door. It was Ashish, his senior assistant. Chirag signalled him to enter and then returned his focus to the file.

"Is something bothering you?" the senior assistant asked, without any filters or inhibitions.

Chirag looked up. He was looking at a friend rather than an employee. Ashish was still confident and direct. He was never the one to sugarcoat things or words.

There were a thousand thoughts in his mind that were bothering him. For a moment, he thought if she should share them. But then, *which one would he share? Where would he begin? And what all could he tell?* Deciding against the idea, he shook his head with a weak smile and returned to his files.

"Then why are we not going home, having dinner?" Ashish was not going to drop the subject.

Chirag was prepared this time. *"Lots to do."* He replied without lifting his head up, pointing towards the stack of files with his left hand.

"*And why can this not be done at home? Or tomorrow?*" He questioned again.

This time Chirag did not reply. He kept working out the numbers the finance department had sent him. An e-commerce platform was not as easy as everyone had told him. It still took him hours to understand his own revenue reports.

Ashish was still standing by the door when Chirag looked up after a couple of minutes. He smiled at the man closest to a friend and gestured for him to take a seat. There was something he would like to ask as well.

"*You said yes!*" Chirag said calmly after Ashish took his usual spot on the sofa. It was not a question, and there was no hint of accusation in it.

Ashish smiled, "*You asked me.*" He knew exactly what they were talking about.

"*I have asked you several times earlier as well—positions that were far more rewarding and lucrative,*" Chirag responded. It was true. Ashish was the man he considered who could replace him when he would think of retirement. He valued his counsel and had, on numerous occasions, offered him positions to lead a department or a country operations unit. And every time, Ashish had declined.

Ashish was still smiling. Both men looked at each other, unable to decipher what the other was thinking. This was not something that occurred frequently. Most of the time the two of them had understood each other perfectly. This was probably an exception.

"*Is everything well?*" Chirag asked with concern when Ashish did not reply.

Ashish's smile broadened, and there was certainly a gleam in his eyes. "*Maybe I met a beautiful young photographer.*"

Chirag took off his reading glasses and placed them on a table in a serious manner before bursting out. When the two men were alone, they often interacted as friends and equals. Chirag knew most of Ashish's family—having met them in real life and in Ashish's stories. Ashish knew about Chirag's past as well, but since he also knew that Chirag did not like to mention it, the two never spoke about it. Though Chirag was anticipating this conversation sooner or later.

Once the men stopped laughing, Ashish added, *"You have changed, man. Rather, you are a changed man ever since you had that fateful dinner."* This time Chirag was silent. He kept smiling, barely keeping himself from blushing, as he took accusations.

"How come we don't eat dinners spreading across five hours?" Ashish added the final question while getting up.

Seeing his friend leave, Chirag replied, *"Have you come to ask me this?"*

Ashish was already at the door, pulling it open. He turned back, the gleam still in his eyes. He held the door ajar and added, *"For now."* Moving to a side as if holding the door for someone, Ashish added, *"You have an unscheduled appointment, and since you want to spend more time in your cabin, let me just invite them here."* He rolled his eyes, looking mockingly at the cabin as he said the last part.

He walked out saying so, leaving Chirag completely confused. Most of the people had already left. He was in the office with just his assistants and the finance team, as per his knowledge. He stood up and started to move towards the door, his curiosity getting the better of him. He could hear a few faint noises of big luggage and rushed footsteps.

Before Chirag had the chance to reach the door of his cabin, a person ran inside. It took him a moment to realize that it was Jiya. She was beaming at him. She left her suitcase at the entrance and flung her big black purse onto the sofa as she ran over to hug him.

Dressed in blue denim jogging pants with a loose peach top and a traveling coat, Jiya held him tightly with her two slender arms, reaching to his back. He closed his eyes and felt his lips curl to a smile as the warmth spread all over his body. He could not think of anything that had happened between the last time she had hugged him and this moment. All the thoughts that had been bothering him became irrelevant. He could not even think of anything but the way he felt at the moment. Even the realization of being in his office had melted away. Nothing else mattered.

The moment lasted for a long time. It could have been a few seconds, a minute, or a few minutes. But then Jiya pulled back. She looked at his deep brown eyes while he looked into her hazel eyes. He could keep looking at her smiling face. He was already feeling a lot happier and relaxed.

Suddenly, Jiya took a step back, and her expression changed. She grabbed the magazine lying on the table and started hitting him with the same. His emotions took a drastic turn as all the sensations returned. Even the worst articles that any print media had published had not hurt him like the currently useless roll of newspaper supplement magazine was hurting him.

"Why is your mobile switched off?" she kept repeating as she hit him a few more times. She had, obviously, been worried. He swiftly dodged her last blow before pulling the magazine out of her grasp after a few frantic attempts. Putting it on the table, he tried to tell her how hectic his day was and lied. Now that she was here, he could not think of not having her around. He did not have the heart to tell her his doubts and fears. Rather, he narrated the schedule that he had had since morning.

Finally, Chirag realized they were still in the office and that he was the boss. He looked towards the door. Ashish had gone, and he could not see anyone else either. He closed the ajar door and sat down, facing Jiya on the sofa.

"How are you here today?" he asked her, choosing from the countless questions he wanted to ask her. In the excitement of seeing her, he even got the sentence wrong. She did not seem to mind, though.

Jiya reached for her big purse and pulled out some takeout. He knew that smell. She had gotten him burgers from his favourite burger shop in the city. He had told her of the times his friends and he had bunked school and had burgers at a particular shop. It was also the place where he had celebrated several of his and his friend's birthdays. His parents had often bought him his favourite burger from the shop during his exams. The smell brought back several fond memories.

She handed him a cold burger and a pack of cold fries she extracted from the brown takeaway bag and added, *"Someone told me that they always preferred a burger when working late."*

NINE

Things are always brighter on a full stomach and a filled heart! Jiya and Chirag were a testament to the statement. She gobbled through her burger—it was her first meal of the day if the five coffees she took to keep herself working were not counted. After a minute, she swallowed the burger and attacked the fries. She kept sneaking glances at Chirag, who was constantly looking at her. It did not matter how she looked or how ravenous she might appear. The thrill of carrying out her plan had kept her from feeling hungry, but now that she had finally arrived, her hunger hit her all at once—stronger than ever.

She told Chirag all about her plan as she reached out for his share of French fries, having finished her own. Everything felt comical now that she narrated it in the third person. It had been extremely unlike her to rush through a shoot or make excuses to leave early. And even though she had not had a minute to herself, she was quite happy with the amount and quality of work she had completed.

She had completed approximately forty per cent of the shoot by the afternoon. She had set up two stage areas, and the call times had been rigorous. She finished shooting the dresses on the mannequins before the end of the day on Friday—her interns were tasked with keeping two dresses ready while she shot the current ones. It made her expenses go up considerably, but getting to share her meal with Chirag made it worth it. Another set of interns was instructed to have two models available for a night shoot. She got hardly any sleep that night and was ready early Saturday morning to resume.

Models were ready by the time she set up her camera and other equipment. Better lights, a lot of planning, and demanding schedules had allowed her to shoot one batch of all the sixteen dresses on mannequins and half a batch of the same dresses on the models.

Her interns were going to take charge on Sunday to review the pictures. They would share the pictures with her before sending the final versions to the designer. It would take the designer at least two days to come back with his feedback, and the shoot could be harmlessly halted till then. She had casually slipped him that she needed to travel in a personal capacity and should be back by Tuesday. Happy to have a batch of pictures delivered to him earlier, he did not bother about Jiya's absence. One of her assistants would be able to resume the shoot on Tuesday. Her other assistant will join us on Friday. And she could always fly back for a day if the designer got impatient or if any other problem arose.

Saturday had gone in a blur. Sleeplessness had caused her to be more irritated than usual. With significantly less time than she usually had, Jiya rushed all over the place to get things done. She did not take any breaks and sustained through the scorching heat of the high-beam lights with coffee. Her work and excitement to travel later during the day had kept Chirag away from her thoughts for a while, but she got worried a little before noon. Checking her phone, expecting to see his usual mid-morning message, she tried calling him. Her panic grew when he did not answer. She tried repeatedly every thirty minutes, but to no avail. Though she could not suppress the ill feeling arising in her abdomen, she decided to use it as an opportunity. She took no breaks and kept her interns on their toes to keep the shoot running. It was the motivation she needed to finish her work faster to go and check on Chirag. It was already three in the afternoon when she paused the shoot.

Jiya kept dialling Chirag's number several times while on her way to the airport. It had still gone to his voicemail. The adrenaline rush she felt from being in the car and making her way to the airport helped keep the negative thoughts at bay. It was probably, again, for the better. She did not trust herself to hide the excitement of meeting him. She knew he was alright, and when she met him soon, he would give her some lame reason for not taking her calls. She could not help but visualize the various settings in which she would surprise him soon.

Finally, the flight landed at Delhi Airport. The route from here was simple. She had the office address where she was going to meet him on Monday. She tried one more time dialling his number, and when it went unanswered, she took a cab to the office address. Her concern had given rise to a bit of anger—she felt an urge to shout at him for being negligent. However, there was another concern that she currently had. Jiya had no clue about Chirag's whereabouts. He had told her earlier in the morning that he had a big meeting scheduled in his e-commerce office. But that meeting would have ended several hours back. She only had the address of his e-commerce office and decided to make the most of what she had rather than dwell on what she didn't know.

With all her luggage, she hailed a cab from the app on her phone to take her to his office. The cab driver was confused as people usually returned from the office at this hour rather than going to it. Moreover, Jiya was not dressed as someone working in a multinational e-commerce firm. The driver's constant glares did not bother her. She was experiencing an overflow of emotions.

While she looked out of the window, beholding all the sights Delhi held for her, she spotted the shop that Chirag had told her of. It was a burger joint that had outlets all over the city. Chirag had spoken about it quite fondly. Jiya asked the already confused driver to halt while she ordered two veg burgers and two packs of large fries. Securing them inside her bag, she returned back to the cab and asked the driver to move as fast as possible.

She had a letter inviting her to Chirag's e-commerce office. The guards were naïve enough to not check the date for her assignment commencement and granted her entry. They made her fill out a lot of registers, issued her a gate pass, and took several minutes going over the contents of her suitcase. Once satisfied, they walked her to the reception, where she was asked to wait indefinitely by the receptionist. Jiya had asked to meet Chirag, and she had no appointment with him. It was quite unusual for people to walk into their office and demand to meet the CEO. The receptionist did not let Jiya enter the office but also did not deny Chirag's presence in the office.

The conclusion spread a wave of relief over her. Though she had suppressed them enough, the negative thoughts still existed within the depths of her mind. Knowing that Chirag gave her heaps of relief. She let out a long sigh, ignoring the receptionist's flustered response.

Jiya paced across the reception, her heels clicking against the marble floor in sharp, agitated beats. She hated how close she was to Chirag—just a few floors above, in the same building—yet completely out of reach. Her fingers curled into fists at her sides, frustration simmering under her skin as the minutes stretched endlessly. She waited patiently for a few minutes before reaching back to the receptionist. If Chirag was busy, she wanted to meet his team—several other men had been with him in the Lonavala hotel; surely, they would recognize her. Moreover, one of them had sent her the email from the generic mailbox. Jiya produced the email for the receptionist to read.

The receptionist was proving to be extremely inefficient. She had tried reaching Chirag's secretary, but the phone kept going unanswered. She had even dropped messages to several of his assistants and waited for them to reply. Though she did not believe it was likely to come. Several people from the staff had already left. Saturdays were not working for everyone—and the employees who did come left as early as possible. The receptionist tried again to contact someone but to no success.

Jiya watched as employees trickled out of the office, chatting casually, their day wrapped up while hers remained in limbo. She clenched her jaw, her eyes darting to the reception desk, hoping for some sign that she would finally be allowed in. But there was none. The receptionist was not even looking at her but was busy with her head bent low over some papers. Frustrated, she paced along the reception and stared at several well-suited men leaving the building after a long day. A few were chatting, while the others were in a rush to end the long day. Unfortunately, Jiya did not recognize a single one of them.

It had been over eight, and the receptionist was packing her things to leave. An angry Jiya stormed to her and asked her to be allowed inside immediately. Politely, the receptionist denied it. While the email on Jiya's phone confirmed her identity and her purpose to visit, the receptionist could not allow anyone into the CEO's office. The maximum that she could have done was to secure an audience with the marketing team. Unfortunately, none of the team members in the department were present in the office.

Ignoring Jiya's protests, the receptionist called the security guard—who would double as the receptionist in the evenings—and handed him over a few tasks.

Chirag and a few others were apparently still working. And though it was not confirmed, they were probably going to work late. The others had been asked to leave. The security guard should patrol all the floors every hour to keep a count of the people in the office.

Jiya raced her tired mind. She could not think much except about meeting Chirag, the burger in her bag, and sleeping soundlessly for several hours. Having spent a week with less sleep, her mind refused to be as witty as it usually was. She tried once more to call Chirag, but his phone was still switched off. She was glad that he was well, but she thought of how she was going to berate him for keeping his phone off. She had already wasted almost twenty minutes waiting for him at the reception—the twenty minutes that they could have spent talking with each other.

There was just one option—she needed to sneak into the building while the guard was otherwise occupied.

This was easy—something she could do with a shut mind and protesting body. Calmly, she took back her seat and started to mark the various doors leading outside the reception lounge. There were three passages leading inward and two leading outward. All the passages were at a little distance from where she sat. Additionally, she had no idea where Chirag was or how to reach him. Deciding to leave her suitcase behind, she looked around a second time. This time she wanted to find a suitable place to secure her luggage. She could not drag a heavy bag with her on a wild goose chase, and neither could she allow the security guard to catch hold of her. If the suitcase was gone, the guard would believe that Jiya had left.

Just as Jiya was evaluating pushing her luggage inside the female washroom, two men approached her from the left side and called out to her. They were maybe a few years younger than her but were dressed in professional suits. Somehow, they knew what she had been thinking. She could not think of how she was going to talk her way out of the situation. What if they had received the message from the receptionist and had come to ask Jiya to leave as Chirag was busy? Or worse. What if there had been a change in the shoot dates and she had missed the communication? Jiya stood up in panic, sweat trickling down her forehead to her sleek jawline.

"*Where is...*" she corrected herself mid-sentence. Taking a deep breath and switching back to her normal self, she spoke in her most professional voice possible, "*Hi, I am Jiya Thakkar. I have a contract with your organization for a product photoshoot coming Monday.*" She extended her right hand, giving her introduction.

Both the men shook her hand in turn and gave her a meek smile. She sensed that they already knew who she was. None of them bothered to give their introductions but exchanged looks with each other before the senior of the two spoke, "*We know who you are. Pleasure to meet you.*" He was polite but businesslike. "*Is there anything we could help you with?*"

Her list was not huge—Chirag, food, and bed. She could probably do away with food. And she had not slept for several days already; one more was not going to make an impact. So maybe they could just bring her to Chirag.

None of her thoughts made their way to her mouth. Sounding as professional and relaxed as possible, Jiya told the men that she had been waiting for some time to meet Chirag. The men looked from Jiya to the security guard and then to the big suitcase resting by the sofa. They walked over to the security guard at the reception and exchanged a few muffled conversations before returning to Jiya.

They spoke. "*Chirag sir was indeed in an important meeting that got over just a few minutes ago. He would be in his room now. We have been asked to escort you while he is being informed of your arrival.*"

The men escorted her to the fifth floor via the elevator from the passage on the left. Her suitcase had been placed behind the reception desk, and Jiya had picked up her large purse as she followed the men. One of the men took a left turn after exiting on the floor and showed her into a large waiting area. It was a cosy and colourful nook in the otherwise bland office. Five-seater sofas with multicoloured cushions looked extremely inviting. Jiya could lie down for a while.

Before Jiya could marvel at the stacks of magazines and newspapers scattered on the table in front, the other man returned with a third man—and this man was familiar. He was Chirag's assistant from the dining room. He had interrupted their dinner and was extremely displeased at leaving Chirag in Jiya's company. Chirag had mentioned that he was a close friend and one of his most trusted employees. Jiya was relieved to see the man—something she had not deemed possible till now. Certainly, their previous encounters had been less than cordial, but she beamed as she approached her.

She walked over and shook hands with the man. There was no need for an introduction. The two men narrated everything that she had told them. Jiya waited for them to complete before adding, "*I am not able to reach him on his mobile. Is he alright?*"

The man nodded an assurance. He was not going to divulge anything personal in front of her or in front of the other two men. Moreover, he did not seem like someone who wanted to reduce the animosity from their encounters. He asked Jiya to wait for a moment while he checked with Chirag.

Jiya thanked the two men as they turned to leave her alone in her cosy nook. She stood eagerly looking in the direction that the assistant had gone, all thoughts of sleep driven away from her mind. He had walked straight to the right and then into a cabin on the left. It had to be just a few steps away—was all the distance between Chirag and herself. She kept fidgeting, shifting her weight from one foot to another, ready to run to the room at a second's notice but at the same time trying to contain her excitement.

She waited for as long as she could. While she was excited at seeing him, she tried guessing his reaction. Would he be happy to see her? Unable to contain herself, she started taking baby steps towards the room. After what appeared to be hours of misery, the door of the cabin opened, and the assistant walked out. He looked in her direction; she had been in full view and was already halfway towards the room. She had an urge to break into a run. This could be the dumbest thing she had done in her entire life. But that did not matter. Every moment after she met Chirag would be worth it.

She could see a faint shadow behind the tinted glass move towards the door as she approached it. And after what seemed like a lifetime, she saw Chirag.

Jiya paused long enough to absorb how he looked. His hair was perfectly combed backwards. His clothes remained wrinkle-free even after a long day at work. But his brown eyes were extremely tired, and he was in too much shock to smile—something he had done in all scenarios she had built in her head of this moment. His handsome face was lined with stress and anxiety. She could have stood by the door, transfixed at the man in front of her, but then she decided to do something even better. Throwing her purse aside, she rushed to give him a hug.

ppp

Sunday passed in a haze, feeling both fleeting and endless at once. Right on time, the intercom in Jiya's room rang at seven-thirty in the morning. She was already awake, putting the final touches on her makeup.

She wore a soft pink kurti with delicate floral patterns over faded blue jeans, the colours blending effortlessly. A contrasting green scarf was loosely wrapped around her neck, adding a touch of vibrancy. Her makeup was minimal—just enough highlighter to bring out her features, but her eyes stole the show. Thick strokes of kohl and liner framed them perfectly, the dark contrast making them stand out even more. A flick of liquid liner added just the right amount of drama, and her mascara-coated lashes curled beautifully, making her eyes look even more intense. It was a look she had perfected over years of shoots—making her often make the models turn their heads.

She snapped the lid shut on her lip gloss and tucked it into her purse, her fingers absentmindedly replacing the receiver on the phone. A wide grin had spread across her face, adding the sparkle in her eyes and a spring in her graceful stride. Slinging her bag over her shoulder and grabbing her camera, she headed for the door. Excitement bubbled inside her—she could not wait to live through her perfect day!

As she stepped out of the elevator and into the lobby, her eyes immediately landed on Chirag. He was seated on one of the lounge sofas, casually flipping through a newspaper. But the moment she walked toward him, he looked up, neatly folded the paper, and rose to his feet.

Chirag had a way of standing out without trying—effortlessly blending charm with understated elegance. He wore a crisp white polo shirt tucked into well-fitted blue jeans, the simple yet classic style emphasizing his lean, athletic build. As Jiya took in his perfectly curated look, a realization struck her—this was the exact combination she had worn on their dinner. He had noticed. He had remembered.

She stopped in her tracks, admiring Chirag. He looked young and charismatic. Jiya admired everything about him—how he radiated with his inner goodness, the slightly loose metallic watch hanging on his wrist, the way he had gently folded the newspaper, and the way he smiled looking at her. But it was his eyes that truly caught her attention—deep brown, rich and striking, with a quiet intelligence that made them impossible to ignore. Against the crisp white of his shirt, they seemed even more intense, adding to the quiet sophistication that came so naturally to him.

Jiya couldn't take her eyes off him—it felt just like the first time she had seen him all those days ago. He hadn't changed at all, still carrying that effortless charm and quiet perfection. She had spent ages picking out the perfect outfit last night and just as long perfecting her hair and makeup this morning. But standing in front of him, none of it seemed to matter. She looked good, sure, but only because she was with the most handsome man she had ever seen. No number of hours of grooming and expensive clothing could outshine the raw magnetic charm that Chirag radiated.

Chirag reached out, walking closer to her when she found herself unable to move under his spell, holding a single lily in his hand. Jiya felt her cheeks flush as she took the flower and tucked it into her bag. Then, he gently took her hand to lead her to his car. He had planned everything so thoughtfully, and even though Jiya had imagined this moment a million times and Chirag didn't know she was coming, he had turned it into something even more beautiful than she had ever dreamed.

Without a word or raising their eyes off each other, they left the lobby together. Everything else was not significant. Chirag handed the parking slip to the guard, who called the valet to bring their car. Jiya stood quietly, his left hand softly holding her right. As they waited in perfect silence, with the early rays of the sun glowing through the morning sky, Jiya gently slipped her hand from his and wrapped it around his arm. It was a moment she had always dreamed of, but she had never had anyone to share it with. Inching a bit closer to him, she rested her head on his shoulder, adding final touches to her surreal start to a dreamy day.

She couldn't stop thinking about the night before. Despite Chirag not having known of the surprise, he had been thrilled to see her. They had settled into his office, taking over an hour to enjoy their burgers, fries, and conversation. It wasn't until the guard knocked around nine that they realized it was time to go. Everyone else had already cleared out, and Chirag had even sent his driver home.

Jiya assisted him in carrying his files to the car while he helped her with her suitcase. After driving her to the hotel, he waited while she checked into her room, followed by sharing a cup of coffee in the hotel restaurant. Chirag seemed genuinely surprised yet delighted to see her. By the end of the evening, she noticed the stress lines on his face had eased significantly. With a lot of difficulty, Jiya suppressed her desire to grab his face between her hands or to give him another hug.

"*What about tomorrow?*" Jiya called out to him as he got up to leave.

"*What about tomorrow?*" he asked in a confused tone.

Jiya got up and started walking with him out of the restaurant. It was a little over eleven—way past his bedtime—and Jiya did not want it to hinder the time they would get the next day. "I am in your city. Would you not show me around?" Her tone was calm and playful.

Chirag looked down at that very moment, hiding the fact that he had just blushed at her words. Goofily he had taken his hand and started stroking his hair—something she noticed he did when thinking on his feet. The two walked silently side by side till they reached the hotel exit.

"*Are you sure you want to see my city?*" He asked her in an extremely amused tone.

Jiya did not answer. Instead, she kept gazing at him, trying to capture every little detail about him with her eyes. But she did not need to answer. They had gone beyond the point of needing to ask questions and receive answers. Even though she was the one to voice it out loud first, they both knew that they were going to spend the day together. Moreover, it was not the city that mattered, but the perspective of the person showing her around was what Jiya looked forward to.

He took a step closer, enough to whisper only to her. "Be ready at seven thirty in the morning," he said, extending his arm to say farewell. Jiya held his hand and pulled him into a warm, lingering hug before turning toward his car. They walked towards the car, Jiya still holding his hand. She stood on the top of the stairs, and he walked to his car. He reached for the car door handle but paused, a thought flickering across his mind. Taking a step closer to her, he turned and called out to her, his voice tinged with a mischievous tone, "*Would not that be a bit early for you?*"

Jiya scrunched her face in an adorable pout, giving him a look of made-up anger that melted too quickly into a broad smile. He took his seat and drove away as smoothly as he had slid into her life. Everything had been worth the second wonderful evening they had shared together. She could not remember walking back to her room or changing into her night suit.

Her phone buzzed and lit as she lay in bed, being too happy to sleep. Chirag had reached his home and reverted with a short message, "*Sleep well. See you soon.*" She closed her eyes and fell into a sound sleep, eager to enter into the next day.

Jiya woke on Sunday feeling extremely happy about something. The lingering warm hug from the previous evening had left a lasting effect. It had to be all real, as she had never dreamt of so much happiness before. Yet, her reality had suddenly been clouded with a surreal quality. She got out of her bed with a jump. It was six forty in the morning. Though she would have liked more time to get ready, she was certain there was nothing that could prevent her from meeting Chirag in under an hour.

She had taken a bath and straightened her hair. Standing in her bathgown over her open suitcase, she could not decide which clothes to wear. In a haste to get everything done quickly, she had not had the time to pack carefully—instead, she had put most of the clothes she had owned into her suitcase. Instead of cutting her packing time short, Jiya had spent hours shifting her clothes from the small suitcase to the medium suitcase and then to the large suitcase, ensuring she had enough space to stay for a few weeks.

She stood in front of the suitcase long enough that she was only left with less than ten minutes to get ready. Without realizing what she was picking, she grabbed a pink floral dress she had bought long ago. She pulled up her favourite faded denim pants to complete her look. There was a bit of running in the room to reach all her accessories—her purse, scarf, earrings, watch, bracelets, ring, and camera. She did not care for a lot of make-up. It might be a long day, and keeping it minimal was the key for such days.

She was applying her lip balm when the receptionist called to inform her that she had a visitor waiting for her in the lobby.

Lost in her own memories, Jiya allowed herself to be led to the passenger's seat of the magnificent white SUV brought by the valet. Chirag had already taken his seat behind the wheel when she returned back to the present. Startled at finding herself in a different world. Sitting on the soft grey seats, with the sleek dashboard shining in front, she marvelled at how much space the car had. Curiously, she kept looking at the different controls on the music controller and the add-ons Chirag had done to personalize his car. It was shining and grand—just like its owner.

Chirag smiled, seeing Jiya's childlike excitement. The hum of the engine ignited excitement for their day ahead as she wore her seat belt and nodded her approval to be driven away.

ﮩﮩﮩ

It took a few minutes for the rhythm to set. Chirag had a wide collection of music CDs in the glove compartment that he asked Jiya to choose from. Most of his collection, Jiya noticed, was of songs and singers she termed as '*Classics*'. Nonetheless, it was some soothing and melodious tunes. She picked out a Bollywood-instrumental one. She wanted music to enhance their conversations but not disturb them.

"*Do you like this?*" she asked for his opinion as the first song played.

Chirag looked at her, smiled, and replied, "*It's perfect.*"

They drove through some posh residential drives in South Delhi—Chirag was providing her with some commentary as they made their way through the clean and green roads. She had asked him before leaving the hotel as to their destination, but Chirag had playfully denied it. He had merely said, *"It is my turn to plan the surprise."*

The silence kept punctuating Chirag's irregular commentary. She sensed that he was thinking before speaking—not wanting to reveal too much about the surprise. Jiya was not sure if he had felt as happy seeing her as she felt at being driven around. In the moments of silence, she busied herself looking out of the window.

There was a soft golden glow illuminating the city. Ordinary things, such as people walking their dogs or people sweeping the fallen leaves off the road, amused her. Everything looked more beautiful and brighter.

Chirag drove through several roads, leading them deeper into the residential colonies. They drove through rows of houses of varied shapes, colours, and appearances before halting by an old and lonely gate. Had the car not stopped, Jiya would not have even noticed the gate. She looked at Chirag with a quizzical look. He beamed as he stepped out.

Together they entered through the gate into a small section of muddy path. Chirag took her hand as he led her to an enormous garden. Surrounded by trees, the place felt like a peaceful hideaway, illuminated by the soft glow of the rising sun. A light mist floated above the dew-covered grass, giving the scene a divine quality. The pathways were quiet, with only a few locals wandering along the winding trails, while the tree leaves rustled gently in the morning breeze.

The crisp air was filled with the scent of blooming flowers and moist earth—thanks to the big pipes running along the perimeter, spraying water. Chirag guided Jiya down the tranquil paths, their footsteps barely making a sound on the gravel. Jiya had not expected such a remarkable place to exist in the middle of the city famous for its pollution index. She noticed the lack of people—had such a place existed in Mumbai, it would already have attracted all the nearby residents and several shooting units on a daily basis.

As they walked deeper in, the serenity was only interrupted by the occasional chirping of birds and the soft rustle of leaves. She squeezed his hand slightly to communicate the freshness she experienced, averse to interrupting the song of the garden.

The garden's low popularity or hidden existence had not only prevented a lot of foot traffic but also helped preserve its natural element. Chirag, on the other hand, seemed to know it like the back of his hand. He led her around the pathways to a secluded corner, near a picturesque pond surrounded by flowering shrubs. Stopping her a few feet away from the water body, Chirag pointed to the other end, towards a family of peacocks. Their iridescent feathers sparkled in the soft morning light as they moved gracefully on the farther end of the pond.

Jiya's eyes widened at the sight; the peacock's beauty was unlike anything she had witnessed earlier. She had never seen peacocks either outside a biodiversity park or this close. She counted; there were seven of them. Chirag whispered in her ear to bring her out of the spell. The peacocks were scattering. Chirag shook the camera in her hand, asking her to click pictures.

Jiya knelt down to snap a few candid photos of the birds. Chirag kept whispering to her, introducing him to his beautiful friends. There were two males and five females. Never having had a chance to observe the birds at such proximity, Jiya had remained ignorant of their existence. She learned that male peacocks had vibrant plumage while the female peacocks, also known as peahens, were less colourful. The males are known to be more friendly, while the females have a natural instinct for camouflage and survival.

Even as Jiya clicked, the two male peacocks and one female peacock were making their way towards the pair. She looked at Chirag, who was smiling back at her. His surprise had certainly given her tough competition. The peacocks strutted proudly, exuding elegance.

Jiya stood in haste, not wanting to disturb the birds. However, Chirag placed a finger to his lips, silently advising her against sudden movement. He then pulled a handful of dried grains from his jeans pocket and handed them to her. Taking another handful, the two kneeled and scattered the seeds at arm's length on the ground. They waited motionless, waiting for the birds to react.

The birds, familiar with Chirag, hesitated only briefly before approaching the seeds and pecking at the ground. Chirag winked at Jiya, who had never experienced such a moment. An overwhelming sense of wonder and appreciation washed over her. He nudged her, urging her to snap a few more pictures before they moved on.

"Did you like them?" Chirag asked Jiya as they exited the garden.

Wide-eyed with having lived through one of the most beautiful experiences of her life, Jiya hugged Chirag. He had made her extremely happy, and she felt like Adam and Eve might have had when they walked through the Garden of Eden, with clothes, of course.

ᐅᐅᐅ

Once back in the car, Chirag again refused to tell her their next destination. Though this time it did not bother Jiya. Rather than getting anxious, she trusted Chirag to have planned something that was worth experiencing in person rather than getting narrated. She kept listening fondly while Chirag narrated how the peacock family in the garden had evolved.

The couple drove through the city. Soon the residential expanses were replaced with shops or commercial properties. Delhi did not have the skyscrapers, which were quite common in Mumbai. However, they passed through a few rows of big villas, and they marvelled at Jiya. There were rows of houses—no, bungalows—as large as Mannat or Jalsa. Having lived in her small studio apartment for the better part of the last decade, she could not help sneaking peeks at the multi-storied bungalows.

Finally, they halted in Connaught Place—something she knew to be the heart of the city. There was not a person from Delhi that Jiya had met who did not tell her some anecdote about Connaught Place or Lajpat Nagar. She was happy simply for identifying the place before Chirag told her.

The large circular roads were empty in the early hours. It had not even been nine yet. The shops in the vast circular structures on both sides of the road were closed. There were a few people making their way through the roads. They entered the interior circular road, giving Jiya a chance to ogle at the circular park, lines of people emerging from the underground metro station, a few street vendors, and the vast white expanse, sitting together in perfect harmony.

Chirag parked in a quiet spot. He asked Jiya to wait as he made a quick trip to a quaint café nestled along the middle circle. Jiya rolled down the windows and quickly captured a few raw clicks. There were very few times when places such as Connaught Place were not crowded. She was happily clicking as the door opened. Chirag was back, holding two cups emanating the aroma of freshly brewed coffee in a travel mug and two pastries.

Jiya had not known she was craving coffee before she took the first sip. It was thick and strong—just the way she liked it. It also tasted of hazelnut. They finished their mini breakfast before moving again. This time, Chirag told her where they were headed.

ϼϼϼ

He took her to Sundar Nursery—a giant nursery. It was big enough to have an entry ticket, several small monuments, two restaurants, a few ponds, a bridge over a stream connecting two ponds, and an area to hold exhibitions, apart from the trees and nursery area.

Chirag showed her around before finding a perfect spot under a tree by the pond to settle down. He had carried a tote bag from his car, from which he pulled out a thick bedsheet to double as their picnic mat. Jiya was tasked with arranging the sheet and pulling out the rest of the items from the bag while he went to get breakfast.

There were no words to describe how Jiya felt. Chirag had thought of everything. There was a pack of disposable tissues, a few disposable spoons, and some old newspapers. This was just like the school picnics she had attended as a child, only better.

Chirag returned soon enough, followed by another man holding out the plates. He had ordered them a wide variety of items for breakfast. There were hot parathas, two plates of chole bhature, some sandwiches, and two glasses of some shakes. Her stomach agreed most to this surprise. She had barely had any food the previous day and could not help but feel extra happy at the smell of the delicious items he had gotten for her.

Without waiting for him, Jiya pulled a plate of Chole Bhature towards her. One did not visit Delhi and did not savour a plateful of these. She had already taken a bite out of her very hot bhature before Chirag could settle down. But it was too hot, and she jumped up and down, feeling the heat in her tongue. Chirag handed her a glass of the cold banana shake and then reached for the bhature on her plate. Carefully he tore it into smaller pieces, allowing it to cool down. He handed her a tissue as she relaxed a bit.

As Chirag made his way through his plate of Chole Bhature, he started telling her a lot of stories about this park. He had lived close to the park with the peacocks as a kid and had several school picnics in Sundar Nursery. He spoke in an animated manner. Clearly, he loved this place. Though Jiya did not interrupt his speech, she felt extremely glad that him sharing all the beautiful memories of his childhood with her.

The sun had risen to almost perpendicular height, and they had already ordered three refills of their lemonades and three bottles of mineral water. Time had passed quite quickly as they shared their childhood stories with each other. But now, when even the tree and proximity to the pond did not prevent the heat from distracting them, they decided to move.

Jiya helped roll up the bedsheet as Chirag carefully collected every piece of trash and threw it into a nearby dustbin. She held the rolled-up bedsheet closer to her heart, giving it a tight squeeze as she looked at him. He was thoughtful. Not only had he opened up to her and shared so much from his life with her, but his gestures had won her over completely.

It was at this point, while holding the bedsheet and looking at Chirag, that Jiya realized that she wanted to hold him for the rest of her life. She was undoubtedly in love with him. Not only did she become fifteen around him, but he encouraged her to be herself—to fly, to believe, to love. And she loved him for all this and so much more.

She had not made all the plans just to surprise him—she wanted to be with him. Their cold burgers from the previous evening had been as special as their first dinner in Lonavala. She could not and did not want to think of a time without him. But she knew he was special.

This was something new. She wanted to hold him forever, but that was it. Yes, she was attracted to him; he was that handsome. But she enjoyed talking with him and just being around him much more. Being with him changed her as well. He made her a better and more thoughtful person.

Her feelings only increased at what happened next. He returned and helped her put the bedsheet in the tote bag. As she picked up her purse and camera off the ground, Chirag asked, "*Do you want a picture?*"

Instinctively, Jiya took off the lid from her camera lens and started looking around for something to capture. She had not decided what she would shoot when Chirag pulled the camera from her hands. He had meant to capture her picture in the garden.

Something that no one knew about Jiya was that she was a terrible poser. Despite spending the majority of her time telling other models how to stand and pose, she felt extremely silly when she took any of those poses. Resisting getting captured, she made an attempt for her camera.

Chirag was not going to give up either. He held the camera high above his head. Jiya jumped a couple of times but was unable to reach it. This turned into a small chase, during which Chirag managed to capture a few candid shots of Jiya.

It had been at least twenty years since she had posed in front of a camera. She had disliked getting clicked in general, but posing was out of the question. The pictures that Chirag took, however, were perfect. They were blurry, shot from weird angles, and did not focus well, but they were perfect. And she looked extremely beautiful in all of them.

The two roamed around for an hour, capturing different things. As Chirag had already captured a few of her pics, Jiya insisted on him being her model. It was a difficult task as she focused a little more on the model than on the picture that she was taking. However, with every click and every step they took together, she felt a little more in love. And the feeling was great.

Soaking with sweat and unable to bear the scorching afternoon heat of the sun, Jiya dragged Chirag to an ice cream vendor by the gates of the nursery. He took a cassata ice cream while buying two ice lollies.

They took the car once more after finishing their ice creams. Chirag's cassata cup proved useful when Jiya's lollies started dripping. Jiya washed her hands before entering the car, excited for the next part of her day. She did not even ask him where they were headed.

ᗄᗄᗄ

Chirag took the car into a parking lot under a metro station. He informed that their next destination was better reached via an auto, and, he stressed, "*When in Delhi, you should travel in an auto!*"

Jiya was slightly sceptical of his statement but corrected herself almost in the first minute of her auto ride. She had taken an auto several times earlier, but this was one ride she would not forget easily. While Delhi roads were not that broken, the auto driver had a knack for finding the speed breaker or the damaged part of the road to drive through it. Twice he brushed past a pedestrian without even a second glance. Jiya was holding Chirag's hand closely to keep her balance and also just holding it.

Luckily, their journey was not long. They exited the auto outside a museum. Chirag led her inside the big ironclad gates and then through the turning on the right. Soon they were standing in front of the planetarium. Chirag bought the tickets, and they were just in time to catch their late afternoon shot.

They both sank into their seats in the giant circular auditorium, under the dome screen. The darkness was punctured with the sparkling stars illuminating the dome. She was still holding his hand, her fingers intertwined with his.

The hall soon filled up with substantial numbers. There were mostly parents accompanying young children. It did not matter. She was with him, under the breathtaking visuals of the distant galaxies. Resting her head on his shoulder, Jiya closed her eyes, waiting for the show to begin.

As the celestial wonders unfolded on the dome above, Jiya raised her head to look up. Chirag looked down at the same time, in response to her head brushing against his face and neck. Their eyes locked. Their proximity was intensified by the dim light. Soon everything melted away except him.

Chirag could not take his eyes off her either. His eyes reflected all the beautiful moments they had lived through during the day. Jiya remembered how he had made her feel. They were close enough to hear the other person breath. Their hands, still holding each other, were growing warmer by the minute. Every second of looking into each other's eyes was casting an unbreakable spell on the two—something that made all their other senses lose their powers.

They sat there, staring at each other, oblivious to anything the recorded show offered. Their connection broke as the lights were turned on. Chirag hastily let go of her hand and stood up as the people around them started doing the same. They exited the building silently, taking another auto to the metro station parking.

They both were silent throughout their journey. Jiya was lost in her thoughts and did not realize when they reached the parking spot. Chirag paid the auto driver and made his way through the untidy rows of parking.

Something had changed, not just for her but for Chirag as well. Jiya had thought of all of the previous times she had fallen in love. While those men had managed to make her feel beautiful. He did not care how she dressed or what he did—which had been quite important in her previous relationships. He had spent an entire day making her laugh, shared his life with her without asking for anything in return, made her transition to the other side of the camera, and celebrated all her craziness.

In all her relationships, the men had done things quite differently. It had mattered to them how she looked. They needed her to have a career but not one to shadow theirs. And despite them forgetting several things, she was always expected to remember. Chirag was different. He was happy just to see her, and she wanted to be with him because that made her happy.

They drove in silence. It was not a long distance, but the traffic had finally caught up with them. Jiya witnessed the famous 'brake-clutch-drive-brake' driving that Delhi was known for. The car clock beeped, indicating the onset of another hour and finally breaking the silence. Both of them turned to see the display panel at the same time—it was six in the evening.

"There is one more place where we could go before the next place," Chirag whispered.

Jiya looked at him and smiled.

ᐁᐁᐁ

The instrumental music filled the silence. It was not uncomfortable. There was nothing more that she could have asked for. Chirag did not speak either as he drove through the crowded lanes. They drove by India Gate, which he pointed towards, before turning into a road leading away from it. A few more turns later, he entered a small alley and parked his car. It was quite empty except for two other parked cars, an overflowing dustbin, and a couple of monkeys.

They exited the car, and Chirag started leading her towards the nearer end. As the monkeys crossed the narrow lane, Jiya slyly walked over to Chirag and stood behind him. She was pretty accustomed to the cats roaming in the Mumbai high-rise societies or the high-breed dogs owned by most of her clients. Monkeys were a completely new territory for her.

They turned right onto the continuation of the alley. However, this was far from being secluded. This one was overflowing with cars lined on both sides, and people gathered over a few stalls.

Chirag walked her over to a particular stall. He purchased a few tokens and then led her to the epicentre around which people stood. Not till she was close enough did Jiya realize that they had come to a street food vendor selling chaat.

While Mumbai had its own variety of street food, Jiya had not had pani puri for over a year. The moments when she could take a stroll on the chowpathy or enjoy dinner at a small shop were rare. There was always some client who wanted to meet for fine dining or other events where she needed to make appearances. She got too tired for the remainder of the time to plan another outing. Mostly, she did not have the people with whom she could go and enjoy. Hence, she was unsure what she was to expect.

Delhi was famous for its chaat. Chirag had resumed his commentary. This particular vendor had been selling chaat for over three decades. Jiya could only imagine how popular it was, considering some items had already been over, and there were at least thirty people in queue for their order.

Careful not to be too close to Jiya, Chirag walked behind her, moving the people aside with his hands. They made their way through the stubborn crowd waiting for their orders to the Pani Puri end of the stall. Handing him the tokens, Chirag asked for his special masala.

Jiya marvelled at the size of the enormous puri. Before she had time to hold it properly, the vendor had prepared another one to be put on her plate. Hastily, Jiya tried to put it in her mouth in its entirety, resulting in breaking the puri half inside and half outside her mouth, spilling the contents over her dress. Chirag handed her tissues while laughing. The vendor, however, was not amused. He was giving Jiya the angry looks for holding the others waiting for their turn.

ᏭᏭᏭ

After finishing two plates of Gol Gappes, which Jiya found were very different from Pani Puri, the two headed back to the car. Chirag resumed his role as the narrator—the effect of the moment they shared in the planetarium had faded slightly. Though they both maintained some physical distance.

There was no secret to where they were headed next—for dinner. Though neither felt hungry, they were not ready to bid farewell. Jiya could travel for several more hours and to several other locations, as long as Chirag was there beside her. Moreover, she was excitedly anticipating what Chirag would have planned.

As Chirag drove through the bustling streets of Delhi, the music changed to a song of his liking. It was the tune of an old movie song. Without realizing it, he started humming the song. It was something new for Jiya. She stared at him in disbelief. He had a good singing voice. It was deep and melodious, and he did not miss any note. Even without a word, he conveyed the emotions of the song. Her stare made him self-conscious. Abruptly, he stopped. But Jiya was not going to let him—she started drumming over the dashboard with her fingers and bangles. They were officially in a jamming session.

The traffic didn't bother them, nor did the string of traffic lights they had to stop at one after another.

Drums, humming, and made-up lyrics, Jiya did not know, added a magical element. She kept shuffling songs, finding ones she believed he might like and the ones that she was familiar with. After thirty minutes, it did not even make a difference if she knew the song or not. They sang and drummed to their heart's content, ignoring the music for the most part.

After a drive that stretched over seventy-five minutes, which Chirag informed should not have taken thirty minutes had the traffic been smooth, he parked the car in the Qutab Minar parking. Promptly getting out of the car, he made his way around to hold open Jiya's door for her.

They went around the Qutab Minar, not entering the gardens, to a quaint building in a corner, illuminated with multicoloured shades of lights emanating from the ground. Chirag held her hand and guided her inside a quiet door to the left, into a spiral staircase.

The restaurant was perched atop a quaint building, offering a stunning panoramic view of the ancient monument. The sun had reached halfway into the horizon, casting a warm, golden glow across the skyline. The darkness engulfed the part of the sky that the sun had just vacated.

Chirag led Jiya to a cosy table near the edge of the terrace, where they could fully appreciate the view. The waiter showed them to the seat, placed a bottle of mineral water, and removed the 'reserved' plaque from the table. Jiya smiled, amazed at how well Chirag had planned every tiny detail. The entire day had been perfect. She had forgotten all about her work, her worries, and even herself, as she enjoyed every second with him.

As they settled, a server arrived with an assortment of pre-selected snacks and two glasses of sparkling champagne. There were delicate plates of paneer tikka, crispy spring rolls, fish fingers, and a colourful assortment of dips and chutneys. Despite having eaten a lot more than her daily quota, Jiya could not resist the delicious-smelling dishes.

There was a tear forming in her eyes as she looked at him. He was a vegetarian and remembered the fish fingers she had told him that she enjoyed and even ordered them. There was another emotion that welled up inside her—it was not love; it was gratitude.

Chirag was no longer just the silent and ruggedly handsome man, and she was no longer fascinated with his looks. He was a perfect gentleman—someone she did not believe to exist. The man-with-the-Midas-touch was bound to have his flaws; she had several of her own—everyone did. And she did not live under a rock either. Jiya had searched through the internet, hoping to get to know his life, when she found heaps of articles articulating his professional success but very little of his personal life. All she could find was that he was divorced.

She had done this research while on her way back from Lonavala to Mumbai. Then none of this mattered as there were no feelings involved. She had seen a flattering man and was smitten with his personality. Now, after knowing him, experiencing the way he treated her, and the way he made her feel, the information had become irrelevant.

Jiya smiled back, thinking how lucky she had been to accept that ad hoc assignment, travel to Lonavala, and meet him. At this moment, as the sun set, bringing an end to their beautiful day, she wished for nothing more than to witness several more sunsets with him.

TEN

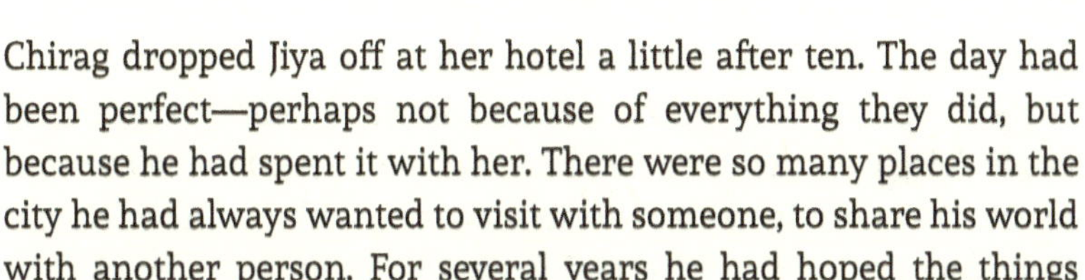

Chirag dropped Jiya off at her hotel a little after ten. The day had been perfect—perhaps not because of everything they did, but because he had spent it with her. There were so many places in the city he had always wanted to visit with someone, to share his world with another person. For several years he had hoped the things would resolve with his daughter so he could take her around. But that never happened, and eventually, Chirag, dejected, let go of his desire completely.

When Jiya had asked him to show her the city through his eyes, he hadn't realized just how much it meant to him. She was becoming the answer to the questions he had. Without realizing how much he was still hoping for this, Chirag had selected his most treasured experiences from his childhood to share with her.

On the drive home after dropping Jiya, his mind kept circling back to her—how she had smiled so often that day, how effortlessly she had laughed. He had felt different, lighter, in a way he couldn't quite explain. He couldn't remember the last time he had eaten so much, talked so freely, or laughed with such abandon. She unlocked a version of him he hadn't even realized existed beneath the suited exterior.

And now, as the city lights blurred past his window, he couldn't help listing all the other places he wanted to take her to. There were so many stories to share, so many places to visit, so many restaurants to try, so many dishes to taste, so many activities to participate in, and so many adventures to experience! All the things that he had not done because he did not have someone to share his joy with, he wanted to do them all with Jiya by his side.

Chirag kept thinking of the future. She was in the city for two weeks, and he needed to plan something for every day at that time.

ᐧᐧᐧ

He couldn't shake off the exhaustion as he got up with the ring of his alarm in the morning. The night before, he had returned late, only to find a stack of files from the previous day waiting for him in his study. Instead of pushing them to the next day, he had chosen to go through them before finally finding his way to his inviting bed.

None of the files were critical or extremely urgent. He could have easily delegated them or done them later. But he did not want work to interfere with his already restricted time with Jiya. The thought of having her in his office and working alongside her made him overlook his fatigue and jump out of his slumber.

He decided on following an indoor workout, followed by a quick breakfast. Despite the late start, he was ready earlier than usual. By the time he took his seat in the car, he was already on a call with his assistants, going over the day's priorities. He wanted time to review a few files before Jiya arrived at the office—because once she did, he had a feeling she would not let him work. He recalled how she had not let Ashish interrupt their conversation the first time they had met. He had no reason to believe that she had changed. Moreover, he did not believe he would be able to work himself knowing she was around.

As a result, Chirag was in his office by eight fifteen in the morning. His assistants were already informed of the same and were waiting for him when he reached. Chirag shared all the notes on the two files he had managed to complete. The briefing ended in ten minutes, which was unusual. Chirag was never known for long meetings, but the first meeting of the day was detailed as he wanted to discuss things in detail to let everyone carry on with their daily tasks.

Usually, he had gone through the files the previous day and had exact pointers with him for discussion. Today, however, was different. He had only managed to read through two files and had only remembered the main headings from them. Unfortunately, he had overlooked a few minor details that his assistants were quick to point out. His senior assistant, Ashish, had let out an audible sigh before stepping in. He offered to postpone their discussion regarding the newly acquired organization, giving Chirag some time to go over the files.

The two men exchanged looks as Ashish left the cabin.

Forcing out all thoughts from his mind, Chirag pulled one of the files open in front of him and started to read through it, keeping a pencil ready to take notes.

ppp

Concentration was proving to be difficult. Chirag had no idea how to resolve the issue, as this was not an issue he had encountered earlier. Lost in the nostalgic lingering emotions from the previous day, he could not help but think of all the places they had visited and how happy Jiya had been. Thinking of the way she looked when she laughed, he could not help but plan the upcoming evenings to spend with her. Every time he found his mind wandering far from the file, he tried to focus back on the open page, which he had read a couple of times without registering anything.

His team had done their homework—digging deep into Jiya's portfolio and analyzing her work. They had raised concerns about her limited experience in digital marketing, but their objections had been half-hearted at best.

Chirag kept looking from the files in front of him to the watch on the wall across from his desk. The primary purpose of the wall clock was to remind Chirag of his scheduled meetings and timely end his overrunning meetings. Currently, it works as a catalyst to fuel his anxiety. Time had seemed to slow down—maybe the clock was not functioning well. It was an unlike scenario.

He noticed that he was acting completely out of character. Not only had he failed to review all the files he was supposed to, but he also overlooked some critical details while working on the two files he had managed to review. This was the first time anything or anyone had come before his work. And to make things worse, since he planned to work more days this week from his e-commerce office, he anticipated a large pile of files from his logistics space waiting in his study each evening.

Pulling up his metaphorical socks and rolling up his real sleeves, Chirag immersed himself in the files. He used a timer technique that an intern had shared with him a few months back, where he would focus on his work for forty-five minutes, at the end of which he would reward himself with fifteen minutes of leisure time. He had never believed he would need to use the technique. But finding himself working against a decreasing time counter on his phone, Chirag felt like giving his school examinations.

By the end of the forty-five minutes, Chirag had managed to rework the two files he had already read through. There were certainly a lot of points that he had overlooked earlier. He took another five minutes to note down the comments from his thoughts. One of their country markets was going through a selective strike. His marketing team had proposed to not operate there as the country was never a high-revenue one. However, his assistants had not agreed and wanted to resolve the problem. Chirag had agreed. They might later face a similar issue in another country—having a solution to such a problem would give them the upper edge.

After finishing writing down his thoughts, Chirag re-read the notes, ensuring he had not missed anything. He was happy with his notes and also had some ideas brewing up in his mind. Mostly he was happy as a simple technique had helped him and made a mental note to thank the intern for sharing it with him. Who knew there was so much to be learned from the newer generation!

Just as he was feeling a bit relaxed at finally having started with his work, there was a knock on the door. The office attendant entered with a fresh stack of files to be added to his existing pile. Chirag forced a smile as the attendant greeted him and left. Chirag's smile was far from sincere and merely out of habit. Going through the files that he had already reviewed had taken long enough; he did not look forward to more files just now.

But when the attendant opened the door to exit the cabin, Chirag heard some voices. He was sure he heard Jiya's voice in the mix. As she was not scheduled to come till eleven, he instinctively looked at the wall clock. It was not even nine-thirty in the morning. He had intentionally scheduled her first meeting at eleven as he wanted her to get some rest. She had, after all, not had much time to sleep during the last few days.

He felt excitement pulse through his body as he heard her voice again—he was not imagining it! He would recognize her voice anytime. And though he knew she was scheduled to be here for work, Chirag could not help but feel happy hearing her voice in his office.

The files were driven out of his mind as in a swift movement he reached the door. Once out of the cabin, he heard Jiya's voice again—loud and clear. He walked into the corridor in the direction that his ears guided him towards.

He reached the intersection point. He could no longer hear her voice and was unsure where to proceed next—whether to turn or to walk straight. Before he could make a choice, he saw two of his assistants emerge from the marketing head's cabin. And they were followed by no one other than Jiya! The sweet odour of her perfume announced her presence before he could see her. And soon he heard her say farewell to the marketing head.

Jiya turned and saw him. She beamed and rushed to meet him. Chirag felt a little self-conscious. He was, after all, in the middle of the corridor of glass cabins. Though things were playing differently in his head than they did in front of him. Jiya came close enough and extended her hand to shake his. It was quite a professional handshake to a curious onlooker; Jiya's wink or the unusual length of the handshake might just have gone unnoticed.

The marketing head emerged seeing his boss standing near his cabin, and so did the occupants of the other cabins. His assistants started introducing Jiya to everyone.

After a lot of hearty handshakes and polite exchanges, Jiya turned back to Chirag. She did not care if others were seeing her. Putting a hand on her stomach and pouting to make her face look cuter, she asked with uncertainty, *"Breakfast?"*

ϷϷϷ

Five of Jiya's interns had flown in the previous day to join her for the shoot. They had followed her around the office as she had entered it, exuding an air of confidence.

She had asked Chirag for breakfast and, without waiting for him to answer, had started walking towards the elevator. Chirag had promptly joined her side, ignoring the looks of all his department heads and assistants. Her interns had followed them silently.

Chirag took her to the cafeteria on the ground floor. The breakfast timings were over, but they had a decent menu selection from the three shops open between seven in the morning and nine at night. Her interns headed for the farthest corner the moment they stepped out of the elevator, while Chirag led her to the nice lounge chairs by the sunlit windows.

Putting her purse down, Jiya walked over to all three outlets, taking her own time to decide what she wanted to eat. And then ordering more than he could believe her to finish, she was back. None of the vendors had taken any money from her as they had seen whom she was accompanying.

Jiya was pretty impressed with this and kept teasing Chirag till the food was delivered.

Seeing the quantity and the way her face lit up, Chirag could not help but wonder if he had not fed her properly the previous evening.

ϷϷϷ

Breakfast was a relaxed one. Neither of them spoke of the previous day. Now that Jiya was in the office in an official capacity, all her attention was focused on work. She kept telling him about the different photographers she knew who were experienced with advertisements and all the conversations she had had with them before coming here. She had done a lot of reading and prep work. However, Chirag was having a difficult time focusing on work talks.

He could not help but notice how the morning sun lit her sharp features. The orange show highlighted the left side of the face, while the lighting overhead gave her right profile the illusion of being sparkly.

She was wearing a loose maroon top with her dirty grey jeans. Her usual stacked bangles were accompanied by some pearl earrings. He knew she had given the 'professional look' a serious thought as well.

She kept on telling him things without needing much response. And even though Chirag wanted to focus on her words, he kept admiring the way she looked, her excitement for the project, or just how perfect she was.

Her interns had finished their respective meals in a normal duration but kept waiting for Jiya as they did not know where to go. One by one, they kept walking around to check she was still there. Jiya, who was sitting with her back turned towards them, had not bothered at all. It was just one of the other things that kept distracting Chirag from focusing on the details of the project that Jiya was telling.

They had a long breakfast. After sandwiches, poha, milkshakes, and dosas, Jiya announced she was ready to leave. She needed the remaining twenty minutes to prepare for the meeting. Chirag obediently dropped her outside the meeting room. His assistants, who had been asked to accompany her at all times in the office premises, had booked a separate room for her for the entire day. Her interns were sitting comfortably while Jiya busied herself arranging her laptop and camera.

Chirag observed her from some distance. He was amazed at the way she was carrying herself—there were no inhibitions or shyness. She commanded his assistants around just as she commanded her interns. She stood next to her laptop, looking at the screen while others rushed around to get her instructions completed.

He had had a lot of doubts about inviting Jiya for the photoshoot. It was not her capability that had caused Chirag to doubt but her style of working. She was an independent and free-spirited artist, whereas his world was way too organized with people in boring pantsuits following the hierarchical order through multiple files and emails. He did not believe she would like it.

But seeing her, Chirag felt she was probably much more comfortable than he was. She dressed differently, but she brought her own creativity, freedom, confidence, talent, and strengths. And despite blending completely into a professional look, her vibrancy and free-spiritedness were adding a beat to his office as well.

Jiya's meeting was scheduled with his sales and marketing team executives. Chirag had never believed in the power of modern advertisements. He believed in developing a product or service of such quality that it could be sold to the first batch of clients. Those clients would act as their brand ambassadors and help spread the word. This method, he believed, was the best way to grow any business. It had worked for him so far. However, the young and more educated recruits of his sales and marketing team did not miss a single chance to point out that it was a lack of a celebrity endorsement or a catchy tagline every time there was a dip in sales.

In the greed of getting to spend more time with Jiya, he had invited her to shoot a proper advertisement campaign. Together, the Sales and Marketing team would reach out to an agency, and the three teams would sign a mutual contract—Chirag's e-commerce business would provide the funds, the agency would provide the concept, and Jiya would shoot it. To make the process smoother, forming a synergy between Jiya and the Sales and Marketing team was paramount to deliver the best results in the agreed duration.

Chirag had chosen to remain out of the meeting. He had always encouraged everyone to get a chance to lead. Moreover, he was not sincerely interested in the outcome. Jiya had managed to enchant him with all her animated conversations over one dinner. She brought a refreshing and unique perspective to life. The more he heard of her views on everything, the more curious he felt to know more. And before he could have given it a rational thought, Chirag had already invited Jiya for the shoot.

Nonetheless, further interactions with her did not deter him from his instinct. She was extremely dedicated to her work and had an appetite to learn and grow.

As Chirag watched Jiya listen through the presentation, he felt a personal click with her on top of the professional one that he had gauged in their first meeting. She was a self-made person and valued talent and hard work above everything else. Though she did a great job at petrifying her team, she was a kind person at heart. At any point in time, she would have a fair idea of any personal problems that her team members might be going through. She would dress as per the mandates dictated in her social circle but valued the simplest things in life. Most importantly, she did not care for the pretence a person might put up but listened patiently to their concerns and emotions.

She clicked in his life, filling the space of a friend, mentor, companion, and so much more.

Click... Click...

Chirag was forced to exit his daydream with his senior assistant actually clicking his fingers in front of his face. Chirag had zoned out of reality and was lost in his thoughts.

"What makes one this happy early on in the day?" Ashish asked in his candid voice that the two men only use it with each other when they are not being overheard.

Chirag had no idea he was smiling. He took a quick look at Jiya, who was sitting down with her head resting on both her hands; he turned his attention to his friend. The action had not been lost on Ashish. He shook his head in disagreement.

"Are you sure this is what you want?" he asked, his voice with the right mix of concern and warning.

Chirag raised his eyebrow in response to the question. He was not sure what they were talking about—Ashish had been one of the strongest advocates for having an advertisement campaign; he would not be objecting to it.

Ashish's brows came quite close as he gave his friend a look that felt like being x-rayed. *"The thing we were discussing before your friend,"* he paused to look at Jiya, *"interrupted us the other day."*

The last five words were devoid of all concern and just a simple accusation. Unsure if he had conveyed his message well enough, Ashish continued, *"The girl is more trouble than you might think."* He paused, thinking if he should ask it out loud. Deciding on whether he would rather give rise to some unwanted behind-the-scenes talks, *"Do you like her enough?"*

Chirag was not offended. It had been apparent to him that he did like her. He liked spending time with her. And he did not see any harm in the same. Smiling while he weighed his words carefully, Chirag took a chance to look back at Jiya—she had stood up and was talking with her hands in constant movement around her stationary body.

"I like spending time with her. She brings out the best in me." He said it out loud for the first time. It did not feel wrong or incorrect in any way. Though it did feel like he was making an excuse to justify himself.

Ashish rolled his eyes with a sigh as loud as voicing his mind on Chirag's words with a raspberry. He did not care for anything less than a sincere conversation with his friend. *"Yes, I get it. She put life into Pinocchio, but does Pinocchio love her?"*

These words had the desired effect on Chirag. Throughout the previous day that he had spent with Jiya, he had no reason to explain why he had arranged all the things that he did. Not only had he taken her to all of his favourite places, even the ones he had not visited himself for several years, but he had also made quite a few calls to get the coffee shop open early and the restaurant to prepare all her favourite items. And sitting in the planetarium holding her hands had made him think of her more than a friend.

But neither was he looking for anything more nor was he going to let him believe that it was anything more. The words even sounded wrong. Shaking his head, Chirag decided to spend his time elsewhere. He needed to clear his thoughts.

Without meeting his friend's eyes and keeping company in his thoughts, Chirag walked out of the room.

ᐅᐅᐅ

Chirag did not want to risk meeting anyone specific. He wished time would pass and provide him with the answers. This was not a good situation to be in—conflicted between what made him feel good versus what made him look good. He walked around the floors of his office without any specific place that he wanted to reach.

He greeted the people he passed by, halted at the pantry areas for casual catch-ups, and even helped out some of the junior analysts in the accounts department. It was not unusual for him to do this. Rather, it had been the most interesting part of owning a business—he could walk up to anyone at any time and start learning.

Though, currently, his intention was just to keep himself occupied.

Chirag had walked up and down several floors, taking random turns. He knew most of his people by name or at least by face. Thus, it was easy to stop at anyone's desk and start talking. He had spent some good time in the accounts department when one of the analysts called out to him.

He looked up in the direction of where he was pointing. Jiya was walking down to where he sat with Ashish—exactly the two people who were capable of messing up his thoughts even further. He was sitting thick in the department. If he were to get up to leave, he would certainly get spotted. Deciding camouflage was his best bet, Chirag continued looking into his file.

The senior assistant and Jiya had not noticed him as they walked to the other end of the room to meet with the head of the accounts department. Chirag saw from the corner of his eyes as his senior assistant spoke with an air of authority while Jiya kept looking around.

"Chirag!" she called out, evidently spotting him. The happiness reached her eyes, replacing the monotony of the boring

conversation she escaped to go to where he sat.

A lot of other heads turned in his direction as well. Firstly, no one had ever heard anyone address him by his first name, especially not loudly through the corridor. Secondly, even though it was not uncommon for Chirag to visit people at their desks and often help them out, he had never sat down for long enough to complete an accounts sheet. Chirag could not think which of the two was causing more heads to turn.

When he saw her approach him and everyone give their attention to the two of them, Chirag knew there was no escape. His senior assistant and the head of the department had followed Jiya. Closing the file and handing it over to the analyst, he listened as she animatedly spoke about her meeting.

He did not care for anything else. It was his moment of clarity.

ᐅᐅᐅ

Jiya had been invited for just the photoshoot. While Chirag's team was discussing their approach to shooting an advertisement campaign through an agency, she had an idea, and most of Jiya's ideas were pretty good. She had read through the company's profile, and through her conversations with Chirag, Jiya had had a good idea of what would be a good advertisement that he would certainly approve of.

Hence, without any extra cost, Jiya offered to do the entire advertisement campaign. Right from conceptualization to sound and editing, her team and she would take care of it.

Her offer was met with a stony silence from everyone. Her interns were too shocked to say anything, while Chirag's employees were unsure if she was joking. Foremost, Jiya did not usually do ad campaigns. And then an entire ad campaign was not just about good pictures; they needed something that the audience would connect with.

However, Jiya was not going to give up. Even as people looked at her with doubt and disbelief, she was sorting out the details in her head. And she liked how they were taking shape.

Jiya decided to share the first draft of her idea on the spot. It was certainly an idea that most people in the room appreciated. The concept was not the problem. She still did not have enough confidence to handle something this big.

The senior assistant, who had joined the meeting post his conversation with Chirag, had felt a sense of déjà vu. Not so long ago, Chirag had had a similar idea to acquire a firm that they were going to reject as a business partner. Though there had not been much work done to formalize the processes in that firm, Ashish had gone through reports of their previous years, and things did look positive. Chirag's whim might have been sudden but had paid well. And just like that, the good idea had come the day after Chirag had had dinner with Jiya; there was no reason for him to doubt this decision being a bad one.

Once the senior assistant supported something, there was little room in the meeting room for doubt. They talked a bit more about Jiya's idea, refining some things.

The meeting ended with an excited Jiya and confusion among the rest of the attendees. It would be the biggest project of her career. Not only was it a different kind of shoot, but if she could deliver it successfully, she could take up more advertising assignments. That would open way more avenues for her.

When Jiya discovered her passion for photography, it started with normal shots such as sunrises, sunsets, flying birds, scarlet skies, city landscapes, and night sky. However, when she started interning with photographers, she soon discovered that her love for art was in the city with a belly full of tasty food. Her only internship with a wildlife photographer had made it quite evident that she was not meant for the outdoors.

She had, then, chosen her specialization with a lot of thought. Fashion photography was the most common niche, and the competition was high. But she did not mind that much. And even years after having had her own setup, her avenues for change were highly limited. No one would ask a fashion photographer to shoot an advertisement, let alone deliver it completely.

She did not wish to miss the opportunity.

Excitedly, she accompanied the senior assistant to the accounts department. She was not going to charge any extra fees, but there would be some extra finances that the organization would need to take care of.

Chirag listened calmly as Jiya narrated the entire scene. And it was not only him; everyone in the section was listening to her. It was not much out of choice than out of politeness and curiosity—they did not want to interrupt someone speaking, and it was interesting to see her talk to their boss. He did not know if it was fortunate or unfortunate that the only thing relevant to him was how excited she was. There would be lots of time later to get judgmental looks—he had been getting them all his life. But he had not met anyone like Jiya before.

Maybe Ashish was not being absurd.

Once she finished her narration, Chirag guided Jiya to a cabin he had booked for her and her team. His Senior Assistant had followed them to their floor. Just as the three left the elevator, Chirag was sure he heard a whisper hidden inside a fake cough that sounded like, *"Pinocchio."*

ᗡᗡᗡ

The rest of the day had been quite busy. Chirag kept dropping in and out of Jiya's room as it was already too cramped. At least that had been his official statement.

The sales team shared with her their targets for the upcoming years and the locations that they wanted the sales to drive from. The Marketing Department Head had formed a small working group that was cramped in the room with Jiya's interns and herself. Two of his assistants had also been asked to join them and cater to all requirements.

Before lunchtime, the large whiteboard in the room had been completely filled with lines, arrows, and scribbles. There were a few charts on the desk containing several discarded versions of their plans. Sketch pens, markers, pencils, erasers, and pens occupied all available surfaces. A few open notebooks lay scattered among all the other items, where everyone noted down the requirements.

Chirag had joined the entire lot for lunch at their cafeteria. After having that few hours with Jiya, his team had become quite positive about the whole idea. It could also be attributed to the fact that when his assistants narrated Jiya's tale to him again, Chirag supported the venture. He had instructed them to do their best, and in case, despite everything that they could do, the campaign failed, he would find funds to cover up the losses.

His approval had certainly increased the confidence in the room. Little did they know that there was no chance that he could deny his approval since it had meant so much to Jiya.

The team worked through the afternoon and well into the evening. Chirag had taken this time to complete a few of his calls. Getting to his pending files had been impossible—every time that he had reached his cabin, he had either been called for an urgent matter or called back in by Jiya.

By tea time, Chirag had given up all hopes of getting any files completed today. However, there were a few discussions he needed to have with his country offices for his logistics firm. Considering how his day had gone, Chirag was not sure if he would be able to make time for those calls later in the week. Hence, he asked his assistants to get the calls scheduled immediately. While Jiya was busy, he could use the time to close his calls. As the shoot would be in the studio from the next day, he would also spend most of his time travelling between his offices and the studio.

It was not until quite late in the evening that Jiya felt content with their one day's effort. His employees were quite excited. They had never worked on such schedules, and working with a renowned photographer was already keeping them motivated. Her interns, however, did not need to be told twice. They packed all their things and their bags and left before she could have a change of heart.

Chirag escorted her to her hotel, where they enjoyed a lot of conversations over dinner before he left for his home.

ꕤꕤꕤ

The next morning, Chirag joined Jiya for breakfast, savouring the quiet moments before the chaos of the day took over. She was still the same vibrant, determined woman, yet something about her had shifted. The playful, relaxed energy she had emitted on Sunday was now replaced with razor-sharp focus. Even as he sat across from her, she barely noticed the sandwich he had ordered for her, too absorbed in firing off questions about the product and his vision.

Their breakfast felt rushed, almost transactional, but Chirag didn't mind. He had seen this version of Jiya yesterday—the woman who lost herself in her work, who lived and breathed creativity until she shaped something extraordinary. It was part of what made her so captivating.

They had rented an SUV, but Chirag had insisted on driving Jiya himself. He wished her luck as he dropped her off at the front gate before starting for his office. As soon as she arrived at the studio she had rented in Delhi, she switched gears completely. Blocking out everything else, Jiya was in her 'Queen' avatar. If she committed to something, she would ensure it got delivered. And there were no shortcuts—there could be some creative solutions, though.

The first step was always to familiarize yourself with the working space. Not only did this allow her to mentally compartmentalize the areas for different utility, but it also helped check if they were missing anything. The space was expansive and well-equipped, giving her full freedom to bring her vision to life. Her team was already there, along with the studio staff, waiting for her lead. She moved through the rooms quickly, scanning the equipment, checking the lighting, and mentally piecing together the framework of the shoot. Every small detail mattered.

Within moments, the studio transformed into a flurry of activity. Jiya stood by the whiteboard, sketching out a rough storyline, and explaining ideas in quick bursts. Her interns, long accustomed to her working style, trailed behind her with notepads, jotting down every word. She tested the lighting, noting the variations she could play with. She ran her fingers over different drapes, carefully selecting the perfect textures and colours to match the mood she envisioned. Every background, every prop, and every minute detail had to be just right.

Hours blurred together. Jiya was relentless and completely immersed in her work. The world outside the studio ceased to exist—she didn't check her phone, didn't pause for a break, didn't even think about food. She was everywhere at once, overseeing setup, adjusting angles, and ensuring everything aligned with the vision she was crafting in her head.

By the time she finally stepped back to take it all in, the studio was already evolving. Half-formed sets stood in place, the whiteboard was no longer just vague ideas, and her team looked completely drained. But Jiya? She was exhilarated. This project was more than just another campaign—it was an opportunity, and it was for Chirag, and she needed it to be her best work yet.

The thought of him sent a jolt through her. When had she last spoken to him? Breakfast felt like a lifetime ago. A flicker of regret settled in, but she pushed it aside—she had done what had to be done.

Her stomach twisted in protest, reminding her that she hadn't eaten all day. She ignored it, pushing open the door to the editing room. There was still more to do before she could call it a day. But before diving in, she finally reached for her phone, only to be met with multiple missed messages from Chirag. A soft smile tugged at her lips.

Her world expanded a little. It was everything in the studio and one man waiting outside for her. The thought brought a big smile to her face.

ELEVEN

After a long, gruelling day at the studio, Jiya had finally captured a series of images that made every bit of the effort worthwhile. Working with Jiya—the photographer—was an exercise in patience. Her meticulous attention to detail and relentless pursuit of perfection kept everyone on their toes. But managing Jiya—the editor—was a different challenge altogether. She was an even harsher critic, scrutinizing her own work with ruthless precision. She edited her work as if the world had shrunk to the hundred-odd pictures now stored on the computer before her, each one demanding her full attention.

The main studio lay cloaked in darkness, the remnants of the day's work scattered like scattered drops of oil in a pool. The beam lights had been shut off, carpets rolled away, and props hastily packed into cardboard boxes lining the edges of the room. If a stranger walked in now, they would have no idea of the magic that had unfolded there just hours ago. Such was the paradox of showbiz—you could conjure breathtaking beauty from nothing, only to erase it just as swiftly.

Most of the crew and technicians had left as soon as the shoot wrapped up for the day, but Jiya remained. Her work was far from over. She had spent hours testing lights against the green screens. She had read through the company's profile and found that it valued the employees and artisans above everything. She would not have expected anything less from a place owned by Chirag. And when they were discussing the details during the meeting in the office, she had an idea. Why not have an advertisement customized for the audience? The purpose would not be to sell the product but to market the skill sets. They would shoot the artisans against a green screen and later overlay it on a video of the native place. The ads would also run in multiple languages.

The team liked the idea. They, however, needed some time and budget to bring the artisans to Delhi for the shoot. That should not be a problem as it would cost less than whatever the ad agency would have coated them. And it was for the same that Jiya and the senior assistant had visited the audit head.

Not only was the advertisement going to be unique, but the team believed they could get some government backing as well. It could also later be expanded into a documentary—to study the business use case. For Jiya, it served three purposes. Foremost, she was certain that Chirag would approve of it. Second, after the initial few days of setting everything, she might get a day or two of rest while the artisans were being brought. She could use that time to travel back to Mumbai. Finally, this was not something that would wrap up in two weeks. She was going to get a lot more of Chirag than they had initially anticipated.

Jiya sat at her desk, the soft glow of the computer screen casting a pale light on her features, sharpening the contours of her concentrated look. This shoot meant more to her than any assignment before. Normally, she would delegate lighting and image sorting to her interns, letting them filter through the first round of selections. But not today. Not for this shoot.

Her interns hovered behind her, shifting their weight from foot to foot, exchanging anxious glances. They longed for the day to end, but Jiya remained unaffected by their silent protests that turned to pleas over time. Her focus was razor-sharp, her scrutiny relentless. Each click of the mouse was a decision, a judgment, and there was no place for any mistake. Every angle, every shadow, every frame held weight, each one a puzzle piece sliding into place to bring out the best picture for the campaign.

It was not just that Jiya wanted to deliver a good piece for Chirag—she did this for herself. Her work was her meditation and connection to the divine. Photography had not been just a career; it had been her language, her expression, her way of making sense of the world. It was way more than a means to earn; it was her means to feel accomplished. And every perfect angle that she shot made her believe in herself. The thought of sharing her experience with Chirag this time had only added quite a lot of excitement and fluttering in her stomach.

Time slipped away unnoticed. The ache in her shoulders had become a dull throb; her body was protesting the long hours she had ignored its need for basic movement. A faint symphony of crickets played outside the partially open window, the night pressing in around her like a silent observer. Her stomach twisted in protest, reminding her that she had skipped lunch. And dinner. But she had always given her preference to the organs in the order of their occurrence in the body, starting from her head. Currently, her mind was focused on the work, and her heart was set to deliver a perfect masterpiece. Her stomach had no standing before the two maestros.

The studio was silent except for the rhythmic clicks of her mouse and the occasional murmurs indicative of the continued presence of her interns. Jiya had always liked working in silence, as it allowed her to focus completely on her tasks. However, after bringing in interns, she understood that she needed them in the room; otherwise, she would end up explaining her process over and over again. The rule, however, was to be present unless asked to interrupt.

Her thoughts drifted to Chirag as she felt her phone buzz a bit in her jeans pocket. Had he stayed late at the office? Had he gone home? Their last exchange had been negligible. His marketing team kept tabs on her progress through her interns; she had no time to call and greet people at regular intervals. However, she wished she could have had that with Chirag. She reached for her phone, hesitating, then set it aside. Work first. The rest could wait.

The soft creak of the studio door barely registered in her consciousness. It was only when the whispering of her interns became prominent that she flicked them a sharp look, silently demanding silence. And then, as if the Universe had taken to answer all her calls, Chirag walked into the monitor room.

Jiya stood up, forgetting all about what she had been looking at a second ago. He carried several boxes—steaming, fragrant, and undeniably filled with pizza. The scent of melted cheese and freshly baked dough hit her senses, and only then did she fully register just how hungry she was.

A smile curled at her lips, warm and unbidden. Without saying a word, she pulled out a chair and set it beside her for him to occupy. Chirag passed three boxes over to the interns and gestured for them to eat as he took a seat beside her holding a box of hot pizza and some garlic bread.

"How did you know I was starving?" she asked, her voice filled with excitement as she hungrily pulled a piece of the garlic bread from the box.

"I heard you were working late," he said, his grin teasing. *"And really, is there anything better than pizza to fuel late-night creativity?"*

They both laughed while Jiya took another piece of the garlic bread with one hand and opened the pizza box with her other.

▷▷▷

Even something as simple as a pizza transformed itself into magic when Jiya and Chirag were together. She did not remember talking as much as she did while having a pizza. Chirag had been right—pizzas were the staple food when there were a lot of late nights involved. They required less thought process, and it was difficult to get a pizza wrong unless someone was hell-bent on using stale items.

Pulling the long strand of cheese off the last slice of pizza to roll between her fingers before finally adding it to her mouth, Jiya remembered what she had been doing. It was like a switch suddenly went off that she took a tissue, wiped her hands, and then pulled the screen a bit closer.

Jiya started navigating between various pictures. She was overcome with the excitement bubbling within her to share her work with him. She was not showing these pictures to Chirag Kapoor—the man who would pay for her work—but to Chirag—someone whose opinion mattered to her. She was keen to show some pictures while hiding some as she felt they were not too good.

Even though Chirag could not have made out the difference and all the pictures looked weird to him as they were all taken in front of a giant green curtain (in his words), he waited patiently and looked through them all. He nodded at all her words, interrupted only once to ask for clarity on something she had said, and, most importantly, gave audio clues at all the correct locations. He was the perfect listener, just as he was perfect with everything else.

Things were always better with a full stomach—Jiya's rule was universal. As Chirag packed the empty boxes and stacked them neatly near the exit, Jiya could not help but feel way better than she had done in the last few hours. Her shoulders did not ache. Her head felt lighter. And Chirag's presence made her want to sing. Being in love was weird; it gave one the confidence to attempt things that they already knew were never meant for them.

They continued looking through the pictures as Jiya walked him through her concept. He did not question her even once on if she would be able to handle it and did not offer any help either. Rather, when she confessed that the idea of delivering the whole giant assignment was scary, he merely said that if he believed there was someone who could do it, it had to be her.

Jiya did not know if it was possible, but she felt a heightened level of emotion for Chirag. Though she had felt the same way in the planetarium and the same way during their dinner in Lonavala. With every moment that they spent together, she had only found her emotions to increase.

So lost was she in her own world that she had lost track of time. When two of her interns came around to collect their water bottles, it was Chirag who reminded her that it was getting late.

She checked the time—thirty minutes until midnight. Her interns had taken an unusually long time to finish their food. It was nothing she had not seen earlier. Unfortunately for them, such late nights were always in Jiya's studio, where they needed to order their own pizza, and there was no other room where they could disappear.

"*I have an SUV waiting outside. My driver can drop them home,*" he offered smoothly, as Jiya asked the two interns if they had booked a cab. Their faces broke into grins at the thought of a pack-up. Jiya was, however, doing some math—five interns, herself, one driver, and their luggage would be difficult to fit. Chirag might have seen through her mind or merely waited before adding, "*And I can drop you.*"

It was difficult to say who was happier—Jiya felt a roar of emotions at the offer; the interns were glad at not having to share any more time with their boss; while Chirag looked a little flushed at his own courage to make the offer. Unsure she would be able to speak, Jiya nodded her head vigorously.

ᏜᏜᏜ

It took Jiya almost thirty minutes to gather her things, her mind running through the list of things she wanted to accomplish the next day. Chirag, being Chirag, had already seen off the interns in the SUV waiting outside the studio. Since they were alone except for the security guards at the gate, Chirag followed Jiya around the studio, holding the items she kept segregating from the heaps lying around.

He helped her place the lights in the corner to avoid accidental collision and roll the long cords. He also found the prized camera that she had forgotten in the main studio hall.

Once Jiya had secured all her belongings safely in her purse in her left hand and held her camera in the other, she turned to confirm that the security guard was properly locking up before she left. After all, it wasn't her studio—it was a rented space, but she was paying for all the props and expensive equipment lying inside. Satisfied that everything was secure, she and Chirag stepped out into the night under the vast starless sky.

They had only taken a few steps towards the side where Chirag had parked his car when it started to rain heavily. Within a few seconds that it took them to realize the sudden change, the intensity of the downpour increased, transforming the paved street into a shimmering ribbon of water streams. Huddled under the building's awning, Chirag pointed out his car, parked a good distance from where they stood. A playful grin spread across his face as he turned to her and asked, "*Ready for a sprint?*"

Jiya smiled broadly. Despite the long hours, Chirag's enthusiasm was infectious, and she could not help but forget her worries about her bag or camera and become, as her team called it, 'fifteen' again. It was as if by magic Chirag knew exactly what she wanted and liked and kept bringing those things to her. Without thinking twice, she dashed out into the rain, eager to catch him off guard.

Chirag dashed after her, just a heartbeat behind as they raced through the puddles. The rain hammered against the pavement, its rhythm blending with their laughter—a melody of joy. Jiya felt a thrilling lightness, each raindrop splashing against her face, neck, and arms, igniting a happiness that had been missing for too long. At that moment, the world faded away; it was just the two of them, running and splashing, wrapped in unbridled happiness.

With every stride, she cast furtive glances at Chirag, who had not only managed to catch up with her but was overtaking her with almost no extra effort. There was something mesmerizing about his movements—confident and graceful. Raindrops trickled down and shone under the heavy night lamps illuminating the otherwise empty campus, just as they had shimmered when she had seen him for the first time. She had admired him since then. His striking features and deep brown eyes captivated her, drawing her almost involuntarily.

As they dashed toward the car, Jiya's heart pounded—not just from the run, but from the exhilaration of the moment. With every step, the space between them seemed to dissolve, an unspoken energy pulling her closer to him, binding them in a shared rush of spontaneity.

It had only taken them a couple of seconds to reach the car. They both laughed as they giggled at their childlike race. Jiya looked at Chirag; he was taming his hair back while his shirt clung to his chest. Despite being drenched himself, he unlocked the car, opened the door for Jiya, and waited for her to sit before circling around to take his seat behind the wheel.

"*We made it!*" She exclaimed while holding back her emotions, her eyes sparkling with sheer joy.

Chirag nodded, his grin wide and genuine. "*We sure did.*" In that moment of shared triumph, Jiya felt like she had not felt in years. She put her camera on the rear seat while dropping her bag under the passenger chair. Leaning back against the comfortable reclined seat, she closed her eyes and kept laughing, thinking of the past few moments. It had been so easy and natural to be herself around him.

Chirag turned on the car heater, cranking up the fans to combat the chill from their soaked clothes. Just then, a jagged bolt of lightning split the sky, followed by a thunderous crash that made them both jump. Jiya looked at him, her laughter replaced with a look of concern. Rains had never been good in Mumbai.

"*Don't worry!*" Chirag reassured her, putting a hand on her shoulder for a moment to comfort her. He then turned on the ignition and pulled his car into the driveway. As they drove away, the rain hammered against the roof of the car, lightning illuminating the dark, tumultuous sky.

ᜉᜉᜉ

Chirag navigated the rain-slicked streets with careful precision, testing different routes in a relentless attempt to get Jiya back to her hotel. He was trying to keep the speed as low as possible owing to the cars rushing past on the waterlogged roads. Even with a tenth of the traffic volumes that the roads supported, they had already found themselves sitting through traffic jams on three roads. The downpour was merciless, hammering against the car roof, turning the city into a maze of flooded roads and standstill traffic. An hour had passed, and they were nowhere nearer to Jiya's accommodation than they had been at the studio.

Jiya could sense the concern rising in Chirag's mind. She, too, was worried thinking of whether the interns had reached or not. The rain had not just managed to sweep away the heat but also the mobile network. And even though she felt as safe as she could, drowsiness was taking over and she longed to sleep before another hectic day.

She turned to look at Chirag. He must have been tired as well but was doing a great job at masking it. "*I could take accommodation in another hotel for the night? If there is one on the way…,*" Jiya suggested, hoping to reduce his stress.

Chirag did not respond. He started searching for nearby hotels in the in-car GPS system.

"*Wait! You don't have to drive me. I'll take a cab. You should get home,*" she insisted. Just like her, he had had a long day as well, and her suggestion to rent a room in another hotel was more out of concern for him than for the pain increasing in her limbs.

Chirag flicked his gaze toward her, something softer replacing the tension in his eyes. "*Don't worry about me. I'll drop you. You won't find a cab at this hour.*"

But Jiya wasn't having it. The idea of him braving this weather just for her didn't sit right with her.

"*Let's go to your place instead,*" she blurted out the first thought that came to her mind. "*The rain might ease up by then, and I can head to the hotel later,*" Jiya added, trying to cover up the sudden suggestion she had shared.

The atmosphere inside the car transformed with Jiya's statement. It suddenly grew silent as it had been in the auto when they were returning from the planetarium. Though Chirag was looking ahead on the road, he did not move his car when the car in front inched forward. There was some honking from the following cars that made him aware.

"*We will reach your hotel soon,*" Chirag said while pointing towards the GPS system that was clearly indicating that they were entering a traffic jam of over thirty minutes and the total time to their destination was a little under an hour.

Jiya turned to him, a teasing glint in her eyes. *"Are you trying to get rid of me? Don't you want me to know where you live?"* She had understood his concerns and reactions, and she had not even meant to say this. But the moment she looked at him, words rushed out of her mouth.

For a beat, he said nothing. The two sat in silence, their senses heightened. Jiya felt her wet clothes sticking to her body as the warm air from the heater rushed past her face and legs. Water dripped through her hair, along her neck and shoulders. And she knew Chirag was experiencing similar things, though she refrained from looking at him. She could hear their deep breathing noises in the stillness of the car, jamming against the downpour on the front glass. She opened her eyes as she felt a jerk—Chirag had waited for the car ahead to leave some gap and then taken a sharp U-turn. There was no jam on the other side, and they slid smoothly along with the other cars following pursuit.

Jiya felt a thrill curl in her chest—an anticipation she hadn't expected. She was excited at getting to see his personal space and spending more time with him.

"Maybe we can watch a movie or something when we get to my place," Chirag said, his voice deliberately casual, letting her know that he was on board with the idea.

Jiya smiled, *"Sounds perfect. As long as you promise to make the popcorn."*

"Deal." His answering grin made her heart stutter.

ᐁᐁᐁ

Chirag's house was a picture of understated elegance—a pristine white independent duplex nestled within a considerable lush, verdant garden. Framed by towering trees and a riot of colourful flowers, the well-kept lawns stretched across three sides of the centrally constructed villa. At the gate, Chirag punched a code into the electronic keypad, and the entrance swung open soundlessly, revealing a driveway that curved toward the back, leading to a discreet garage. A stone pathway meandered around the perimeter, thoughtfully laid to provide an easy stroll without disturbing the softness of the grass.

Chirag drove to the garage and parked his white SUV in front of it. Jiya stepped out of the car holding her bag. The garage's roof was providing shelter against the rain. However, the heavy scent of the rain-soaked earth and fresh blooming flowers rushed to her nostrils. The rain, which had not reduced to a pacified sprinkle, coated all the leaves and petals spread throughout, adding a renewed freshness.

Chirag led her swiftly to the back entrance, sliding open the large glass doors with practised ease. The moment they stepped inside, they were met with an exuberant welcome—two golden retrievers, Scout and Molly, bounded toward them, barking joyfully, their tails wagging in a blur of excitement. The dogs nearly toppled Chirag in their enthusiasm, jumping up to greet him.

A slightly breathless Binu Bhaiya appeared behind them, attempting—unsuccessfully—to corral the ecstatic canines. Rubbing his dogs in turns, Chirag made introductions. Scout and Molly were his friends, fitness pals, and partners in crime. Binu Bhaiya had been with him for almost a decade. He managed everything from cooking and cleaning to caring for Scout and Molly. He lived in a cosy outhouse by the garage, always within reach, always dependable.

Scout and Molly had rushed to sniff Jiya when she entered. She did not have a lot of prior experience with dogs. She did not feel scared of them but was not sure how to approach them either. Chirag held her hand as he guided her to a lounge chair and pulled another one close to hers. He affectionately ruffled the dogs' ears, calming their restlessness.

The golden retrievers were now making turns around each of them, squeezing through under their legs and around their chairs. Scout had stopped barking, but Molly was still not welcoming to Jiya.

"*Rub her,*" Chirag said as he did the same.

Jiya had never owned a dog, and the dogs she had met of late were owned by her rich clients. They were always too well-behaved and had their own attending staff. She had never had to '*rub*' any of them. Rather, if her clients did not keep fussing over them, Jiya might not even notice their presence on her shoots.

Scout and Molly were nothing like them—with their tails wagging vigorously, they kept moving around without a pause. She looked at the various chewed toys and balls scattered on the floor. Binu bhaiya was moving around collecting them.

"*Do you trust me?*" Chirag asked, extending his hand to take hers.

After a moment's hesitation, Jiya nodded slowly, giving her hand in his, her eyes closed as Molly and Scout had come too close to sniff the extended hands. With Chirag guiding her, she found herself patting Scout's head, feeling the softness of her fur beneath her fingertips.

"*There you go,*" Chirag encouraged, watching her with a soft smile. Molly's playful spirit erupted as she barked her disagreement, clearly upset that Scout was receiving attention from both of them.

Releasing Jiya's hand, Chirag lifted Molly into his arms, showering her with affection that elicited joyful barks from her. It did not take another moment for the dogs to consider Jiya a part of their family and neither for Jiya to fall in love with them. She sat for long minutes, not concerned for the time or being partially soaked, rubbing both the dogs in turns.

But then Jiya's serene moment was broken by a sudden sneeze, reminding her of her drenched state. The chilly air was becoming more pronounced now that she was inside, the change in temperature highlighting her discomfort. Binu Bhaiya had brought a few towels before leaving.

Chirag handed a towel to Jiya, motioning for her to follow him inside. He led her into an expansive main living area, followed by both the playful golden retrievers. Jiya was struck by the elegance and comfort she found herself in.

The living room was large and square-shaped, fitted with plush bottle-green sofas that lined the walls, creating an inviting atmosphere. These sofas were positioned for convivial conversations, and the presence of two central tables hinted at the frequent business discussions that unfolded here. And even when the room was warm enough to host fifteen people at once, Jiya was surprised at how warm she felt there.

She turned to her right, glancing at the dining area that was seamlessly connected to the living room through a porous curtain. It was dominated by a magnificent antique wooden table, surrounded by sturdy benches instead of typical chairs. The browns of the table offered a striking contrast to the plush greens of the sofas, enhancing the room's aura of rustic charm.

Jiya felt she had entered a movie set from the moment she had walked in. Chirag moved confidently around the house, adjusting the lighting and increasing the heating to make the space even more comfortable. Jiya tried her best to keep up, her curiosity running faster than she could.

As they passed, her gaze was drawn to a beautifully crafted staircase on one side of the dining area. Jiya's eyes followed the wooden staircase as it led to the visible upper floor, lined with bookshelves filled with countless volumes.

She felt slightly out of place; this was not a home she could have ever imagined, let alone dreamed of. Everything was meticulously designed and maintained, and she could not think of anyone calling it their home.

Chirag noticed her bemusement and smiled at her bemused expression. He walked a few steps ahead before turning back to gently pull her along. He led her to a room on the opposite side of the dining area—the guest bedroom. Just like everything else in the house, it was designed with a lot of thought. It housed a king-size bed with plush linens, a study desk, a large wall mirror with a small dressing table, and an ottoman by the window. He showed her the attached washroom before excusing himself and allowing Jiya to step inside.

Jiya gasped at everything in the room. It was almost the size of her studio in Mumbai. She pinched herself, half expecting to wake up. The room was more luxurious and better maintained than even the finest seven-star hotels she had visited. She jumped, as she had pinched herself a little too harshly, when Chirag knocked gently on the already ajar door, entering with a pair of folded clothes.

"*I got something for you to change into,*" he said firmly, trying his best not to laugh at her goofiness.

ϷϷϷ

Chirag's musk lingered on his oversized t-shirt and track pants. The soft fabric felt rich and warm against her skin. It had been large enough for her to feel a little lost but comfortable in it like she did when he hugged her. As she pulled on the track pants, which sagged comically around her hips, a smile broke across her face; their size only added to her charm. Dressed in his clothes, she felt an unexpected closeness to him, as if he were beside her. Never even in her wildest dreams, and they could be quite wild, had she ever imagined being at his house and wearing his clothes.

Stepping out of the guest room, Jiya made her way to the dining area, her damp hair still clinging to her shoulders, which added a certain charm to her already delicate appearance. She had spent a few minutes in front of the mirror before stepping out, making sure she looked beautiful and not funny. Pulling up her sleeves and folding the pants to reveal her ankles, she felt she looked good enough.

As she wandered around, she noticed the entrance to the kitchen just under the staircase, something she had overlooked in her earlier explorations. The sweet, comforting scent wafted through the air, guiding her toward Chirag. There he was, having already changed into a solid t-shirt and black track pants, standing in the spacious kitchen before the island slab, pouring down something into mugs. These had been the final two straws of Jiya's unsuccessful attempts to restrain herself from falling even more for Chirag.

First, he did not just have a big and beautiful house, but he had also successfully managed to make it a home. It was warm and comfortable in all aspects. Second, he was working in the kitchen.

Steam rose gracefully from the pot, carrying the rich, chocolatey aroma that filled the kitchen. As Jiya entered, their eyes met, and they both smiled. Chirag's gaze softened as he took in her appearance: his oversized clothes draping her frame, her hair still damp, and a faint blush warming her cheeks from the cosy atmosphere of his home. She looked undeniably adorable, and he couldn't help but feel some butterflies that were running in her stomach.

Chirag immediately looked away and asked, "*Hot chocolate?*" She nodded, and he handed her one of the cups that he had just filled.

As she reached for the mug he offered, their fingers just brushed against each other, sending a delightful shiver down her spine. There was a rage of emotions and sensations in all parts of her body. Her head felt light, her heart was running at a speed at least three times higher than its normal speed, blood rushed to all parts of her body, making her feel hot all of a sudden, and the sensation of touching his fingers lingered on her fingers.

Jiya held the mug between both her palms; she did not want to break Chirag's mug, feeling the odd sensations that she was experiencing at the moment. As she took the first sip, the taste melted in her mouth. The hot chocolate had a hint of vanilla and hazelnut. It was hot enough to spread its aroma with the vapours but not too hot to burn her mouth. It was not too sweet and neither too less sweet—just perfect.

As the warmth and the sweetness spread from her tongue to the rest of her body, she kept looking at Chirag, who was still not meeting her eyes. He first poured himself another mug of hot chocolate, took a few sips, went to fill the pan with water, wiped the slab clean, and returned back to his hot chocolate.

It was this moment that stretched beyond her expectations and, meanwhile, was as small as it could be. She had seen a man a couple of days ago—someone who was too handsome. She desired to meet him. But the moment she did meet him, her carnal desires had taken a back seat, and her conversations were driven by sheer admiration and curiosity. She loved the way he was, how he made her feel, and how he treated her. And it was this moment where all her desires were gaining a strong hold on her—she wanted it all with him. She did not want to spend time with him or have some meaningless relationship with him—she wanted him.

They both stood in silence, sipping their hot chocolates.

ϷϷϷ

Jiya and Chirag settled onto the sofa in the living room after finishing their drinks. Molly and Scout sprawled comfortably and lazily on the ground by their feet, reducing their voices to whispers.

"I love this!" Jiya exclaimed all of a sudden.

"Hot chocolate?" Chirag asked with a playful grin, pulling a few cushions to support his limbs as he turned to face her.

Jiya turned her head to look at him, smiling back. She took a moment to keep looking at him before answering, *"And good company."*

Her heart raced from looking into his eyes. The exchange felt heavy with unspoken feelings, the kind that hung in the air like the delicious scent of chocolate.

"So, how do you like my house?" Chirag asked, breaking the momentary silence, his tone light yet genuine.

"It's beautiful," Jiya responded, glancing around in appreciation. She pulled a few cushions as well to support her back as she turned to face him. *"I can't believe you've managed to make it feel so warm and inviting,"* she added.

"Believe it or not, I spend most of my time here. It's my haven away from... everything else." He sighed softly, looking around as if taking in the memories that filled the space. "I wanted it to reflect who I am—not just a showcase of success but a place where anyone stepping inside feels at home."

"Mission accomplished," she said, her voice sincere. *"Being here with you, I feel... at home."*

She had been sincere and truthful. She had never felt at home before except at her parents' house. And it could be the exhaustion, the traffic, the rain, or the hot chocolate, but she wanted to tell him.

Everything. Truthfully.

They sat side by side on the sofa, looking at each other with a few cushions separating their torsos, knees almost touching, the quiet atmosphere punctuated only by the occasional crackle of the old fan in need of repair and the gentle cadence of rain drumming softly against the windows.

As they relaxed, Chirag began to explain the layout of his house. They were both too tired to do a house tour at this time. "*The ground floor isn't used much,*" he said, his voice calm and steady, a soothing lull against the backdrop of the rain. "*The first floor is where I spend most of my time—my room, my home office, a small workout space, and my daughter's room are all up there.*"

He paused, growing conscious of what he had said. Suddenly the statement had led to doors for several unwanted thoughts to gain entrance. There was a huge age difference between the two of them. There was a lot of difference in their lifestyles. He was divorced. He had a daughter. And despite everything above, he was sitting close to Jiya at two thirty in the middle of the night.

It became awkward for both of them. Jiya had known that he had been married. It still did not change how she felt for him. But it was definitely weird hearing it out loud. They both shifted a bit apart. Chirag had turned his face upwards and closed his eyes as his head rested on the sofa.

Finally, the heaviness grew too profound to bear. Jiya moved away her own fears and insecurities, placing a gentle hand on Chirag's left knee.

"*We do not have to talk about them if you do not want to,*" she whispered to him in a calm voice.

Slowly Chirag opened his eyes and turned his head to look at her. She smiled reassuringly at him. It was probably the best for both of them to stop the conversation at this point.

Giving him a reassuring smile, Jiya got up to move around. She needed the moment and the uncomfortable silence to pass. Everything had become too real too soon. She had too many thoughts in her mind that she needed to clear out-she had admitted to knowing about his past; she had seen how upset it had made him; the mere mention of his family had brought an eerie silence between them; and despite what she might say, it hurt her to know that there was someone else he cared for.

"*Jiya...*" Chirag called out. His eyes were slowly turning red with the effort of controlling his emotions. He closed his eyes, but not before Jiya saw through his struggles.

He sounded normal but she saw the pained look in his eyes. Her intuition told her that any further communication might cause more problems between them, but she could not simply walk away. Not from him.

She stopped where she was and looked back at him with a weak smile. She might have stood still but there was a total mess in her mind. And then, in an instant, she knew something that would communicate better than all the words combined. Jiya paused for a second, came over to Chirag, bent down, and whispered, "*It's alright.*"

She started to inch away but then changed her mind. Leaning in closer one more time, she kissed his gently on his forehead.

TWELVE

Jiya had pulled away just as unexpectedly as she had come closer. Chirag heard her move back and sit at some distance. He kept his eyes closed as all his worries left, and an unexpected calmness spread over him.

He had not realized how much the empty room hurt him. It reminded him of all his failed attempts at having a relationship with his daughter. And somehow, Jiya was not the person he wanted to discuss this with. She had been the reason for his smiles, and he did not have the heart to drag her into his sorrows.

They sat in silence, but now the silence was not been awkward as it had been a little while back. Chirag opened his eyes gradually as he felt the lingering touch of her lips fade from his forehead. Jiya had moved to the adjacent couch, and Molly had accompanied her. Jiya was fondly stroking Molly's head as the half-asleep retriever attempted to find the softest piece of earth by Jiya's feet.

"*What does she like?*" Jiya asked unexpectedly. He was glad for her to break the silence, as he wanted to keep talking to her.

He contorted his face, making a funny imitation to think, before saying, "*Running around squirrels. And music, I guess.*"

Jiya's face lit up at the mention of music. She sat with a jump, startling Molly into suspicion. They had, not long ago, jammed to the music tunes. He had told her about owning a small collection. Jiya remembered that at the mention of music and was after him to show it to her.

Chirag did not need much persuasion. He quickly made a dash to his study and brought a medium-sized bag. He brought it to Jiya and pulled out an old cassette player from the bag.

He had liked music from a young age and had started collecting since he was pretty young. That was the time when people had to buy the audiocassettes from the shops. Each cassette had two sides, and some four or five songs could be recorded on one side of the tape. Jiya had vague memories of her parents fidgeting through such cassettes.

She was surprised when Chirag pulled off the cover from the hidden cabinet under the television to show approximately a hundred audiocassettes he had secured in their covers.

Jiya rushed to the cabinet and started checking out cassettes randomly. She pulled out a few cassettes, went over them, and read through the narratives on some of them before either putting them back or separating them on the floor. His collection was very dear to him. He had never told anyone where he kept it, and only Binu bhaiya was allowed to clean it in his presence. But sharing it with Jiya was very soothing. He was finally relieved at seeing her childlike curiosity and excitement at reading through the cassettes.

"I will keep them back. I promise." Jiya had read through his thoughts. He could not help but think if he was this easy to read or she was this good. He shook his head with a smile to let her know he would happily share it all with her.

Jiya brought a couple of cassettes and asked Chirag to play certain songs from each of them. A few of the songs were the ones they had already jammed on in the car. Chirag kept playing the songs one by one. Most of the songs had a peppy beat to them. And every time a new song played, Jiya would jump up and down in excitement, playing the invisible drums with her hand.

In a couple of songs, Jiya had completely lost herself in the music. She ran around the room, waving her hands and legs in all directions. She transformed into a stage performer, cabaret dancer, drummer, disco enthusiast, and classical performer in a short span of time.

Her energy was so infectious that even Scout had left his slumber and looked up. He was one of the laziest dogs, and nothing but food or long walks could get him to not sleep. Jiya's dance had done the deed better than anything else.

She danced all over the room and even got close to Molly and Scout, pulling them into her performance. Within seconds, there were three dancing beings in the room. Molly and Scout scurried all over the room behind Jiya.

Soon it did not matter which song played. The three were full of energy and ready to perform. Jiya sang her own lyrics, danced at her own rhythm, and raced across the room with Molly and Scout. And during the silence when Chirag would change the cassette or forward to a specific song, Jiya would keep up the performance.

When a particularly famous song played, Jiya and the dogs started moving around in circles around the two tables. Chirag kept craning his neck to keep them in view. During one of the turns, Jiya grabbed his hand with both her hands and pulled him into their performance.

Chirag did not have a dancing bone. He had never danced in his life—not as a kid or in college. But at this moment, he wanted to dance, except that he did not know how. He stood surrounded by the three beings very important to him and clapped for every step and hop they did.

Jiya understood him once more. She raised his hands high and showed him to move them up and down. And just like that, the four of them were running around the room and dancing.

For the first time in a long while, Jiya felt a deep, comforting warmth spreading through her chest. It was not just the joy of the moment or the thrill of the dance. It was the quiet realization that this—the laughter, the playful banter, the simple togetherness—was something she had been missing. Something she had been searching for, perhaps unknowingly, in all her travels and work.

Being with Chirag, even in the simplicity of the moment, felt right. It felt like home—something she had never experienced.

🐾🐾🐾

Jiya and Chirag, far from all their worries, had settled on the floors, laughing and sharing stories while petting the tired dogs. None of them felt sleepy—it was just like the first time that they had dinner.

At half past three in the morning, Chirag realized that keeping Jiya up any longer would jeopardize their assignment. The businessman in him chided his decision. As the fatigue from their playful evening settled in, Jiya found the idea of retiring to bed increasingly appealing. Chirag roused his two dogs, who shared his room and led them to the stairs. They swiftly bounded up, well-trained, and disappeared into their room. Jiya followed them to the base of the staircase.

Standing there, the air between them was thick with unspoken words and feelings. Without a word, she stepped closer, wrapping her arms around his waist and pressing her head against his chest. For a moment, Chirag froze, taken aback by the sudden closeness. Then, instinctively, he encircled her with his arms, pulling her gently into a warm embrace.

The warmth of her body against his was both comforting and electrifying. He could feel her heartbeat—steady and strong—echoing the way his own heart raced at their closeness. The scent of her hair, still faintly damp from the rain, enveloped him, and he closed his eyes, savouring the moment.

There was a deep longing within him, something he had fought hard to suppress. The softness of her body pressed against his, the way she fit so perfectly in his arms, stirred emotions he hadn't allowed himself to feel in years.

For those few precious seconds, everything else faded away—their age difference, his fears, her insecurities, and the complexities of their lives. All that mattered was the warmth of her presence, as if she belonged there, two pieces of a puzzle finally united. And he knew that Jiya had meant so much more to him than anyone else. It was not just how she had added spark to his life but also the way she made him a better person. He wanted to do better and bigger things for her—to bring the world to her and to give her all the happiness the world had to offer.

He gently loosened his grip, pulling back just enough to meet her gaze. Jiya's eyes were closed, her face serene, and he could sense that she felt the same comfort, the same unspoken connection.

"Goodnight, Jiya," he whispered into her hair, his voice rough with emotion.

ꞵꞵꞵ

Jiya awoke with a heavy head, the kind of sleep that leaves you feeling as though all the worries of the world have been washed away. It took her some time to think about why her head hurt. Slowly, things started coming back to her, and a smile spread through her lips. Eating pizza. Meeting Scout and Molly. Dancing.

She jumped out of bed, realizing that she was in Chirag's house. It was a little over eight, and she had woken up out of habit that she had adopted since knowing Chirag. Though she could have slept for a few more hours, she did not want to miss any chance to spend time with him.

The soft clatter of pans from the kitchen stirred her from her peaceful slumber. Morning light streamed gently through the translucent curtains, casting a warm, golden glow across the room. With a smile, she pushed the curtains aside and gazed out at the lush garden, where vibrant trees and blooming flowers filled her with quiet joy.

Chirag had been thoughtful enough to leave a spare toothbrush and toothpaste for her. After freshening up, she followed the delicious aroma wafting from the kitchen. The clattering of the utensils and the fresh aroma could mean only one thing—Chirag was already up. She brushed her teeth in a rush, and fixing her slept-in hair with her fingers, she rushed to the kitchen.

As she entered, she found Chirag by the stove, flipping pancakes with a skilful ease that made her smile. Watching him so at home in his element filled her heart with a warmth she hadn't anticipated.

"Good morning," she greeted him, her voice still soft with sleep.

Chirag turned, a smile lighting up his face as he saw her. "Good morning. I hope you're hungry," he said, nodding towards the two pancakes that he was cooking on the stove.

Jiya beamed with immense pride. Her perfect man seemed to be getting even more perfect—if that were even possible. Here was a man who excelled at work, displayed gentle kindness, had two amazing dogs, and owned a wonderful collection of audiocassettes. He knew the best dining spots in the city, treated her like a princess, encouraged her to take charge at work, and cooked for her!

As she stopped across from the island counter, she noticed his t-shirt—too loose for her—slipping slightly off her left shoulder. It swayed gently with her movements, adding a casual charm to her appearance.

Chirag, standing by the stove, had just finished pouring a steaming cup of coffee. He smiled as he handed her a mug, winking playfully. Jiya stepped closer and cleared some space on the countertop. With a swift motion, she hoisted herself onto the counter, a twinkle in her eyes as she watched him.

Holding the hot cup between her palms, she lifted it to her lips, gazing lovingly into his hazel eyes from up close. Having a lot to be distracted with, she didn't realize how hot the coffee was and took a large sip. The hot fluid burned her lips and mouth. She spit out the coffee on the side and kept the mug back on the table with a thud. The burning sensation did not even let her scream, and silent tears came down her eyes.

Chirag let go of the spatula and pulled out a glass of water at a magical speed. Holding the glass as she drank a few sips of water, he moved in close to her. Placing the glass back, he started to pat her head to comfort her. He restricted her hands to open as he leaned in closer to inspect her mouth. Her tongue was a little red, but apart from that, there seemed to be no harm done.

Holding both her hands in restraint, Chirag moved in even closer to her. Her knees were pressed against his left leg, and his arm was brushing against her shoulders as he held her hands in his. As he raised his head a little, he found his face extremely close to hers—her warm exhales rushing past his left cheek. The sound of her inhales was causing a dizzying effect on him.

Trying to break free of the moment, Chirag raised himself to his full height and let go of her hands. Though the closeness had made them both incapable of moving. Her hands stayed where he had held them, and his hands were an inch above hers. His nose was close to her eyes, and she had raised her head slightly to keep gazing into his.

As their eyes locked, a magnetic pull drew them closer, suspending the moment in time. Jiya's heart raced in her chest, each beat quickening with anticipation. The air around them crackled with an electric tension that was almost tangible.

Their faces drew closer, the magnetic pull guiding their movements. Jiya's eyes fluttered shut as Chirag's lips brushed softly against hers. The initial contact was gentle and tentative, the warmth of his lips surprisingly tender against her own. They pulled apart a few times before finding their equilibrium. A thrill ran through her as his touch sent tingles across her skin, and she felt the reassuring pressure of his lips as his fingers found their way to her hands.

Chirag could feel the subtle taste of coffee lingering on her lips, a hint of rich, roasted beans blending with the sweet warmth of her breath. He kept closing his eyes to experience the moment and then opening them to have a look at her. His hands found their way to intertwine his fingers with hers.

Chirag could feel a slight tremor in Jiya's hands, a testament to the depth of her feelings mirroring his own.

As they finally broke apart, their breaths came in hot, heavy gasps, fingers still intertwined, their foreheads resting gently against each other. Jiya slipped her left hand from his grip and wrapped it around his neck for support. When her eyes finally opened, she met Chirag's gaze once more. They were both breathless, overwhelmed by the moment they had just shared, longing for it to last forever while feeling almost weak in the presence of their powerful emotions for one another. She closed her eyes once more, tears trickling down her cheeks—of happiness rather than of the pain that no longer existed—and smiled.

"*Dad?*"

In a moment that redefined his life, Chirag heard the voice he longed to hear every day. It had taken him several hours and days to sort through his emotions. But in the moment that he had accepted his feelings, he heard the voice that brought back all the chaos. It was the voice that reminded him that his life had no space for a new relationship.

It had probably been years since his daughter had addressed him as 'dad.' He felt conflicted about whether to feel happy about it or upset about what Jiya might have said if it had not been for his daughter interrupting.

Still holding Jiya's hand, he instinctively took a step back. The surge of adrenaline, coupled with the sudden movement, made him slightly dizzy. Jiya climbed down from the countertop and steadied him with both hands.

With his eyes closed, his heart skipped a beat at the sound of her voice. The deep longing to be near Jiya, a yearning that had begun the moment their eyes first met, had blossomed into this pure moment—one where he finally acknowledged his feelings, certain they were mutual. But now, that precious moment had been abruptly interrupted.

Slowly, he opened his eyes. Jiya stood too close, blocking his view of the door. He took his hands off her arms that he had held for support and moved slightly to his left to see his only daughter, Mukti, standing at the door of the kitchen.

"*Mukti,*" Chirag stammered, his face flushing of all colour. As he stood there, looking at the horror and disgust reflected on his daughter's face, his world came crashing.

He stood in the kitchen, surrounded by two women with whom he shared profound connections, yet at that moment, he wished he was sharing this time with just one of them. It was a strange and conflicting emotion to think of choosing one over the other, and there was nothing that could help him make the decision.

From the very first time he laid eyes on Jiya, he felt a genuine connection with her and had finally come to terms with his feelings for her. Yet he couldn't shake the feeling of unworthiness, knowing he had let her go the moment he heard his daughter's voice.

On the other hand, he had prayed every night for a morning like this, when he could cook breakfast for his daughter. And now that the moment had come, he did not feel happy at seeing her or being addressed by her. Not only did her voice have an accusatory tone, but she had also caught him in the one moment since she had left him that he did not yearn for her return.

Jiya saw the horror spread across Chirag's face. She had not registered any sound in the wake of the moment. Trying to see what had caused him to step back, Jiya turned to face the intruder.

The person standing in the doorway shocked Jiya much more than it shocked Chirag.

"*Jiya*," Mukti exclaimed in anger.

The kitchen fell into an excruciatingly awkward silence. Jiya's eyes met Mukti's, who stood frozen, her expression a mix of shock and disbelief. Mukti, who had been one of the most talented persons that Jiya had ever met, was her assistant for almost a year. She was the last person Jiya had expected to meet. And the same horror was reflected on Mukti's face as well.

Then the realization dawned on her. Jiya's face flushed with a mix of embarrassment and anger. The weight of the situation hit her hard, and she struggled to regain her composure. Her heart raced as she looked around, trying to find a way out of the uncomfortable situation. It had to be a bad dream or a prank in bad taste.

She was not being intruded on by Mukti, but she was the intruder between Mukti and Chirag. Mukti was Chirag's daughter.

Things became too real a little too fast. The bubble that she had been living in for a while burst open. Without a word, Jiya pulled herself out of Chirag's hold and walked out of the kitchen, her movements hurried and disjointed. She barely registered Chirag's half-hearted attempts to stop her as she rushed past Mukti, whose eyes followed her in stunned silence.

The feelings that had been pure and raw only a few moments ago were all wrong. The warmth that had spread over her body when she had been around Chirag melted away, and she felt nothing but the tip of a thousand cold and pointed needles pinching every inch of her body. Everything felt wrong.

Jiya made her way to the guest room, her mind reeling with emotions and convoluted thoughts. She quickly gathered her belongings – whatever she could grab, her hands shaking slightly as she collected her things. The weight of the unexpected revelation was too much for her to bear at that moment.

With a final glance at the room where she had woken up feeling extremely loved and at home only a few minutes back, Jiya walked out. Everything had suddenly become strange and unfamiliar. Keeping her head down to hide the tears that would not stop leaking out of her eyes, Jiya made her way to the main door. She met Scout and Molly, who had been enjoying their morning walk in the garden with Binu bhaiya. Both the dogs rushed to greet their new friend, but Jiya was out of the main gate before either of the two could catch up with her.

THIRTEEN

Jiya had walked for several minutes, walking aimlessly through roads and alleys. She had no idea of how long it had been since she had walked out of Chirag's house, whom she had crossed, or where she had reached. She felt numb. All her strength and effort had gone into blocking a single thought out of his mind—that Mukti was. It was too much for her to process. She could not bring herself to even think of it.

She stopped at the end when her legs went numb with exhaustion. Jiya looked all around and was unable to identify anything around her. She was standing on a road with a large park on one side and a row of buildings on the other side. She did not care to look for any signboards—that was not important. For the first time in her life, she felt lost, and it had little to do with not knowing where she was physically.

Grateful at finding a lamp post surrounded by some shrubs, she sank on the ground, resting her back against the lamp post and facing the road but not looking. She allowed the numbness to take over. Her feet were radiating a lot of heat after having done a fair share of work, her stomach growled timidly with hunger, and her clothes—she blocked the thought of her clothes as she did not want to think of the person.

The numbness was getting replaced with anger. She felt angry at the passersby for continuing their lives as if hers had not just crumbled down, at her parents for letting her choose the profession, at her old boyfriends for being the jerks that they were, at her assistants who were just incompetent, at herself for being stupid to believe she had any chance at some great love, and at him. She did not want to think of him, but he was no longer a thought. He had become a part of her existence. She felt extremely angry at him. It had all been his fault.

It had been him who had dived into the pool to ruin her shoot. It had been him who had interested her with all his talks on their first dinner. It had been he who suggested she take the assignment for his firm. It had been he who took her around Delhi. It had been him who kept lingering in the studio. It had been he who took her to his house. It had been he who had crept slowly into her heart and life.

He had first become an important part of her life and then broken her heart.

When the sun reached high enough to not let her sit and blame him for everything, Jiya was forced to register her surroundings. Her earlier confident self took charge. She got up and looked around. It did not matter if she did not know where she was; she was looking around for some vehicle. She could not see any taxis, and there were only a few autos that barely registered her presence. Jiya felt angry at the city—a stupid city with its stupid peacocks and stupid gardens but no transport.

Pulling out her phone, which was thankfully in her pocket, she booked a cab to the hotel she was staying at. No wonder people here were so disconnected as convenience came into the city at the cost of isolation.

Jiya reached her hotel in the same fit of rage. Mechanically, she walked over to the reception and demanded a second key card. Her senses were still failing to register anything. Without having any memory of anything from the cab ride or her walk to her room, she banged the room shut after her and collapsed on her bed.

Numbness had brought a friend—pain—and they were taking turns playing hide and seek in her body. There were moments when she hit something and did not even register the contact and others, like now, when she lay still but felt a piercing pain. Currently, she feels pain and heaviness in her heart. Giving in to an urge to scream and shout, she sat up and let out a howl. Venting out her anger by punching through her sheets, she let the tears out. Upheaved by her own actions, idiotic spring on the mattresses and the silk-soft satin linens, she slid to the floor.

Everything in the city was working against her. She did not want any of it. Without any further thought, she pulled out her suitcase from the cupboard and started throwing all her things inside. She needed to leave now!

ᐅᐅᐅ

Her return to Mumbai was anything but easy. She had left a lot of things behind—her camera, a pair of clothes, a few accessories in the hotel room, her happiness, her peace of mind, and her strength. The pain of leaving all those behind and more, especially after a few days of feeling as if she had struck the jackpot of life, gnawed at her constantly. She hailed a cab from outside of the Mumbai airport and reached her studio. Thankful for all her interns being busy with shoots, she took the opportunity to head into her room and lock herself inside.

Her studio apartment had two rooms and a bathroom. The larger room was one entered from the main door. It had a vast space that resembled the shape of the block that looked like the 'Z' block in a game of Tetris, with a very small balcony on one side. The idea was to provide some privacy with a means of a curtain. There was a smaller second room that should have doubled as a storage unit. Since it had been all that Jiya could afford when she had moved into the city, she had found different uses for the different portions of the apartment.

You entered into the studio to be welcomed with a wide collection of items and a few chairs. There was a small kitchen unit. The upper half of the Z was crammed with a kitchen slab holding a single stove that had not been used for months, a few plates, bowls, and spoons, a microwave oven, and a water dispenser. Most of her meals were shared with her interns—there was no way she would cook for all of them, and she found little point in cooking just for herself. As a result, the kitchen had only the items that she needed. The second part of the section had a table with her high-graphics desktop to work on, her storage units holding all her cameras, lenses, and lighting equipment, and a few more chairs.

Since she knew she would use the space to work more than for her personal time, she had put on a thin mattress and covered it with a couple of bedsheets to make a comfortable bed for herself. She had a small cabinet stuffed on the other end, which consisted of her clothes and accessories. Her few books, an empty vase reminiscent of a plant she had once brought to nurture, and her first camera were always displayed on top of the cabinet. There was a small window that Jiya had installed after purchasing the apartment on the opposite end of her bed, with a wall-mounted AC unit to keep her cool.

While she did have a proper room in her parent's home, this felt much more comfortable as it was her own. Jiya entered her studio and felt alien to the place that had always comforted her. Everywhere she sat or moved, thinking about him or about the trip to Delhi, was alienating her from the place. The room, which had once brought her joy, was making her miserable.

Tearing herself away from almost everything, Jiya went to her room and closed the door to anything and everything else.

༔༔༔

Rahul, Jiya's second assistant, had had the worst two days of his life. He, along with the team, had managed to wrap up the shoot in Dubai a bit earlier than scheduled to reach Mumbai back in time. He had landed on Monday evening and had just enough time to share a meal with his parents before falling asleep. Thank God, his parents were in Mumbai itself; else, like Mukti, he would have needed extra days to visit them, which would not have fared well with Jiya.

He coordinated with the interns and reached the shoot studio on Tuesday morning. To everyone's surprise, the designer had decided to pay a visit. He had been impressed with the pictures that Jiya had sent him, but those pictures had given him more ideas. He now wanted the entire storyline to be redesigned and the shoot redone. He was happy to pay more, but he wanted to meet Jiya before changing any terms. Hence, Rahul was stuck with redoing the shoot in less time and with the original budget—which they had already surpassed owing to Jiya's other project that required the rest of the team, models, and rented equipment to work double shifts.

He was in touch with Mukti, who kept suggesting him over the phone. She, too, had not been able to get in touch with Jiya. Jiya had not replied to Mukti's texts either. If it was not for the five interns who were accompanying Jiya to Delhi, her two assistants might have believed her to be dead already.

Rahul had managed quite a bit of the changed requirements for a couple of days when the designer found out that Jiya had not yet returned from her absence. He was not sure if the designer had tried to call Jiya, but when he had made an appearance on the shoot, he certainly was not happy.

The next morning became even worse—the interns in Delhi were called to inform us that Jiya's room was empty. She had not slept in the hotel at night and had not returned in the morning either. They had no clue about her whereabouts and did not have any instructions on their next tasks. They had rented a studio for two weeks, and the firm for which they were there to shoot a campaign had a scheduled meeting with Jiya to check on the progress.

Gosh! Rahul could not believe his luck. He called Mukti to check if she could fly to Delhi and handle the situation. But Mukti's phone was switched off. He kept trying to reach either Jiya or Mukti throughout the day, but no one picked up his call. The designer had sent his own team to keep a tab on the shoot. It was not until later that evening that the interns called to inform that Jiya had left. Apparently, she arrived at the hotel sometime around noon, checked herself out, and left without a word.

This was not like Jiya. Rahul could not help but hope the entire thing to be a dream. He might just be on the flight back from Dubai. But despite what he hoped for, his nightmare just kept stretching.

ᕽᕽᕽ

Two days had passed since Jiya had left Delhi. Rahul had waited for some time to hear back from her, but when she did not call for two days, he grew worried. Luckily, the contract that she had taken from the firm in Delhi had called only a few times before telling them they were happy to extend the timelines. Rahul had enough time to complete the shoot for the designer and then travel to Delhi to pick up where Jiya left off.

But where was Jiya? No one had heard from her. It appeared to be the time to take the matter to the authorities. He went to the studio after the day's shoot. The assistants and a few of the interns knew the code to the key secure box outside her studio. Pulling out the key, he entered with two other interns. Things looked as dishevelled as they usually did.

He was not sure what they were looking for, but Rahul was sure they would need identification to lodge a complaint. As he walked to the door to Jiya's room, aware that he was invading her privacy, he heard the sound of the AC running. No one but Jiya ever entered her bedroom, and it was not a likely case that she would leave the AC running before leaving for Delhi. *Would she? Or was there an intruder?*

Rahul put a finger to his lips, gesturing the interns to stay silent. He grabbed a light stand lying on the floor and wielded it as a sword, ready to strike to defend himself, if needed. The interns grabbed what they could find—a used bedsheet and a paperweight ball. They tiptoed to the door separately, Jiya's workspace and her personal space. In slow motion, Rahul turned the handle, and to his surprise, the door fell ajar with a slight creak. A musky smell of a room that had not seen sunlight for days rushed to burn their nose hair along with the sound of slow breathing.

The room was dark, but they could make out someone in there. Rahul asked one of the interns to turn on the torchlight on his phone as he gripped the light stand firmly with both hands.

The light illuminated the small space. The three people were torn between curiosity at checking Jiya's off-limits bedroom and finding the intruder. As the intern shone the light around, the three of them were left stunned to spot. It was Jiya. She definitely looked bad, and her room was littered with several toffee and chocolate wrappers and a few empty beer bottles, but it was her. And she had been sleeping.

ᗤᗤᗤ

It took Jiya two proper meals a day and another night's sleep before she could comprehend what she was being told. She had lost track of the number of days she had locked herself into the room. She refused to go out. She had raided her stock of chocolates and a few beers from the fridge to survive. She had not left her bed except to use the washroom. She had merely woken up, screamed, shouted, wept, eaten some chocolates, drunk some beer, slept, and then repeated. Sometimes she would skip a few of the steps as well.

The three people had come raiding her home and found her asleep. One of the men had shaken her out of her slumber. The light was on, and it was too bright. She asked to get it closed. Slowly she recognized the three men to be her assistant and two interns. Rahul pulled a chair from the studio and sat while getting Jiya to rest against the wall. He kept asking her questions to which she had no answers.

Her life had seemingly been divided into two halves—one before she visited Lonavala and the other after returning from Delhi. She had blocked most of the time between the two points. And since the second part of her life was just beginning, she had nothing to tell. However she must have looked really bad as the interns maintained their distance during the entire length of their stay, and Rahul ordered her plenty of food. When he could not get any answers, he did the best he could to be useful—he made her eat dinner and stocked her mini refrigerator with a lot of good food. He even stayed the night, sleeping in the studio, not trusting to leave Jiya in the state that he had found her in.

He returned every morning, and now that the studio was open, the other interns dropped in as well. He must have already instructed them, Jiya was thankful, for they did not comment on her state or appearance or ask her questions; not even the interns she had left in Delhi. Jiya had managed to take a shower and put on some new clothes, though returning to work was still something pretty far away.

Two interns were asked to stay in the studio at all times. They were there on Rahul's instructions to take care of her and keep him informed on her well-being. They also kept sharing pictures from the shoot with Jiya. It was the only way that her team felt she could return back to being her old self. When the interns thought she had been sleeping, she had overheard them say that they preferred the older, bossy version of their queen to the defeated one. She also heard some weird speculations, many of which involved a certain individual she was still not ready to think of.

But all the care that Rahul and her team had shown her made Jiya snap out of her shell. She was grateful to all of them and made all possible efforts to work. It was really difficult, but she was trying.

On Saturday, she decided to video call the designer. It was Rahul's idea—he wanted her to just switch on the camera. The designer, who believed that Jiya had ditched him, grew genuinely concerned about her health. He did not say anything, but from that point on, his behaviour changed. He let Rahul work out the details and work with less scrutiny.

ᐅᐅᐅ

Jiya spent the most unproductive week of her life. The fashion designer was satisfied having seen Jiya. She still did not believe she could step out of her studio and go to the shoot, but she offered to help edit the pictures. This was her way to escape—there was still her professional voice, however, diminished, inside her head. When she looked at the pictures, the voice-guided her to give suggestions, and that, she realized, was the only thought that kept her from thinking anything else.

Gradually she left her room and started spending time in her studio. The heavy cloud of grief and pain that accompanied her everywhere kept her on the edge. Her frustration bubbled to the surface at the smallest of things—whether it was a misplaced prop, some spilt drink, or the lighting not being perfect. Every minor inconvenience, even when she only heard about it, felt like an insurmountable obstacle, and she found herself snapping at her team more than usual.

Her assistant, Rahul, tried his best to manage the situation. He had not just been a friend to her but had emerged as a saviour. The designer, now convinced of Jiya's illness but continued involvement, put more faith in him. Rahul did some experiments of his own, a few of which gave great results. He kept a constant tab on Jiya as well. Once when he did mention that he had not been able to get in touch with Mukti, he saw Jiya's expression change and did not mention it again. Though, Jiya knew, he would keep making attempts to contact her as well.

Making a mental note to help Rahul establish his independent setup, Jiya made a few calls. She struggled with existing every day. Basic tasks such as combing and drinking water ached as well. She felt angry all the time. And though work helped her block all the unwanted things and thoughts, she was just not herself anymore. Jiya had decided to take a break. She wanted to go back home, spend time with her mother, maybe visit someplace where no one knew her, and think about what she wanted. However, her interns need not suffer because of this, and since Rahul was already shouldering more responsibility than needed, she knew he was ready. And she was going to help him before she took a break.

Most of the time during the day went in a whirlpool of emotions. She could not help getting angry about everything. And even after she had taken two trips to the nearby grocery shop to stock up on some basic items, she did not trust herself to be in the shoot. There was just one person on the planet who could have calmed the storm that was swirling inside Jiya, and that person had not called, not even texted. Not to mention that she had blocked his number and deleted all the logs.

The designer's shoot finally finished. All the pictures were delivered. Despite the hiccups and the constant changing demands from the designer, the shoot had only been extended to ten days. Jiya had already cancelled her subsequent shoots or passed them to her previous assistants.

Rahul had taken some time before addressing the big problem—there was an incomplete shoot in Delhi. Since they were under a contract, this needed to be done. He called the people from the marketing team of the e-commerce business they were contracted by and communicated the dates. And even when Jiya knew that Rahul had done the right thing, his actions resulted in the biggest argument between the two. She got into the worst rage that anyone had ever seen her in the moment she heard what he did. Banging her fists on walls, throwing things around, and breaking items, she was quite clear on her stand. She was not returning to Delhi, and she knew that the firm would not take any legal action—at least she expected that much courtesy from him.

However, she could not explain either of the reasons to Rahul or his team.

ᐅᐅᐅ

A month passed. Jiya's mood had improved slightly over the past weeks—though no one could really tell as she had avoided being with her team ever since hearing Rahul's decision—but she still kept herself at a distance from everyone. Her once vibrant and collaborative spirit had turned into a cold, solitary focus. She spoke only when necessary, her interactions curt and to the point, and this suited her just fine. The less she had to engage, the better.

Rahul had taken the five interns who had initially accompanied Jiya and a few others to resume and complete the shoot. He had called occasionally to check in on her, but the two had never discussed work. Things had changed drastically between them and Rahul, who usually had gotten along well with Jiya, had understood that the Delhi shoot was much more than a mere assignment. His intuition made him take it even more.

Quite honestly, Rahul had not found the shoot anything complex. Yes, they had all been accustomed to working with living people, and shooting objects was challenging as one could not shout instructions for them to move for better light. He had to make changes, move back to the camera, go back to make more changes, and so on. Adding inclinations or angles was a challenge in itself. However, nothing that could not be done. The good thing was the objects did not move of their own accord, giving him enough time to shoot them.

Another good thing was that the firm's team had collected all of Jiya's notes and items from the studio when the shoot halted. Already familiar with her style, it had not taken him much time to understand the storyline.

Jiya's idea had been great—she had decided to mix advertisement with the company motto. Her photoshoot and video ad were with the real artisans posing alongside their products. While he loved her idea and vision, he made one change—he did not want to do the photoshoot in a closed studio and use CGI. Rather, he was confident that he could do a much better job in real locations.

He presented his idea to the board, and to his utter surprise, not only did they all agree, but they also offered to pay the costs of the travel and other expenses at all locations.

▷▷▷

Chirag raised his head after he heard a knock on the door. He checked the wall clock across his seat out of habit, then as a necessity. The silence in the office was indicative enough of the fact it was over eight in the evening. He had already been in the office for over eleven hours.

As he let go of the pencil in his hand and pushed himself away from the desk an inch, the pain in his limbs and back became evident. He had had his last meeting around three in the afternoon with the photographer who proposed to shoot in the outdoor locations. It had been a brilliant idea. Chirag had left the meeting without a word, having slid a note to one of his assistants, reading a single word, '*approved*'. Since then, he had been in his room, going over multiple files.

The extended strain had caused his limbs to freeze, and he felt the pain as he did his best to stretch. He was an old man.

His door opened slightly as his senior assistant, Ashish, walked in. Chirag smiled briefly before returning his attention back to the file open in front of him.

Though he had his eyes bent, he was not really reading anything. He waited for his senior assistant to begin, but when no words came, he was forced to close the file. It had been rude of him to have a file open in front of him at all times. This technique had worked for him—people did not ask any questions and kept the conversations short, assuming he was working. And though Ashish would have understood this long back, the two men had never discussed the same.

Rather, Ashish had called him not long after Mukti had left his home that morning. Mukti had screamed and raged and shouted at him before storming out. Before Chirag could get the keys to his car, her cab had driven out of the curb and left. Helpless, Chirag had only managed to call Amita and inform her of everything that had happened. He mentioned he had been with a friend when Mukti walked in. Something did not let him admit how close.

He had called Mukti several times before giving up. If there had been any scope for him to have any kind of relationship with her, he had lost it—lost it all for one moment of closeness with Jiya. Jiya—he could not help but remember how perfect and innocent she had looked that morning. No matter how much he tried, he could not forget her laughter. He remembered how she ran after him that day in Sundar Nursery or when they sat a little too lost in each other in the planetarium. It had been since then that he had wanted to grab her and hold her forever. He wanted more than anything to hold her hand, longed to kiss her tender lips and to kiss her forehead.

He had been warned, and every time, he had ignored the warning. The few times that he was forced to confront his feelings for her, he had merely denied it to be anything more than friendship. And though he wished more than anything for Mukti to not have witnessed the kiss, he was glad he had that one moment before Jiya left forever. After all, she was way too perfect to be with a man like him.

Chirag had sat in his living room, with the cook cleaning the remains of the burnt breakfast and Scout and Molly lying on his feet, when his phone rang. It was Ashish. He had been informed by Jiya's assistants that she was missing. She did not return the previous evening; she had not answered when the interns knocked, and when the hotel manager had opened the door on their request, the bed had not been slept in.

He did not worry, for he knew where she was last night. And she probably needed some time to process things before going back to the hotel. He had asked Ashish to keep him apprised of the situation. But as he had not worried a bit, Ashish had known that something was wrong. Later in the afternoon, Ashish called to inform us that Jiya had left.

Chirag had been pacing in his room when he took the call. He sat down on his bed with a thud, knowing it was all over. He had not spoken about her with anyone again, though his instructions were clear. It was she who would do the shoot in her own time. His team was not to force her or her team for any timelines. Additionally, they would pay for any expenses.

Chirag looked up expectantly at his friend. He was sitting comfortably on the sofa—where Jiya had sat not so long ago. Chirag forced a smile on his face and folded his hands, gesturing Ashish had all his attention.

Ashish took his time. The two friends sat in silence with a smile on both their faces. Neither of them was in a hurry. And though they made it look quite casual, Chirag knew that Ashish had some serious things to discuss. Else he would not have stayed up late to talk.

"*So?*" Chirag asked, cueing his friend to speak.

"*Why can't you just go and bring her back?*" Ashish asked bluntly. He had never been the kind to sugarcoat. Moreover, it had been two months since whatever had happened between Jiya and Chirag. He had understood that the two had been together when she was presumed missing and then she had just left. Something would have happened. And it was not like Chirag to make a mistake twice—he would not have let Jiya walk away since he had already lost everything once when Amita had gone. Something had happened, or he was still in denial of his feelings. The latter was less likely as he had been pining for two months.

Chirag did not respond. He let out a sigh before walking over to the sofa and taking the spot he had taken when Jiya had sat there. Sooner or later he would need to answer. And no matter how much he wanted to escape from the fact, he had to face it.

He barely opened his lips and whispered, "*She did not deserve to be with me.*"

Ashish's expression changed. He looked at his friend accusatorily and blurted out, "*She was not good enough for you?*"

The words shocked Chirag as much as they had shocked Ashish. Chirag shook his head vigorously before clarifying himself, "*She was too good for me. She needed someone who would be worthy of her. Not someone—*" he broke off mid-sentence. Turning his gaze away, he completed, "*-Not someone like me who turned his back on his family.*"

Ashish waited patiently for Chirag to turn back. There was a long silence. But when Chirag did turn back to look at his friend, Ashish was standing. He looked visibly angry. Without the kindness that Chirag thought would come, he was berated, "*And you fix that by turning your back again on a second chance to have a family?*"

"*You do not understand.*" Chirag pleaded, but his voice rose slightly.

Ashish sighed. He had known Chirag to be a very sensible man—yes, we all have our demons, and Chirag had him—but he could not have ever believed him to be someone to throw away the chance at happiness.

He said, "*Maybe I do not. But you do not see. You did not see how her face lit up every time she spoke to you. You did not see how she risked her career and personal safety just to spend one extra day with you. You did not see how being with her made you a livelier person. And when you do not see, I do not understand.*" He said that all in a single breath and turned to leave. He halted at the door, turning back for a closing sentence, "*Maybe I should leave too, just like she did.*"

Ashish had grabbed the door handle to pull when Chirag called out, "*I.*" He stuttered for a moment before completing, "*I need a favour.*"

ϷϷϷ

The doorbell rang for a third time before Jiya walked out to answer it. She had stopped putting the key out in the lockbox. Most of her interns had gone out with Rahul, and she had dismissed the remaining until their return. Jiya had found a good space that Rahul could use as his personal studio. It was way bigger than her small apartment and was equipped with the basics. It would need some renovation, but once done, she envisioned it to be perfect as per his taste and style.

She had not taken any more assignments and hence did not need the interns poking around. She could not take any more assignments as she had left her most prized camera in Delhi. While the interns had returned with the rest of the equipment, her camera had not been at the hotel or in the studio. And she did not think she would get it back.

Jiya had taken a walk down the beach one evening with another of her cameras. It was not bad. It had been the one she had purchased when she was assisting other photographers. There has been a great advancement in technology since then. It might be the camera, or it could just be that she had lost her talent, but the pictures were no longer the same as those from her best camera. She did end up, however, taking a few pictures of a bakery that had opened near the beach and some of the children playing at the beach.

When the doorbell rang again, she got irritated. Her temper was getting better, and she had managed not to shout at anyone since having the row with Rahul—but that was primarily due to the fact that she had dismissed everyone the very next day. Whoever was at the door was close to testing how much better she had become at controlling herself.

Jiya trudged to the door. She opened it to find herself facing three interns. Her temper was rising slightly. One of them had a bag while the other two stood a step behind the first one.

"*What?*" She said in her no-nonsense voice.

Terrified, the intern held out the bag and spoke, "*This is for you.*"

If only her interns were not dead scared of her, she might have believed it all to be a prank. But it was not a prank, and the interns were shivering in fear at her raised voice.

She pulled the bag from his outstretched hand and started looking for the zipper to open. "*What is it? Who sent it?*" she asked impatiently.

The intern shivered for a second before speaking, "*I think it is your camera. The Delhi clients sent it.*"

Jiya pulled out her camera at the same time as the intern spoke the words. It was not a camera. It was her camera. The same camera she had left.

She did not want to complete that thought. In the last two months, Jiya had trained her brain to not think about him. Why should she think about someone who had not bothered about her even for a second? He had not called. He had not messaged.

After her initial phase of screaming and shouting had subsided, the void had been filled with a lot of negative thoughts. She kept getting reels and stories about men cheating on women or going out with multiple women at the same time. Who knew how many people a billionaire like him went out with? Was she just a count?

She did not want an answer to that. So, she trained her brain to block everything about Delhi. She never met anyone. She did not take any assignment. She did not fly there. She did not get her heart broken.

Ignoring the actual physical pain she felt in her chest, Jiya banged the door shut without a response. She put the camera on a chair and sat down across the room, staring at the camera, transfixed.

ꯅꯅꯅ

Mukti had not had any easier time than Jiya or Chirag. Her mother had insisted she meet him while she was visiting Delhi for a friend's engagement. She had flown in from Dubai the previous evening and only on her mother's insistence had taken the first flight to Delhi. She took a cab to the hotel and then immediately to the address that her mother had texted her.

She was not sure what she was anticipating. Maybe some breakfast? But she had breakfast where she was staying. They might not be as rich as the Richie Rich man she had for a father, but her mother and she had enough to meet their needs.

Reluctantly, Mukti had walked past the front lawn and into the house. The door was open. She thought of all the things that could have prevented her from witnessing what she had witnessed next—her own reluctance to meet the man, her anger towards the man, her feeling out of place at his rich, rich house. Yet, she had found the door open and had walked in. The living room was empty. She called out softly, "Hello?" No one responded.

She moved around a bit and could smell some freshly brewed coffee. She moved tentatively in the direction from where the smell came and soon found herself standing in the doorway of the kitchen. And she was not alone.

Her father was standing too close to a woman. She had her arms on his back while he held her waist, and the two were kissing. They let go, and the woman relaxed her body a little. She turned her face a little to the right. And that was when Mukti let out a gasp. Her father had been snogging her mentor Jiya.

The scene was as vivid in her mind as it had been on the day when she had witnessed it. A tear trickled down her cheek as she found herself reliving it for the thousandth time. With each subsequent time that she was forced to relive the moment, she hated the man even more. He was never there for her mother. He was never there for her. And he had somehow managed to creep into her work—where she felt happy. He had not just managed to creep in but poison it as well. *He was making out with Jiya—who would be, what? Half his age? How could he even think of such a thing?*

Mukti had barely managed to stay through the remainder of her friend's engagement before returning back to Indore. She had not told her mother what she had witnessed. But she had refused to go back to Mumbai.

Her mother had tried to talk to her, but Mukti's decision was final.

As the days passed, Mukti couldn't help but relive the memory. Each time it was as gruesome as the first. She felt as disgusted, if not more. And after a few days, it was no longer just the memory that tormented her. Her brain started creating more scenes that led to or followed the one she witnessed. She thought of them holding each other in an embrace and mocking Mukti and her mom.

Every time she would have that nightmare, Mukti would scream for her mom. Amita had a fair idea of what Mukti might have witnessed considering the way she had reacted. However, she did not pry or force Mukti to share before she was ready. But one evening, she shared. She told everything that she had seen, everything she had done, and everything that tormented her.

Amita had put a hand on her head as she listened through the entire narrative. To Mukti's surprise, nothing shocked her.

"It does not bother you?" she asked through her tears.

Amita thought for a while, holding her daughter's resting head on her lap, and replied, *"Honestly, not really. Yes, there is a tiny bit of me that thinks what life would have been had he not been crazy for his work, but that tiny bit is not naïve."*

Mukti was not sure what her mother was referring to. Amita understood and continued, *"He is your father, and he was my husband, but I never thought that he had never dated before this and would not date after."* Amita paused, allowing her daughter to process before adding, "*He is crazy for his work but not about celibacy.*"

She laughed at her joke before excusing herself to get Mukti a snack.

Her mother's words changed a lot of things. Firstly, her nightmares stopped. She still could not control having to relive the moment, but it did not prove to be harder than it already was. Jiya and Chirag did not mock anyone. Moreover, now that she thought about it, Jiya had been as stunned as she was to see her. She had stormed out even before Mukti could. It all pointed to the fact that Jiya would not have known either. How would she? Mukti was never keen on discussing her father with anyone or having any contact with him. Everyone in her college and team had believed that she did not have a father, and they had never bothered with any details.

They all did love her mother's roasted namkeen mixture, though.

ᖰᖰᖰ

It was late one evening when the bell rang. Mukti was in her room, reading one of her books. Now that she refused to return to work, she had a lot of time to do the things she had been putting off for more than three years.

She heard her mother open the door and then close it. Then she could hear voices, and she believed she recognized one of the voices.

Mukti rushed out of her room to find Rahul, her fellow assistant, sitting in the hall with an older man. Rahul stood up to see his friend, and they both rushed to give each other a side hug.

The other man, Amita introduced, was Ashish. Ashish was one of the longest-serving employees of Chirag's firm. He was a very dear friend of Chirag as well. Rather, it had been Ashish, Amita recalled fondly, who had often called her to inform her that Chirag had to leave for another city or country and would not be back for a few days.

Ashish had not known Amita much. He knew her as Chirag's wife, but there had been next to no social events where he could have had the opportunity to know her as a person. He had seen the markers of the broken marriage from a distance and seen the gap between the couple convert into cracks before drifting them apart completely. He had tried to warn Chirag of the signs, but since then, he had just been an employee; he had not been as assertive as he could be now. And a part of him felt that all Amita and Chirag needed was to have a talk.

Anyway, that was a lost cause and water under the bridge. He had come here to return Mukti's bag. She had apparently left it at Chirag's house. Since Rahul needed to capture some artisans in Indore, Ashish thought to accompany him. It turned out Rahul knew Mukti. Rather, they had both worked together with Jiya.

Before their flight had landed in Indore, Ashish had understood everything that had happened on the day when Jiya disappeared and Mukti left her bag. Chirag had asked Ashish to ensure the bag was returned to her.

ϼϼϼ

Rahul asked Mukti to help him out with the shots. She was not sure—it was Jiya's project and for her father's firm. However, she had not told anyone except her mother that Jiya had been sending across her salary even when Mukti had not shown up for work. She felt it was her chance to settle the dues from her end and then formally quit.

"I do not think I would be much help." Mukti tried to decline politely. *"After all, it would be some old-school narrative."* She added a reason not to let Rahul read into the truth.

But it was Ashish who replied, *"Actually, as I understand, it is quite interesting and innovative."*

Rahul confirmed. He told of Jiya's concept and how they were shooting with real people in real locations. They were targeting advertisements in seven local languages, two national, and one international campaign. The entire thing was massive, and the entire project would stretch for a couple of months.

Mukti was surprised. *"I do not believe my Father would approve of this."*

It was Rahul's turn to be surprised. Mukti realized a second too late her mistake. She paused for a moment before letting him know that Chirag was her biological father. She made sure to stress that he and her mother were separated for years.

Despite the last bit, Rahul had found the information quite interesting. He kept asking her if she had helped their team get the contract. Mukti had no idea how this had happened. Rather, she had been so focused on being miserable that she had not given this a thought—how did the two come in contact?

It was again Ashish who came to the rescue. *"They met in Lonavala,"* he added.

Both Mukti and Rahul had known that Jiya had taken up an ad hoc assignment in Lonavala as a scheduled assignment had gotten cancelled. Ashish told them how they had met each other and how Jiya had impressed everyone.

"She was managing everything independently. Models, equipment, hotel staff..." He paused, laughing at his recollection before adding, *"Even us!"* This was nothing new for Mukti or Rahul - they had seen Jiya in this avatar almost everyday.

Ashish told about the extremely long dinner that Jiya and Chirag had shared, which had somehow resulted in Chirag offering her the assignment. And though Chirag had been opposed to the idea of a professional advertisement campaign shot till then, something about Jiya had convinced him. Not only the advertisement, but Chirag also changed as a person after meeting her. Ashish told them about the distributors whom they were going to reject and had made the decision two weeks in advance, but after meeting Jiya, Chirag had ended up acquiring the firm.

"He changed. Your father." Ashish added, turning to Mukti. *"He had had the same routine for several years now. Anything that could bring him joy scared him, and he never tried it."* Ashish was not just telling Mukti; he was thinking about the struggles that he had seen his friend live through. His intent was not to guilt Mukti into anything but to introduce him to her father as the man Ashish had known him to be.

"But with Jiya, he was different." Ashish continued. *"He was happy and alive. Unlike I had seen him for years, or more. Her energy was infectious."*

The last line worked as a cue for Rahul. He had no context of the subtext and the years of history behind the conversation, but in the last line, he started talking about how miserable Jiya had been. He had meant it as a genuine concern for someone they all knew. But Mukti and Ashish had very different reactions.

Ashish was happy for his friend. Though he did not need a confirmation to tell that Jiya had been as much smitten with Chirag as Chirag had been with her. Yet, if someone wanted proof, this would work well.

Meanwhile, Mukti was feeling sad. Jiya had been her mentor, her teacher, and her friend. She was strict and crazy in all ways, but Mukti had learned so much from her. Based on everything she heard, she had chosen to be more miserable than to be the reason behind Mukti's unhappiness.

The topic was closed intentionally. The three spent the day together. Ashish took them to the distributors' offices in and around Indore, where Mukti, Rahul, and their team took the pictures. Rahul would stay on for two more days to complete the shoot, but Ashish returned back, hoping to talk some sense into his friend.

ᗡᗡᗡ

Mukti spent her evening thinking about a lot of things. She had pulled out the box filled with cards, pictures, bracelets, and a few toys—everything that Chirag had sent over. She had refused to touch them, and her mother had stored them in a big box in the attic.

She went through each of the items—birthday cards, cards wishing her the best of luck before her exams or competitions, bracelets and toys for her birthdays, and a few handwritten notes.

She could not help but notice that he had always tried to make a connection to her even when she had made it quite clear that she was not interested. This contradicted her theory—a man who wanted to be a part of her life would not go the extra mile to find her mentor and use her to get to Mukti.

Did Mukti judge him a little too soon and a little too harshly?

She thought back on the calls she had not received, the messages she had deleted before reading through, and the efforts she had never acknowledged. She knew her mother had been in touch with her father, and Mukti had always disapproved of that as well. But there were only a certain number of times one could tell their mother not to do something before mothers did it anyway.

Every time she found her becoming soft, she could only do her best to remember the day in his kitchen—he was with Jiya, and she had clearly spent the night! This was the first time that she had seen him with another woman, but who knew Jiya was the first? She could have been one of the many! She forced herself to think of the worst—he was not just cheating on her mother but had also hurt Jiya, who had been her mentor for long.

Mukti felt conflicted. She heard Ashish talk about how Jiya had made a positive impact on Chirag and then Rahul had told her of how difficult it had become to work with Jiya. Though Mukti had not shared the reason behind the transition, she could string it all together.

Two people, who might not have been made for each other but came together to be better together, and now, she was the reason behind their sadness and misery. But the thought of them being together made her miserable.

Her nightmares were now getting replaced with self-doubt.

ᑭᑭᑭ

It was another week before Mukti was ready to share the latest reason for her sleep-deprived nights. Unlike what she had earlier believed, Chirag might not have known at all of Jiya's connection with Mukti. The two might have met innocently and fallen in love. While the idea was absurd and she was not ready to accept it either, it was at least a reason for her to give him the benefit of the doubt.

Amita agreed. She was stroking her daughter's head again, and Mukti's head rested on her mother's lap. It was her safe haven.

They had formed a new ritual in their lives. Every evening, Mukti would find her mother, and rest her head on her mother's lap while Amita would tell her anecdotes from her childhood—stories about her grandparents, her school, her friends, and some of her dad. Mukti had heard a few of the stories while some were new to her. Most of the stories concerning Chirag were definitely unheard of. She had intentionally blocked anything related to him from reaching her.

Now that she heard her mother tell her, her self-doubt grew. What if he had not been as bad as Mukti had made him out in her head?

Thoughts would fill up Mukti's mind to the extent that she could not decide what next. She would listen till the point she could without exploding and then vent out the thoughts that plagued her.

Her mother would patiently listen, providing some fixes. Usually, they would end up singing some songs or laughing at some of her childhood blunders.

It was not until a day later that Amita sat her daughter down and then asked her to face her fears to eradicate them completely.

When Mukti had asked what she meant by it, Amita announced that she would invite Chirag to their house. It was time they sat down and conversed like the broken family that they were.

ᗛᗛᗛ

Chirag stepped into the cosy home, an unexpected warmth settling over him. He greeted his former wife with a brief, formal hug—stiff on his part, but effortlessly warm from hers. It had been years since he had last seen her, yet she looked just as he remembered, only now there was a new radiance about her—the kind that came with being at peace.

Amita, too, had almost forgotten just how handsome her ex-husband was. It had been his charm and presence that had drawn her in all those years ago, and time had done little to change that. He still carried that same quiet charisma.

Chirag had come prepared, bringing small gifts—thoughtful tokens of appreciation for being welcomed into their lives. Amita accepted them with grace, without a trace of resentment. Mukti, however, kept her distance, watching silently, still unsure of what to make of it all.

They sat together for hours, reminiscing about the best moments of their past. It was mainly filled with Amita chatting and Chirag providing the fillers. Mukti had accepted to take a seat but refused to contribute in any way. The times Chirag had been absent no longer held weight between them, and neither felt the need to bring those up. Those gaps had lost their sharp edges, fading into something unspoken and forgotten.

Dinner was simple yet comforting for Chirag, enriched by Amita's cooking and the even rarer pleasure of shared company. They gathered in the small living room, surrounded by family photographs—silent reminders of a life that Mukti and Amita had continued without him. The conversation flowed easily at first, filled with light-hearted nostalgia and casual chatter. But as the meal came to an end, an unspoken tension started to set in.

Amita set down her glass, meeting Chirag's gaze with quiet intensity. "*Chirag,*" she asked, her voice steady and deliberate, "*do you love Jiya?*"

The question hung in the air. Both Chirag and Mukti were caught off guard. Chirag had almost forgotten Amita's uncanny ability to cut through pretence and get straight to the heart of things. And Mukti had never expected her mother to ask her father something so direct—something she herself could not think without feeling violated.

Chirag sat stunned, his breath hitching as the question hung in the air. He hadn't expected this. His hand froze in mid-air, holding the fork carrying the grains of rice mixed with dal. There were a few choices he had made that fateful day. He had to choose whether he wanted to look for Jiya or for Mukti. And regardless of how much it pained him, he knew in a choice between anything and Mukti, he would always choose his daughter.

The second choice was driven by the first one. Even after making the choice, he could not explain the reason for his heartache. He had spent several moments lying awake at night before it came to him. He loved her unlike he had loved anyone before her, and he was not going to love anyone like that ever. And because he loved her, it made him see things clearly—he could not think of himself.

He was a middle-aged man with a failed marriage and a lifetime of mistakes he was still trying to fix. Jiya was young and talented, standing on the edge of infinite possibilities. She could move to another country, dive into new adventures, and maybe even bungee jump off a cliff halfway across the world. He wouldn't be the one to hold her back.

There was a simple answer to Amita's question. He closed his eyes as his fingers dropped the fork. Taking a deep breath, his mind raced back to those moments with Jiya—her laughter, the way she had made him feel alive again, the way her hair fell on her face, her dedication to her work, how naturally she had bonded with his dogs, and the painful silence that followed her departure. Yes, he loved her. He loved her deeply, more than he had allowed himself to admit.

He opened his eyes, his gaze landing on Mukti. She was watching him with a mix of hope and fear, waiting for his answer. And in that moment, he understood something with heartbreaking clarity.

Loving Jiya wasn't the question. Admitting it was.

So, he lowered his eyes, burying the truth where no one could reach it.

Amita did not need an answer. She had spent years listening to Chirag's silence. For a small moment, she felt a sharp tinge as she had once hoped for the emotions that Chirag felt for Jiya for him to feel for her, but that sensation passed as soon as it had come. That was a long time in the past and did not matter. Amita and Mukti had together created their separate world filled with their joy. For years they had not bothered to care for what happened to him. They had moved out into their world, leaving his world distraught.

And after all these years, when he had found a person he cared for, over his businesses, it was not fair for them to deprive him of a chance at his happiness.

Gently placing a palm over his hand, she said, "*Love is complicated, Chirag. I never stopped loving you, and you never stopped loving Mukti.*" Chirag looked at her in shock.

Amita smiled and added, "*My love did not stop me from building a happier and healthier life for Mukti and myself. Your love for Mukti should not stop you either.*"

Chirag's eyes widened as he stared back, completely stunned. He had various thoughts running through his head and Amita seemed to read through them. She shook her head, and with a kind smile on her face, added "*The damage here is too much. Even though I wish more than anything for Mukti to have a proper family, I am sorry. We have to make the best of what we have. Though you can build whatever you want to with a new person - with Jiya!*"

At the words, Amita turned to Mukti. Her kind eyes conveyed more than just words. Mukti had remained silent throughout, and if she was going to speak, this might not be the proper place. Her mother had already helped her see things better. She had come a long way from hating the man to accepting that he was a bad father but, maybe, not a bad human being. Most importantly, Jiya deserved to stay happy. And if Jiya was happy with him, Amita and Mukti should find a way to be happy for both of them.

Reluctantly, Mukti nodded.

Happy to see her daughter grow, Amita added, "*From what I hear, Jiya is a great person. Don't lose her!*"

The former couple looked at each other with understanding in their eyes. They might not have been able to lead their lives as a couple or be the partners each desired, but they had started as good friends and were still good friends.

FOURTEEN

At the end of the delightful evening they had spent together, Mukti did something unexpected. She invited Chirag to spend a few days with them in Indore. He had not anticipated anything of the sort and was taken aback by the unexpected invitation. Amita's words made Mukti think about her issues with her father. She realized that she had blamed him for everything and never gotten to know him for who he was. Not that it would change anything from the past, but it would prevent the poison of her parents' relationship from seeping into her relationships. And for the first time in her adult life, she wanted to spend time with her father.

Even while trying to make amends, Mukti had remained a little aloof. Chirag had noticed that she hesitated with every sentence and was evidently trying for a future; she would still blame him for the past. But this in itself was more than he could have asked for. Suddenly he saw his little girl in a new light. She had grown up. And he was happy to have a chance to be a part of her life going forward. If he could have that, nothing from the past would matter, not that he could forgive himself for not being there for her.

Chirag would not have believed her had Mukti suggested that he stay in Amita's house. However, he graciously agreed to extend his stay for a week. He checked himself into a hotel at some distance from Amita's house but close enough that he could reach it before a pizza would. His life had taken an unexpected turn. Maybe it was time to retire. He could live in a city like Indore, enjoy the things it offered, and sometimes, come and visit Mukti—that would be his dream life.

The only problem was that this dream had come at the cost of another one—a dream that had been woven with open eyes with someone else. But Chirag knew better than to let that reflect on his face or ever mention Jiya's name.

The happiness that filled his heart through the course of the day left Chirag as he found himself alone in his room. He felt a void inside him that no matter what he did, did not fix. He lay on his bed, holding an open book to his chest, lost in his thoughts. Amita had very easily asked him about Jiya, and since then, he had lain awake each night thinking over her words. It was probably for the best that he was no longer in contact with her.

Chirag had called her a couple of times after Mukti had left. He had no idea that Mukti was Jiya's assistant until Mukti told him before storming out of his house. He did not even know she had relocated to Mumbai or was working as an assistant to a photographer.

The light of how wrong his actions had been dawned on him. Mukti's words, harsh but true, had changed the way he looked at the moments he shared with Jiya and at himself. None of it made him feel good anymore. *Jiya was significantly younger than him. Her world was as different from his as possible. She had her whole future lined up in front of her. Just because she was confident, charming, extroverted, and extremely beautiful, he had found himself attracted to her. But that was no reason to sentence her to a life of despair.*

Mukti's words reverberated through his mind. Was he engaging Jiya so he could leave her, just as he had left Amita?

That was true! He saw a reflection of his crazy workaholic self in Jiya. What would happen when the initial spark would die? Jiya would spend days away from home for her shoots. And many times, he would have to travel as well. When would they then meet or spend time together? Would they end up fighting just like Amita and Chirag? Would the initial spell break, and would Jiya see the whole thing as a mistake?

There were more questions than answers. But Chirag was not looking for any answers. If the answers were something that resonated with his fears, it would break his heart. Moreover, the answers mattered no more. Jiya had made her choice, and he had made his. She would become the best in her field and find a person worthy of her, while he could retire and spend more time with his daughter. And somewhere, deep in his heart, he could lock up all the memories of the moments and conversations he had shared with her.

ᛒᛒᛒ

The first day passed quietly. Chirag visited Amita's home in the late evening hours. After a small talk over coffee, Mukti showed him around the neighbourhood. They walked through the lively streets, and she pointed out the spots that she had frequented as a teenager—the quaint coffee shop where she had spent hours every day working on some project or another, a small bookstore that would order all the books she requested, and the community park where she had played with her friends for hours during their childhood.

There existed a perfect little world for Amita and Mukti, which Chirag had not been a part of. Chirag could sense the hesitation as Mukti allowed him access to the same. He appreciated all her efforts and knew that he needed to work even more to win her trust.

He could not help but feel a rush of gratitude towards Amita. Through all the years, he had not believed her to be wrong. Yes, he had hoped that she had intervened when things were becoming tough for her to manage—yet, she was not wrong. She had done all she could until she could. And when she could hold no more, everything had crumbled down. And despite his negligence and putting her through all that, she had convinced Mukti to invite him and get to know him. The regret over his mistakes towards Amita grew multifold.

As the two walked through the streets of the neighbourhood, Chirag spotted several known landmarks. Of course, he had never been to this part of the city earlier, but he had a few pictures that Amita had sent him of Mukti. The park where Mukti had participated in a dance competition when she was younger, was no longer fit for anything of the sort. It had been divided and converted into a mini cricket pitch and a mini football court. There were a few swings cramped in the side. Though the fencing had remained the same as the one depicted on his bedside picture of Mukti dancing. The community club had been repainted. He could not have recognized it to be the same building where Mukti had won her swimming competition if the board had not been the same as in the picture of her that he kept in his study.

For Chirag, it was all surreal. He had spent so much time staring at those pictures, wishing he could be there. And now that he finally was, it felt almost dreamlike. He saw his daughter in a new light. As a toddler, Mukti loved to colour. She would take her crayons with her everywhere and start colouring over anything. He had not had his house painted until he sold it to move to his current home. To him, his daughter was still that little girl with crayons. He could not imagine her dancing winning swimming competitions or becoming a photographer.

Not only had her career choices changed, but she had also changed in several aspects. Mukti was no longer the young girl he had missed out on raising, but a young woman with her own life, routines, choices, and space. She was hardworking and made her own decisions.

He was so proud of her.

ᐅᐅᐅ

Each day of the following week Mukti took Chirag to a specific part of the city – one day she showed him her college campus, another time a famous restaurant that she had frequented and some local tourist points. He could sense she was still weary of his presence, yet she made constant efforts.

Their meetings were short – not spanning over a couple of hours each day. This format worked well for both. After some time, Mukti would grow tired of chaperoning him through the city or remember some bitter memory associated with him. Meanwhile, having been absent from her life for too long, Chirag would run out of ways of communicating with her. Additionally, he knew he was still under probation. Happy at what he was getting, Chirag would arrive promptly to pick her up at tea time and the two would share an early dinner together before he dropped her back to the house.

Chirag had the rest of the day to wait for the next time he would meet her. He had counted the number of times he had made her laugh. Ironically, she was a master at telling jokes. This was something he had never known. He spent hours reading and learning jokes to tell her when he would see her next. There had been a total of seven times when he felt that she had genuinely laughed, and they had together made a memory.

There were some things that disturbed him as well. For instance, Mukti had absolutely refused to let him pay for her. She had insisted on paying or splitting the bill every time. She had also not introduced him to her friends when they spotted the two of them together one evening. It was unsettling, but Chirag had decided not to let these things come in the way of their newly formed relationship. He was not going to give up.

Amita had kept herself busy through all these evenings. She had been heavily involved in several things. She took tuition for the neighbouring children. She was a part of two different women's groups that met regularly every alternate week. She was also a member of the RWA committee for her neighbourhood. Moreover, she had also become a devotee and visited the nearby temple every day to offer her services. It was all in addition to her regular job, which was already keeping her quite preoccupied.

One day when she joined the two, she explained that after Mukti left for Mumbai, her life had suddenly become quite empty. She needed to get out of the house in order to survive through the periods of loneliness.

Chirag was left awestruck. He felt quite insignificant. There were magazines and newspapers waiting to write about him—describing him to be some genius who had everything figured out. Seeing how Amita and Mukti had shaped their lives, he felt all his merits and achievements diminish. When Amita had asked him about his life, he could not think of a third sentence to describe his routine—he worked, and he took care of his health.

Even though he had known the reason for their separation from the moment they had stopped talking while remaining under a single roof, he had never made amends. Their departure had given him the excuse to dig a deeper hole and bury himself in it. It did not matter what reasons or excuses he had given at that time; the truth was that his life was in vain. There was no one except Scout and Molly whom he could talk to. Ashish was as close to a friend as he had. And it did not matter how many birthdays or anniversaries his employees invited him to; he did not have a single person to share a slice of cake with.

Mostly he was amazed with the warmth with which Amita had graciously invited him to her home and life. He no longer felt like a man not welcomed. He was definitely still far from being Mukti's father or even friend, but at least she did not turn away at the sight of him.

Chirag would return each night to his hotel room, having inched a little closer to Mukti, with a heart full of satisfaction.

ϷϷϷ

Each day had passed in a rush. Even though it had been difficult for him to wait each morning for the evening to dawn, his last day of stay in Indore had already come. Chirag had explicitly asked not to be disturbed under any circumstances. He would wake up and take an unusually long walk followed by breakfast. He would then take his own time to get ready and follow up on the world news. He would roam around till lunch and after lunch, he would cuddle inside his blanket watching any movie on the television. His work had left him with no time to watch television, and he realized it was something that he could talk with Mukti about. She had told him about some of her favourite movies on their first day, and he had made it a point to ask her opinion on the movie that he had seen earlier that day.

On the last day of Chirag's stay in Indore, Mukti had planned a dinner for him. She had gradually warmed a bit towards him, and Amita told him that the grand dinner was all her idea. She had invited him to the most expensive restaurant in the city. Chirag was a bit taken aback by the choice, knowing Mukti wasn't one to indulge in such luxuries, but he went along with it.

To add to the list of surprises, she asked him to get a box of chocolates of a particular brand and flavour. Chirag was extremely confused at such a specific request, but he was highly delighted to run across the city trying to find the chocolates. It was the first time in forever that his daughter had asked him for something, and he was going to get those chocolates for her. The task, however, took him longer than expected, scouring through shops and making calls until he finally tracked them down. He found himself wondering if Mukti was testing him, perhaps to see how far he was willing to go for her. The thought made him more determined to not disappoint her.

Finally securing the chocolates in a bag in his hands, Chirag looked at himself in the mirror. To go the extra mile, he purchased two flower bouquets—the lilies for Amita and the sunflowers for Mukti. He had gone a little overboard and got himself a new blazer for the occasion—his father-daughter dinner date!

He felt a strange mixture of anticipation and unease as Chirag reached the restaurant. Mukti had booked a private cabin for them. When Chirag gave his name, the waiter escorted him to the furthest inner section of the restaurant. He could tell that there were only five tables, as there were five smaller alcoves attached to the larger oval space. Each of the alcoves was hidden behind a partition, not allowing any pair of prying eyes to get more than the intrinsic design of the wooden partition in place. There was a small handle on one side of the partition that he believed provided the entry point into the space beyond.

The private cabin, Chirag considered, offered an exquisite private dining experience in a quiet and intimate setting. As the waiter walked him to one of the alcoves, he took a deep breath before pushing the handle gently. He was careful not to exert a lot of pressure—the partition might break, the door might make a lot of noise, or Mukti might get scared. There were too many possibilities.

But the sight that greeted him stopped him in his tracks. Out of the several possibilities he had considered, he was not prepared to witness what he saw with his eyes.

Mukti sat on the farthest end, facing the wooden partition. She was dressed elegantly in a midnight blue bodycon dress. She was laughing at something as he opened the partition door. And she wasn't alone. Seated beside her, looking just as surprised as he felt, was Jiya.

Chirag's heart skipped a beat. For a moment, he simply stood there, unable to process what he saw. His eyes locked onto Jiya's beautiful hazel ones, and he saw the same emotion mirrored in them. She had no idea of his presence either. The room seemed to close in around them. It was just like the first time that they had both laid eyes on each other—they were both unable to shift their gaze or speak anything.

Jiya had been taken in by surprise as Chirag walked in. Mukti had called her seven days earlier and requested her to come to Indore. She had refused to say more on the call, and Jiya presumed it might have been for a project.

Even weeks after their last meeting, Jiya was not able to concentrate on her work, and Mukti had not returned either. She had wanted to call Mukti up and check up on her but could not get herself to do it. Her other assistant and interns had frequently asked about Mukti—she had stopped picking their calls either, and gradually learned to move on when Jiya refused to say anything either.

This was not good for both of them. Mukti had been one of the most promising people Jiya had had as an assistant. She did not even know the extent to which she had been dependent on Mukti—Mukti was the person she would call whenever she needed anything; Mukti took care of most accounts; Mukti was well connected with several of her former assistants; and most importantly, Mukti had a natural talent.

Jiya had a few assignments lined up, but she was getting her assistant and interns to complete those. Even on the two occasions, she managed to pull herself out of bed and into the studio, she had failed to do anything. It had been as if she had not just left her camera at Chirag's house but also her soul. She could not focus, could not eat, and could not even think.

It took her over three weeks to get out of her house after she returned to Delhi. Every time she would close her eyes, she would see the accusatory look on Mukti's face from the day in Chirag's kitchen.

She had no idea of where her career was going. She did not care for any work. And she had no personal life. Hence, when Mukti called her, she had not even picked up the call in the first two times. She did not feel brave enough to talk to her just then. But Mukti was persistent. She also knew Jiya, having worked together for almost two years. She kept calling, and Jiya eventually picked up.

The idea of travelling to Indore without a reason was absurd. Jiya had not managed to visit a salon or even buy vegetables from a vendor on the street. She was in no condition to go to Indore. But Mukti persisted again. She called Jiya multiple times each day, until the day before yesterday when Jiya gave in.

Jiya reached Indore sometime in the afternoon. She could not have taken a morning flight even if her life depended on it—not that she slept in late anymore—but because she needed time to fix herself.

When she looked into the mirror after weeks, she saw the haunting reflection look back. Her face had grown dull and dirty. She had lost quite a lot of weight. There were dark circles under her eyes due to the lack of sleep and puffiness over her eyes due to all the tears she had cried. Her hair was dishevelled. Her clothes were wrinkled, and she was sure that she was not smelling good.

Her bedroom had been a complete mess. She had even refused to step out into the hall that doubled as her studio. She lay on her bed throughout the day and night, smoking, screaming, crying, or throwing anything she could hold.

Deciding it was probably an attempt from Mukti's end to mend things, Jiya had agreed to go to Indore. She did not care whom Mukti was related to. They could obviously not work together anymore but there was no rule about the two of them not moving on with their lives. If there was a project in Indore, Jiya would take it as her chance to take control of her life. And she would help Mukti set up her own base or be the assistant to some other photographer. Hopefully, she had wished there would be no mention of Chirag during the Indore visit.

Chirag could not take his eyes off Jiya. She looked quite different from the last time he had seen her—she had lost a lot of weight; her face and eyes had lost their sparkle; and she was not smiling. She looked sad and kind of guarded as she looked back at him. But she was still beautiful—in her flowing golden dress.

He did not want to and could not take his eyes off her. She was the most beautiful woman in the world.

A loud voice in his head chided him for his thoughts. Apparently, the feelings he had had were not completely gone. They had merely decided to mellow down in her absence, and now that she was back, they roared inside his mind and heart. As the feelings grew stronger, so did a voice in his head. It chided him, reminding him that there was no future for the two of them together. He caught hold of the wall—was he imagining her? He blinked a couple of times and tried to push his nail into the palm of his hand.

It was not a dream. She was as real as the pain he felt. Chirag broke the eye contact with a jerk and turned to leave.

Mukti, sensing that her plan was going to backfire, immediately got up and walked over to Chirag. "*Dad, wait!*" She ordered him to stop.

Even during the seven days that Chirag had spent trying to get to know his daughter, Mukti had never once addressed him as '*Dad*'. It had been years since he had been addressed like that. And just like that, there was a surge of another emotion in him. He stopped.

Gently Mukti took his hand into hers and led him towards the table. Chirag shook his head, trying to silently communicate his disapproval of the idea. But she would not let go of his hand.

Jiya saw the scene. The sharp pain that she had felt in her chest intermittently for the last few weeks had returned. She had spent days endlessly worrying over how he had been. And despite the amount of pain that she was in, she had prayed for him to get what made him happy—his family—even if that came at a cost to her.

She was happy to see them together. She saw the teardrop swell up in his eyes as Mukti called out to him. Not being a mom yet, she could not relate to his feelings but having known him, she knew that it meant a great deal to him.

Finding herself intruding on a personal family moment, Jiya decided to excuse herself. There had been some kind of a miscommunication—maybe Chirag had had no idea of her presence and had merely come to meet his daughter. Maybe Mukti had gotten something messed up. After Jiya had reached Indore, Mukti asked Jiya to join her for dinner. She had also asked her to wear a party dress. There could be several explanations, but the fact would remain that Jiya needed to distance herself from the restaurant—from Chirag.

She picked up her purse and got to leave.

"*Jee!*" Mukti called out, using the nickname she fondly used for her. Mukti had followed Jiya's work for a long time. Jiya's story of becoming a successful photographer intrigued her. Once she was satisfied with the photographs she had taken, Mukti did not delay another second to send those to Jiya and ask to be her intern.

Jiya reciprocated those sentiments. She had liked Mukti's work, and that was high praise, as Jiya rarely liked a novice's photographs.

There were a few hundred letters that Jiya received monthly—each containing photographs and long letters. Jiya made it a priority to take time during her busy schedule to go through the letters. She would invite most people to be her interns. She had not forgotten the several letters that she had written to secure her internships. But rarely did someone stand out exceptionally.

Mukti definitely had the makings of a fine photographer. With the correct training and experience, she could even become a better photographer than Jiya herself.

She stopped, facing the door. The reason behind the heavy feeling she felt in her chest dawned on her. Mukti was one of the three people that Jiya had taken a personal interest in. While she might have had several interns and a handful of assistants, three of the applications she had received throughout her career had intrigued her. Mukti was one of them.

That day in Chirag's kitchen, not only had Jiya lost him but also Mukti.

Mukti let go of Chirag's hand. It was time that she addressed the elephant in the room—the reason to bring them both together under false pretext.

She walked over to the table and pulled out a chair for Chirag on one side while asking Jiya to take her seat facing Chirag on the other side. She guided him to his seat, right across from Jiya. The table was set with exquisite attention to detail, candles flickering softly in the dim light, and the faint sound of music played in the background. But all of that faded into the background as Chirag sat down, his heart racing.

Neither of them felt comfortable, and neither of them could leave. They were both complying for Mukti, whom they both genuinely cared about. However, now that their eye contact was broken, they were far more determined to keep it that way. Chirag kept looking at the box of chocolates that he held in his hands, and Jiya kept looking at the plate in front of her.

Mukti looked between the two of them, her expression softening. *"Before one of us gets angry or someone walks out,"* Mukti began, her voice steady but slightly animated, *"there's something I need to say. And I need both of you to listen."*

Chirag looked at her while Jiya nodded. They were both giving her their attention.

"I apologize for lying to both of you." Mukti held Chirag's right hand with her left and Jiya's left hand with her right. She continued,

"*But I had no other way of bringing you both in the same room.*"

Jiya had sunk her eyes to her knees. She refused to look up, scared of being lost in Chirag's deep brown eyes. Time had lost its relevance. She felt like it had been years since she had been with him, and yet, she would lie if she were to deny the existence of butterflies as she had when she saw him for the first time.

Mukti continued her monologue, "*You are both important to me, but over the last few days, I have realized that you are both extremely important to each other. And it is not fair that you stay apart.*" She looked from Chirag to Jiya.

Chirag was holding her hand firmly. He tried to pull it apart on hearing her words, attempting to leave, but she gave him a stern look and held his hand even tighter. Mukti had more to add, "*Especially not on my account!*" She stared back at him in determination and shook her head.

There was a moment of pause. No one said anything. The three of them sat on one side of the table, holding hands as if playing some game.

"*I've watched both of you over these past few days, and I've seen the impact of whatever happened between you both. Dad, you've changed—Jiya's presence in your life brought something good out in you, something no one has ever seen before. But after she left, it's like you have stopped living.*" She took a long breath, giving him a staring look.

"*And Jiya... I've seen how much pain you've been in, trying to keep going, wasting your life with smoking, screaming and breaking things but clearly suffering. And all this because of me?*"

Jiya gently pulled her hand from Mukti's grasp. She looked up. Words were rushing out from her stomach but getting stuck in her throat. It took her a second to realize that she was feeling angry.

She stood up, looked at Chirag, and then back at Mukti. Her gaze was no longer gentle but fierce. "*It is not because of you! Some things are not meant to be.*" She might have looked at Mukti while saying them, but the words were meant for Chirag.

She was upset; rather, she was extremely angry about his actions. *He could have done something—anything—to change the outcome of the events from that day. He could have taken a stand; he could have stood beside her. He could have come to Mumbai.* Yes, he had called her four times on the day she had walked out. But she had been in no state to pick up his call then. She had walked all over the city before reaching her hotel. She had no idea how she walked there or for how long she had been on the roads. One of the interns had rushed to meet her. She was allowed to be led to her room, where she collected some money and took a cab to the airport. She bought a ticket for the next flight out of Delhi to Mumbai and left.

Every second since then, she had wished she had not done that. But Chirag had not given her a reason to behave differently. He could have asked her to stay. He could have called her the next day. He would have found a way to talk to her if he had really wanted to. At least, he could have messaged her, '*Let us not meet again*' or '*It's over.*'

But he had done nothing of that sort. Jiya had spent hours thinking that she and the connection they shared had meant nothing to him.

Did he not feel what she did? The questions had haunted her all these weeks. Yes, she understood that he had longed to be with his family, and it was a wicked coincidence that Mukti turned out to be his daughter. She did not wish to replace Mukti. Surely he would have enough place in his heart and life to have them both in his life.

Jiya's audible words had the reverse effect on Chirag. He was surrounded by his fears all the time. Jiya was working with Mukti. He had been married and divorced while she was still making it big in her career. He was too old for her. She needed a man who could be with her and be like her.

He had no idea why she had decided to play along, but he knew that regardless of what he told anyone else, he had fallen hopelessly in love with her. *Her smile, her eyes, her voice, her mannerisms*—everything of hers was dear to him. He had envisioned several things they would do together or places they would go for vacation.

Through all the things, he had, quite conveniently, forgotten that she was another individual. She had her own priorities and life.

He saw all his fears materialize right in front of him. He did not pull his hand out of Mukti's but stood up to look straight into Jiya's fired gaze and added, *"There are a lot of things needed to make things work—you need to have things in common. Different work, different lifestyle, different habits, and different choices are not components of a lasting relationship."*

Chirag's words made Jiya even angrier. She could not believe what he had just said.

"So, you do not think I am good enough for you, Mr. Rich-and-Perfect?" Jiya shouted directly at Chirag. He got up as well, though calm in action, to reply. The two had almost forgotten that Mukti was in the same room.

He had let go of Mukti's hand and was holding the table for balance. *"I am saying that I am not good enough. What do I have to give you? Two successful businesses—that you don't need and a failed marriage?"* He was matching her energy and tone, *"You have your full life in front of you. What would you get with me?"*

Jiya threw her purse on the floor. Mukti had already instructed the staff to not disturb the meeting unless asked. She was quite glad of having anticipated some shouting. She had taken a step back and was enjoying the view, ready to break up a fight if things got a little overheated.

She had asked Chirag to get Jiya's favourite chocolates. Without being noticed, she had slid them from his side of the table to hers.

Jiya took some time to think of the counter. *"Thank you, but I can decide for myself!"*

"Exactly." Chirag added, *"You need to choose the best for yourself. Just because I love you does not mean you have to spend the rest of your life with me."*

Jiya froze the moment the words left Chirag's lips. *"Just because I love you..."* The rest of his sentence faded into the background; the room fell silent around her as those three words echoed in her endlessly. Her anger, the fury that had been boiling just seconds before, suddenly dissipated, replaced by an overwhelming wave of emotion.

Chirag was still speaking, listing all the reasons why their relationship wouldn't work, why he wasn't good enough for her. He said something about the age difference, his failed marriage, his daughter, his daughter being Jiya's assistant, and several other things. Jiya heard those words but none of them meant anything. she stood there, as transfixed as she had been on seeing him for the first time getting out the pool. Everything that had happened since that moment had beautiful led them two to be here. It was all perfect and it was perfect together.

Jiya's entire being was focused on the revelation that had just come from him—the confession she had longed to hear but never expected. He loved her. Despite everything, he loved her. All those days locked up in her studio bedroom, she had come up with a thousand reasons why he didn't want anything more with her. Maybe she was just a distraction, a fling—just like the few men had been for her. And everything that she had felt was only in her head. Being away from him hurt, but believing that he didn't feel the same hurt so much more. To make things worse, she had never felt an instant connection with anyone-she had never felt as safe with anyone. Probably it was better not having felt those emotions for now that she knew how it felt, she was not able to exist without him.

But she was wrong. He was the ruggedly-handsome, genuinely hardworking and the soft-hearted gentleman she had believed him to be. While she had been thinking he had not felt the connection that she did, he had been safeguarding her interests. Her heart began to race, and her eyes softened as they locked onto Chirag's. He was still advocating his points, his voice steady but tinged with the pain of someone who truly believed he was doing the right thing by letting her go. Jiya saw through them now, saw the fear behind his words, the vulnerability in his eyes.

She took a step forward, around the table, then another, closing the distance between them. Chirag paused, noticing her movement, his eyes flickering with confusion. "*Jiya...?*" he began, but he didn't get the chance to finish, if he had intended to say anything more.

Jiya kept fondly gazing into his eyes as she walked right next to him. He was just trying to be the perfect gentleman that he was—how could she have not seen it? Of course, he would have thought he was doing it all for her! He cared for her. No, he loved her! She could not imagine how she had spent all the days without him. The sudden change of emotions had made her slightly confused. There was a part of him that wanted to hit him to put her through all the misery. And there was another part of her that wanted to hit him for wasting his time on talking now. However, the biggest part of her wanted to hold him and never let go.

In one swift motion, Jiya closed the gap between them, cupping his face in her hands. The words she needed to say were tumbling through her mind, but there was only one way to convey them properly. Chirag had stopped talking. She saw him quiver slightly at the warmth of her hands on his face. She had felt an electric pulse run across her body as well. For a second the two stood there, holding each other before Jiya let go of his face, put her arms around his torso, leaned in and pressed her head against his heart-pulling him into a tight embrace.

The touch of her skin on his face and the feeling on her head on his heart had driven everything out of Chirag's mind. He had forgotten everything that he had thought over the last few weeks. Things rolled back to the last time they had been this close-in his kitchen on that morning. Chirag had known for sometime that Jiya liked him and that he reciprocated her feelings. He also knew that these feelings had only grown with every day that they had known each other. For the weeks that they had been away, he might not have seen her but knew without having been told that she would have been a mess. She would have reverted to her older schedule-sleepless nights, endless work and habits that only made it worse. Yet, he had resisted the urge of messaging or calling her. Despite what Ashish had said or Amita had told him, he did not trust himself with relationships. Somehow, even without meaning to, he had caused pain to all those people who had loved him. Jiya did not need to get added to the list. Moreover, despite how strongly he had felt for her, he would always have a family with Mukti. Jiya did not need all that. She deserved someone better-someone who cherished her, someone who would walk by her side through all the thicks and thins of life, someone who knew how lucky he was to have her, someone who would cross the oceans to be by her side and move mountains if she wished. Most importantly, someone who was only hers.

Yet, the moment she had leaned in closer and held him in her arms, had completed his world for him. He had had the perfect week with Mukti and Amita-something he had longed for so long. It was even better than what he had wished for. And yet, he could not help feel incomplete. While he had forced himself to not think of her during the hours he spent walking around the city, watching movies, working out, reading articles, meeting new people or simply breathing, he could not help her from sliding into his dreams. Every night he had thought of her-walking to her, sharing meals together, seeing her work, taking her to his favourite places, taking vacations together and so much that he would not even admit to. Whatever the circumstances may have been, Mukti had returned to his life only after Jiya had come into it. He credited this happiness to her, even though she was not there to share it with him.

All the reasons he had accumulated for keeping her away from him had dissipated as her head touched his chest. He was complete. Everything felt better and brighter. Overcome with emotions, Chirag closed his eyes, pulling her closer to him. He was going weak in the knees. He remembered the first time she had hugged him in the hotel lobby in Lonavala. That seemed like a lifetime away—a lot had happened since then. A lot had changed in the last few weeks but even more had remained the same. He still felt a wave of warmth ripple through his body at her touch. Her slow breathing spread joy across his chest. His hands reached out to stroke her hair.

Neither of them spoke, for words could not even begin to convey the emotions they were both experiencing.

Mukti had silently walked out of the room, giving them both time and space to reconnect. She had decided to make use of the time to order dinner. Her plan seemed to have worked.

She had been miserable without her work. While she had refused to work with Amita or return to Mumbai, Amita had allowed her some time to take a break. But when the break was extended, Amita got her to look out for other opportunities. Mukti was able to get some smaller projects in other cities, but she felt she did them only half-heartedly.

It was not until one day when her mother sat her down, and the two had a talk. Amita told her how difficult it had been for both of them to survive in the new city when they had moved there. And yet, there was one thing that kept them going—love! Amita loved Mukti and wanted to provide her with the best life she possibly could. Hence, the longer hours and extra tuition were never a bother. Likewise, Mukti was extremely attached to her mother. She would call her at least three times a day and try to simplify Amita's life as much as possible.

When they were both together, the challenges did not seem to bother them. And just like they both needed each other in their lives, so did Jiya and Chirag.

Amita explained how Chirag always wanted to be a dad to Mukti in all the years, but Amita knew he was just too attached to his work. She did not want his money or fame to sidetrack Mukti, and she did not want him to hurt her either. Hence, she had refused to take any help from him. And Mukti needed to give him the respect he deserved, if not the love.

Similarly, Mukti had obviously found Jiya difficult to work with initially, but she had always looked out for Mukti. Jiya had given her several independent projects and encouraged her to network. Over the course of their time together, Mukti had started to understand and even appreciate Jiya's methods and attitude. She may look complex but was a very simple and straightforward person. There were several things that she could have taken care of, like basic organization of her space, focusing on her personal relationships, but she was way too focused on her work to care for anything else. Through all their time together, Mukti knew she had learned so much than she might have had, if she was working with any other photographer. And in more ways than she could count, she had started to look upto Jiya.

The idea of her father being with a woman she considered a close friend was absurd. In ways that she could explain, she felt violated. She could not even answer the reason why did she feel that way when she had never considered Chirag to be her father. And Jiya - Mukti had seen the way Jiya felt about relationships; she had seen the few men Jiya had been on "casual" dates with, without seeing them ever again. It would definitely help if she found someone she wanted to settle down with - it would help the assistants and interns much more.

Then what would the harm be if two people, who might be different in the way they looked or appeared, were together?

Amita's words had made Mukti think, and she had then decided to not intervene. Chirag had been away from her life for her liking. And if he found happiness with someone, it was not her place to intervene. For Jiya, she realized that had the same situation been with any other man, Mukti would have been happy. *Then why not if that man was Chirag?*

Chirag had not mentioned Jiya's name or anything remotely related during his week with Mukti. Though she could see his face drop or him becoming silent every time she mentioned her work. Having spent some time with her, she also found him to be a good person. He had made his mistakes, but then, who did not make mistakes? Sometimes, we struggle to forgive others for things we wouldn't even consider mistakes if we had done them ourselves. And though she did not think he could be a permanent part of her family, it did not mean he could not have his own.

On the pretext of spending some more time with him, she got him to stay. The next part was more challenging—to convince Jiya to visit Indore. Rahul, Jiya's other assistant and Mukti's friend had told her how miserable Jiya had been. She had not touched the camera at all and rarely ate anything. She was following the textbook definition of grieving.

The thought of seeing Jiya again or even talking to her made Mukti uncomfortable. But it was something that she needed to do. She knew that Jiya had a soft corner for her. She kept pinging Jiya and called her at odd hours until she finally picked up the call. She asked Jiya about a local assignment - something she had taken up to avoid returning back to Mumbai. It had gone miserably. Though the details were not meant for Jiya. Mukti needed her to be intrigued enough to agree to come.

Amita believed that if the two of them could talk, things would resolve themselves. And that is what happened.

ᐅᐅᐅ

The silence in the room was quite comforting. They both stood holding each other, without a word. Jiya looked up after a while. Tears had silently trickled down her cheeks creating small wet patches on his shirt. She looked at him with moist eyes and a shaky smile. His face was calm, free from all his negative emotions. He looked extremely handsome.

Chirag opened his eyes feeling Jiya's head move. He looked down into her perfect hazel eyes. She was smiling. And though he had known her to look impeccable at all times, her teary eyes look with hair sticking to his coat was winning his heart. Chirag hesitated for a moment, overwhelmed by all her emotions, but then pulled her into a tighter embrace. She was not a person; she was his home. Home is not a place but a feeling. Despite having a big bungalow to call his, Chirag had only felt happy there the day she had visited, laughing and playing with Scout and Molly. Otherwise, it had just been a structure of bricks and cement.

"I don't care about the businesses, the differences, or the past." Jiya whispered gently. As she spoke, her voice didn't just break the silence—it created something new. Her soft lips brushed against his freshly shaven chin, and with every word, every delicate touch, a

storm of emotions stirred between them. She had not broken free of the embrace but was whispering the words into his neck, "*I love you too.*"

It was not a statement. It was everything this could muster before raising her heels to reach a little higher. Unable to contain her emotions, she planted a firm kiss on his cheeks. It was as abrupt to end as it had been to start. There was more that she wanted to tell him, "*I do not want a part of you-I want the whole of you, with all your problems and stupid overthinking issues.*"

She was looking straight into his eyes. Both of them could not help but grin. Jiya continued, "*As long as we can share our meals and plan dates at the planetarium, we will figure out the rest of the details.*"

She knew he agreed as she felt him pull her a little closer.

Chirag looked at her, still trying to process what was happening. There were so many words forming in his mind - he wanted to promise her the world and it was not a promise that people made for the sake of making it. He loved her so much that he wanted to do everything that he could. But, he could even find the words. This moment was all he wanted. He agreed—with her by his side, he could win any battle. He rested his head on hers, closing his eyes in an attempt to freeze the moment.

In a moment of complete surrender, Jiya had won. Chirag had closed his eyes, but there was a soothing smile on his face. Without a thought, she leaned in and pressed her lips to his, silencing whatever lingering doubts he might have. The outpouring of their emotions had simplified everything. Her brain was releasing so many happy juices that she felt she might explode with happiness. She felt so much lighter than she did in weeks.

It was as if the last couple of weeks had had the reverse affect on both of them. There were a lot of discussions that they needed to have, a lot of fights with each other and with the rest of the world, a lot of adjustments to be made, and a lot of things that they would need to work on, but overall, things were going to be worth it because they were going to be together!

Epilogue

The gallery buzzed with quiet conversations, the soft hum of admiration filling the air as people moved between the photographs lining the walls. Warm golden lights illuminated Mukti's work—her perspective was raw, honest, and deeply moving. Jiya took a deep breath, trying to focus on the art, but her eyes kept drifting toward the entrance.

Where was he?

She glanced at her phone, thumb hovering over the dial button before she decided against calling him again. The last time she had, his response had been an infuriatingly calm "I'm on my way, Jiya." That had been twenty minutes ago.

"*Where are you? How could you be late today?*" she muttered under her breath, willing him to magically appear.

She adjusted the pleats of her saree, the yellow fabric shimmering under the soft lights, its multicoloured blouse adding a playful contrast. She wasn't used to sarees—had never imagined herself in one, really—but when she had unwrapped it on her birthday, carefully selected and gifted by Chirag, she had loved everything about it. Tonight, she wanted to surprise him and could not wait to see his reaction.

A familiar set of hurried footsteps echoed down the corridor, and before she even turned, she knew.

Chirag was here.

He strode toward her in a dark blue suit—the one she had chosen for him—with his hair neatly gelled, just the way she liked. He added a shine to the dimly lit gallery with his heavenly presence. Her irritation melted away as she took him in, her lips curving into a smile. He placed a hand on his heart on seeing her, silently conveying how stunning she looked.

This man... her daily dose of happiness. The reason everything felt right.

"*You're late,*" she whispered teasingly as he finally reached her.

"*Am I?*" He countered, slightly breathless, with a playful grin, flashing that smile that always made her heart stumble.

And just like that, all was forgiven.

Chirag reached into his pocket, pulling out a small velvet box. Without a word, he flipped it open, revealing a delicate pair of silver earrings. "*For Mukti,*" he explained, his voice laced with something tender, and uncertain. It had only been eight months since they had all made amends and decided to continue as an extremely weird family. "*Do you think she would like these?*"

Jiya exhaled softly, touched by the gesture. It was these little things—the thoughtfulness, the attention to detail—that made her fall for him, over and over again. She nodded frivolously to register her approval.

She looked up to escort her into the exhibition hall when she noticed the flicker of hesitation in his eyes. His fingers curled around something else in his pocket, something he hadn't yet revealed.

"*Chirag?*" she prompted, stepping closer.

He swallowed, shifting on his feet. "*There's... something else,*" he admitted.

For the first time since she had met him, Chirag looked uncertain. Nervous.

And then, he slowly pulled out another velvet box—smaller, heavier.

Jiya's breath hitched.

With a quiet snap, the lid lifted, revealing a ring—a simple, elegant band, no extravagant diamonds, just a single, understated ruby nestled in the centre. It was perfect.

"*I...*" Chirag started, then let out a small, self-deprecating chuckle. "*I had a whole speech planned, you know. Something smooth. Romantic. But standing here now, I just...*"

He met her gaze, and suddenly, words weren't necessary.

Jiya felt her heart stutter. The world around them—the murmuring guests, the art, the ambient music—faded into insignificance.

"*I don't know how I lived all these years without knowing you, but now that I do,*" he said finally, his voice steady despite the emotion behind it. "*I don't want another day without you.*"

Jiya felt the sting of unshed tears.

"*Do you think you can tolerate me for the rest of your life?*"

For a brief second, she just looked at him. Looked at the man who had become her home in ways she had never imagined. She saw the love and sincerity etched into his features.

Then, with a trembling smile, she whispered, "*Yes.*", letting a few tears drop out of the corner of her eyes.

Chirag let out a breath he hadn't realized he was holding, a grin breaking across his face as he slipped the ring onto her finger. Jiya looked from his deep blue eyes to the big red stone sparkling on her shaking fingers and then pulled him into a tight hug.

The moment felt infinite.

And as the world slowly seeped back in—the sounds of the gallery, the distant applause for Mukti's work, the warm glow of celebration—Jiya realized something.

This wasn't the end of their story.

It was just the beginning.